THE VOICE OF

Aliette Nouvelle

THE VOICE OF

Aliette Nouvelle

JOHN BROOKE

NUAGE
EDITIONS

Cover design by Terry Gallagher/Doowah Design.
Cover photograph by Vivian Kellner.
Photograph of John Brooke by René De Carufel.
Printed and bound in Canada by Veilleux Impression à Demande Inc.

Acknowledgements
The character Jacques Normand is modelled after Jacques Mesrine. Historical background and quotations have been gleaned from Mesrine's own memoir, *L'instinct de Mort*, Éditions Champ Libres, Paris, 1984, and from the reportage, *Mesrine...ou La Dernière Cavale*, by Guy Adamik, Le Carrousel-FN, Paris, 1984.

Excerpt from *Duino Elegies*, 6th by Rainer Maria Rilke, edited and translated by Stephen Mitchell. Vintage International, New York, 1989.

Excerpt from *The Satanic Verses* by Salman Rushdie. Vintage (Random House), Great Britain, 1998.

We acknowledge the support of The Canada Council for the Arts and the Manitoba Arts Council for our publishing program.

Canadian Cataloguing in Publication Data

Brooke, John, 1951–
    The voice of Aliette Nouvelle

ISBN 0-92183365-2

    I. Title.

PS8553.R6542V64 1999   C813'.54   C99-901334-3
PR9199.3.B6968V64 1999

Nuage Editions, P.O. Box 206, RPO Corydon
Winnipeg, Manitoba, R3M 3S7

For Annie

1ST PART

"For whenever the hero stormed through the stations of love, each heartbeat intended for him lifted him up, beyond it; and, turning away, he stood there at the end of all smiles—transfigured."

Rainer Maria Rilke
Duino Elegies

"How does newness come into the world? How is it born? Of what fusions, translations, conjoinings is it made?"

Salman Rushdie
The Satanic Verses

PROLOGUE

Her voice? It was light but it carried.
"*Messieurs!*"

It had a high register, an almost musical quality that could cut through the noise of a day.

"Lay down your weapons and walk slowly out!"

What I mean, it was delicate but absolute, as if your *maman* were calling you in for supper.

"Please believe me when I say that you are surrounded and you have no chance!"

No, I can't think what it must have been like being at the receiving end. It was weird enough for us, out on the street taking orders. It would always seem to pull the rug out from under this basic thing...this edge, this readiness to fight. It's the way we're trained, you know?

"Resistance will only be one more mistake!"

If nothing else, you would have to stick your neck out, just for a second, to get a look at her.

"There are no options, *messieurs!*"

You'd see a girlish woman standing there. In a way she was quite dangerous. I mean to the process. But I believe it came from her heart—because it sounded like home, like the whole world was touching your ears. Something like that.

"Why create more trouble than you already have?"

I think she provoked them. Made them feel weak. Made them feel more stupid than they already were. Now, whether knowingly or not, well, that was the hard part whenever you tried to get a handle on the voice of Aliette Nouvelle. Sure helped her get things done though. *Ah, oui.* That was the day the Normand thing started—not that any of us knew as much at the time.

She's called us in, see—it was always that way, after she'd done the rest of it alone—and she's got us in an alley down by the docks. She's standing off in the long shadows. It's spring, but still a bit cool out, and that blue mac is buttoned right up to her little white neck; her blonde hair is tucked up inside the rim of her beret. Except a strand that falls across her temple, which only adds to that girlish way she comes across. Or maybe that day she was more like some school-teacher, just so trim and correct and in control. But she's no damn schoolteacher and everyone knows it, not the least the poor slobs she's got pinned behind this one door.

She points—here, then there—and we all move, up along the roof and into corners, and you can just see flashes of those silver-blue eyes, getting it all sorted out as she keeps calling to them with that voice of hers, telling them they might as well pack it in. When we're all where we're meant to be, it's like she smiles at these guys right through the door.

"I mean now, *messieurs!*...We are waiting, if you please!"

It must be horrible. These are tough guys we're talking about. Drug business. Very bad. They don't want to hear a voice like that.

And after about a five count the three of them come flying out, guns blazing, and we get to work. Us men. The Inspector, she turns and walks away somewhere. Leaves us to it, like always—like her part's done.

It's over fast. One of them is down, the other two are standing there with this expression: not pissed off or even scared; just looking around the place, like, "Where the hell...?"

I go to fetch her. She's down the way, standing by a fence. Some woman's on a porch hanging up her wash—heard the shooting, ready to scream. You can see it: she's got a blotchy face. The Inspector's got her hand up like a traffic cop, holding her, suspended, keeping the scream at bay, bobbing there inside the woman's jerking throat. Not a word. Just a hand. And a look. But then, watching their two faces—it's that thing between women, isn't it?

Time stops, but the scream finally dissolves back inside the woman.

Then the Commissaire's car comes screaming into the alley.

We walk back to the scene. The Commissaire's all business, the way he always is. Has his foot pressed against the dead one's shoulder, holding him halfway rolled over as he looks into the face. His shoe is a polished black, thickly embossed brogue. It leaves a grimy print on the dead man's suit, which seems a shame because it's a perfectly decent suit. Staring down at this unfortunate soul, he mutters, "Inspector Nouvelle…"

"I'm here."

Just like that. Like she's here and the rest of us aren't at all.

The Commissaire lets the dead guy drop back down on his face and turns. "Ah… Inspector," shaking her hand, "once again you impress."

She smiles. Her eyes light up—this time more icy than silver. She steps forward, chooses a clean spot on the body's shoulder and rolls it over with her own shoe just to see for herself.

Her shoe looks like a librarian's. But her ankle is pretty nice.

1

THEORY OF THE EASTBOUND MAN

There is not much of the macabre in this story, no gory forensics to speak of, very little of the rude or violent. The mystery was mostly imaginary, a case of mistaken identities. But it was pivotal and bears telling. It happened in the second part of my life, when I was thirty-five. We were into the 90s and the world was changing. France was trying to, but it had such a reputation to uphold.

I'm from the west but I worked in the east, in a city on the Rhine. It was mid-sized and dull: museums dedicated to cars, fabrics, the railway and wallpaper, of all things. These places, however, reflected an ongoing prosperity down through the years and in those days auto manufacture, heavy machinery, chemicals and fertilizer served to keep most people working. Before being French, it had been part of the Swiss Calvinist enclave. A mural depicting the Virtues, on the terra cotta facade over the door to City Hall, bore witness to the pervading moral fibre. After that it was mainly a history of being traded back and forth between France and Germany (the place had been occupied and severely battered during the last war) and one could hear this heritage at every corner, where the Alsatian dialect paid unfelt homage to the erstwhile conquerors across the Rhine. I picked up a bit of it, but usually stuck to proper French. A civil servant ought to.

The offices of the *Police Judiciaire* (PJ) were on the third (properly called second) floor of a time-stained building in rue des Bon Enfants in the heart of the old quarter. Those of us who worked there always said "*la Brigade.*" A pair of neo-classical columns guarded the door. One walked up eight wide stone steps to enter. The ground floor (back down again, but not quite to basement level) housed a small morgue, the "shop" where our two forensics technicians known as the IJ or *Identité Judiciaire* kept their cameras, dusting materials and other devices for gathering physical evidence, a row of detention cells that were quiet and lonely, and a murky garage where two overworked mechanics called Joël and Paul did their best. Main and first floors belonged to the Urban Police—your basic police station, often a busy, clattering place. SU (*Sûreté Urbaine*), headed by Commissaire Duque, handled the more or less straightforward crimes: B&E's, hit and run's, hookers, petty drugs, people beating and sometimes even killing each other inside the home. If the robbery, abandoned pedestrian, purchased sex, drug deal or murder had wrinkles that could not readily be smoothed, the case was sent upstairs to a less hectic domain where our cadre of eleven PJ investigators—also called the Criminal Brigade—specialized in the full range of modern crime that ran from art theft to drug conspiracy, organized gangs to white collar fraud, and those violent crimes which tended toward terrorism. Mine was a corner office overlooking the cobblestone quadrangle. It was nothing special when it came to views, the quad having more or less completed its devolution from stately courtyard to trashy parking lot; but it got the sun at the end of the day, affording a richer quality of light which I have always enjoyed. In a pot on the file cabinet was a shamrock, in the process of flowering on the day this thing started, and on the walls my framed poster of a sweaty Johnny Hallyday the day he gave his legendary impromptu solo concert in front of the Acadian fresco in Nantes, as well as two photos of that city's port (Nantes being my hometown).

I was preparing my report. I won't say I'm proud of it because there are many who say it's a neurosis, but I have always been the organized type when it comes to keeping track. I kept a jar of pencils on the corner of my desk, each of them absolutely sharp. I was reaching for one when there came a knock. "*Oui...?*"

The door opened, revealing Louis Moreau, my Commissaire, coming to present me with another file. He was accompanied by one of my lesser-known colleagues, a gangly man prone to shaving rash named Claude Néon who spent most of his time with the Anti-Gangs group. Claude was carrying a whole stack of files. The boss stepped forward with that tight smile of his, and dropped a picture of a man on my desk. He was roughly shaven, double-chinned, clearly heading toward middle age, but with a jaunty, smirking attitude that made one notice. It was the face of Jacques Normand, stuck front and centre on a yellowed Wanted poster. I was not sure if reputations lapsed like driver's permits and love affairs, but I did recall the faded smile of France's former Public Enemy Number One.

"You know this man, of course..."

Yes, yes, I knew Jacques Normand; anyone old enough to vote would have at least some acquaintance with the man. I had grown up hearing his name at my parents' dining-room table. The less credible papers out of Paris had taken delight in splashing his brutal exploits all over their weekend editions. Seeing him there at my fingertips made me remember the puzzling mixture of horror and adulation those stories brought forth from everyone including my parents and so many of the boys I had thought I was in love with. It was always odd the way my love could change just watching someone looking at a picture; discussions of "our Jacques"—so dubbed by the breathless journalists—always seemed to make people shrink and become much less than they were. What was there to admire? The man was breaking the law and hurting people. But by the time I got to the Police Academy, Le Grand Jaki Normand had long since disappeared. Into Spain, perhaps, or back to Canada, where he had done some time, or maybe to hell, which must be where Public Enemies go after they leave this earth. Although there remained the occasional crime reporter who still felt a need to invoke his name as a touchstone for criminal accomplishment, I had assumed as I began my career—if, indeed, I ever thought about it at all—that the Normand file was closed. Now here was my Commissaire, with a gleam in his eye as he handed me a picture of a ghost. "I remember him," I said. "He was a bad one."

"My dear Inspector, Jaki Normand was the worst. And the best. A remarkable man...the Carlylean great man! He affected people."

"You had dealings with him back in Paris?"

"Dealings? I had champagne!"

Champagne! That induced an involuntary tightening. I braced myself. "Oh...really?"

"I tracked him, and put him behind bars twice. We drank together the second time I arrested him. He let me in the front door and we shared a glass together. No shooting that day, just champagne. In a perverse way Jacques Normand made my career. But he escaped again...and disappeared into the woodwork."

"Yes, he's been quiet for a long time."

"Ten years. But time is not a consideration, Inspector. Not for someone like our Jacques or me or for you."

"Me?" Yes; he was looking at me with that fondness again.

"You, Inspector. I believe you were born to the breed. He's all yours..."

All I could do was study the Wanted poster and try not to appear too dubious. I liked Louis Moreau, and owed much to his good advice and encouragement. "Monsieur Commissaire," I ventured after a suitable silence, "I'm flattered. But what if he's dead? or somewhere in a forest in Canada? or...with all respect, I would never call Jacques Normand a missing person—"

"And I wouldn't let you."

"...but this is not really my kind of operation. I mean to say, I was trained for—"

"You were trained for this."

In point of fact, I had been trained for anti-gang work—like the silent Claude Néon, hovering, gawking, his mouth thrust forward like some kind of expectant dromedary as he held his stack of files. But in a small brigade training cedes to the situation at hand, and I had, shortly after arrival, been slotted onto the *Mondaine*, or Morals, beat, whose concerns were things such as prostitution and narcotics. From there, mainly because no judge has the power to bring a suspect back from Switzerland, a quick and easy fifty kilometres down the road, I'd become, for all intents and purposes, a one-woman border patrol whose unmarked territory ran along both sides, and if need be, into Germany. My specialty was the drug trade, but only because I was responding to the demand. Zurich was fast becoming a world-class junk haven. But I had also made my presence felt in bringing to ground everyone from crooked bankers to hired guns, importers of illegal immigrants and carriers of improperly carted wine. That's French ground I refer to.

There were complaints: routinely, by those who thought their rights had been abused; and occasionally, but more pertinent to my professional standing, by those who believed my catches belonged to them. This is inevitable when systems overlap and jealousy gets the better of good sense. No, not everyone liked me. Who could expect that? Generally speaking, however, my work brought praise upon the balding but tautly dapper, sixtyish head of our Principal Commissaire, Louis Moreau, and so, upon myself.

Good words came often from the Judges of Instruction in our city who mediated between police and court in all criminal enquiries; sometimes, cautiously, from the court itself, represented by the Procureur and his Substitutes—prosecutors who stood to inherit the system if they could keep it intact; more than once from the much feared but always respected NF, the Divisional Commissaire who ruled us and the rest of the region from the larger, more glamorous city to the north; and therefore, also—but cryptically, almost invisibly— from the unknown men at the Quai d'Orfèvres in Paris, police mandarins who run the *Service de Police Judiciaire* for the Minister of the Interior.

Although the police universe was wide, I have to say that Inspector Nouvelle was what some might call a star—and rising.

And Louis Moreau's fond look usually carried a certain basic truth which I had learned to appreciate. But that afternoon his eyes were wider and brighter than I had seen them in a long while. This bothered me—rubbed something inside the wrong way. A police thing, not a woman thing—no worries there. Well, I had earned the right to push the matter and responded accordingly. "But he's been quiet for all these years. He really could be dead!"

"No. He's here…in this city."

I told him with my own bright eyes that he would have to tell me more.

"Inspector, I'm a cop…like you." He smiled, the stocky but still tight mass of body relaxing slightly as he rested his behind against the edge of my desk. "Le Grand Jacques was something left unfinished in my work. My life's work, if you know what I mean, and I think by this point you do."

Yes.

"Do you think I came to this place for the good of my health?"

No.

"Do you think, perhaps, I was shunted out here for the sake of my pension?"

No.

My responses were silent—and subtle, made with my eyes, my body—but they communicated clearly enough, and gave him the responses he sought. I knew that Louis Moreau had been highly regarded for his work against the gangs in the streets of Paris and could easily have stayed in Paris; that he could well, even now, have been sitting behind one of those polished windows on the Quai.

"A man makes decisions…"

Indeed.

"…When Jacques disappeared from Paris, I didn't go running after him. There's no need to run after anybody…that's another thing you seem to have learned quite well."

I nodded once more: *merci.*

He continued. "I had a sense of where he might be, so I followed him." The smile returned, not for me this time, but for a memory. "Bonnie and Clyde, in one man, but fifty years later, right here in the most sophisticated country in the world! What I like to call a magnificent aberration…"

I was meant to endorse that, and did.

"The country loved him and he needed that love. *Alors,*" a shrug, "he never left France. He couldn't. If he ever left he'd be lost, because he would be no one. But here, he could hide forever and he would always be our Public Enemy Number One. If nothing else, there would be the story…on the streets, in the hearts of the people. I knew the man. I knew he was here in France. He had to be."

"But here?" It was Claude. His first words.

"East… He came east," answering Claude, but keeping his eyes on me. This one was for me. "When he was inside writing his memoirs, like most men he ended up looking for the meaning in his life. For his soul, if you will. That's eastward, Inspector. East was his direction, and this was the logical place. Perhaps that's why you came here as well. Fate's a strange thing, isn't it?"

I did not answer that. Looking through the rimless lenses and into eyes that were blue like mine—but a deeper hue, richer, like his experience and showing no signs of age—I acknowledged the logic of the theory of the eastbound man, then tried to bring the briefing down to a more practical level. "Where should I look then? He's not working with anyone. Not dealing anything, or stealing anything. I'd know it…I'd have brought this thing to you long ago if that was the case." I gave the face of Jacques Normand three brisk taps and challenged my Commissaire to disagree.

"There's no gang. He's alone…he has to be alone. It's the only way he could hope to exist at this point." Turning to Claude Néon, who stepped obediently forward, Louis Moreau patted the stack of files. "Have a look at this stuff…it's all there."

I took the top one from under Claude's oily nose and opened it. "But this is from downstairs…"

"They all are—except this…" handing over the single item he had been kneading and bending as he had spoken his piece. "Perhaps you'll recognize it."

I glanced and did. It was an unsolved drug shooting from a couple of years ago. So? I did not follow. The rest were B&E's. What could he possibly want?

"It's clear to me," he said. "I know it will be clear to you." The look was meaningful, that tight smile absolutely confident. And I knew him well enough to sense that behind the words, eyes and smile he was asking: do this for me. It was more than a request. It was a compliment, perhaps the finest one an old cop could extend. Of course I would have to try.

I reconsidered the famous face. "I seem to remember more of a shine."

"Don't we all?" mused Louis Moreau. "Time will do unkind things to a man's face, but the soul of the man—especially that man— is eternal." Now he pulled an old volume from his pocket and presented it. "This might help you bridge the gap."

I read: *Dans les traces marginales*. It was a memoir, dog-eared, yellowed, and heavy—closing in on eight hundred pages. The back cover displayed the same face as that on the Wanted poster, but cleaned up and smiling a brighter, more roguish smile. His popular face, his Sunday face. As I pondered it, the boss clasped my shoulder—like a comrade. "He's out there waiting for you, Inspector. Find him. If anyone can pick up his trail and put him away for good this time, it's you."

"I'll do my best."

He bowed. Then, as an afterthought, added, "Claude here is at your service." And he left.

Thanks…

My well-acknowledged talent was finding and communicating with those who existed between the morass of police and underworld systems which tended to bring justice to a halt or turn it into a diplomatic mess. Whoever they might happen to be, my "people," as I have always called them, were effective—because I knew how to work with them. This usually allowed me to work alone. And clean; rarely would you find the standard issue 7.65 mm Saint Étienne pistol packed in my valise (although neglect of this sort is quite against the rules). If force was required, it was supplied according to my specifications. Whatever I may have accomplished of any value, however, was done pretty much alone, well before any shooting had to start.

So, as Inspector Claude Néon stood there in front of me, my thoughts changed course. He had been along with some of the other boys to help finish a case here and there; but in five? six? years—I was honestly not sure how long he had been around, only that it was not as long as I—it was our first real face to face. One reason, beyond the different lines of work, was that I had always suspected him of liking me. The wrong kind of like. Because this Claude Néon was too thin. His brown eyes seemed to bounce around in their sockets with a nervousness I could not find interesting and which I felt no urge to calm. And the smell of him, now that we were alone together, was a bit too close, a little too much like myself on all the wrong days. I held nothing against him, but he was not my type at all and so I had kept my distance. Now here he was: at my service.

"Well, Claude," I ventured, careful not to send the wrong signals, resting in neutral as I tried to imagine working with him, "…Jaki Normand: he's out there waiting for us."

"Is there anything I can get you?"

"I don't think so. We'll start on this tomorrow." So saying, I rose, opened my valise, and dropped in the Normand Wanted poster, the memoir and the file on the dead drug dealer no one had accounted for. I left the rest of the files waiting in his skinny arms.

"May I offer you a ride home?"

"No thank you. I prefer to walk. *À demain*..." As I stepped past, I could feel his eyes on the back of my neck. Every woman knows this sensation.

"I look forward to working with you. I've wanted to for a long time. They talk about your instincts."

I turned. "Really, Claude? That's very nice. We'll see how it goes. *Salut*." Then I left the office.

2

PIAF & ME

I lived beside the Parc de la République, opposite the *rond-point*, on the northernmost edge of the quarter—strictly speaking, just outside its boundaries. To get there, I always followed the lanes that wound and jogged, the narrowest streets and the shadiest avenues. It was basic to my routine and I had covered them all. I could do the most whimsical variations and still end up at the same place, each morning and every evening, a journey from one edge of my life to the other— thinking, dreaming, looking in all the shop windows which never seemed to change. There was a red garlic press sitting in the window of the *quincaillerie*: a red garlic press with dust on it, and I had been feeling I might stop and buy it. Someone had to.

But that evening, with Jacques Normand tucked inside my valise, I had other things on my mind. I had a sense of something big. I was thinking about the Commissaire and telling myself: yes, why not me? He's going, finally (he was past the official age), and he has given me this to help him in the leaving. We had been working toward it, unspoken but steadily since the first day. Had we not? Yes. From amongst all of us, all of a generation—middle thirties, early forties— I was in line to succeed. Certainly, Paris could parachute someone in. That would not surprise me in the least. But Louis Moreau had chosen me. So yes: why not me? It was about time.

Just past Madame Chong's *épicerie* the way opened onto the *rond-point* where five streets met and mixed. The traffic cop who worked it was a good-looking man (a horsy quality that attracted), always busy but never too much so to extend a smile as he shepherded me across to the other side. Some days his smile seemed to carry weight. And some days I returned it in kind. That evening he smiled in such a way and so did I, enjoying his spinning pantomime as I took the final steps out of the public domain of my work and into the private territories of my home.

There was Piaf, out on my balcony, waiting to welcome me. After the Commissaire's odd intimations about fate, I appreciated an old friend's uncomplicated *salut*. Having grown up in a city on the other side of the country, having listened carefully to my father and disagreed with my mother, having split from my sister, friends and world to become a cop, having had six boyfriends and one abortion, having reached the delicate age of thirty-five, this was where that fate had brought me.

My apartment was at the top: third floor. There was a garden below, spreading to the fence along the edge of the park. Madame Camus, the landlady, offered it to everyone, but Mademoiselle Nouvelle never sat there; I preferred looking down from above. So did Piaf, although at this point he had little choice. After fifteen fine years, his selection had come down to a basic in or out. There would be no more climbing, no more pathetic birds or rodents to be carried home and placed proudly at my feet. Piaf's hunting days were over, while my own had just taken a turn the likes of which I had never thought to dream. Jacques Normand! I tucked the outlaw under my arm as I fiddled with my keys, calling, "*Salut*, Piaf!"

I have to say there were not that many friends. There had been a few, at different points in a life in a new city; but when people paired up, married, had children, the focus always seemed to shift away. And I was a cop. Someone different. Even with friends the first reaction was always one step back.

So I called my father instead.

"Papa...please! Of course I'm ready for something like that...I wouldn't have got it if I wasn't ready for it!" I had chosen to tell my father because after eight years on the service my mother had yet to approve my choice of careers. Besides, it had always been Papa who had gone to fetch those weekend papers. The downside was that all too often his love and encouraging words were undermined by questions which left me wondering if he knew me at all. "His name is Moreau...

Yes, he knows the business inside out... Yes! and he hunted Jacques Normand for years. Mmm...I'm sure he has some stories to tell. In fact I know he does. But underneath it all, this Normand's just another criminal. They all are. No...! Papa! Stop it! You know, he's probably dead. It's just the fact he gave it to me that—*Oui*...a feather in my cap, *c'est ça*..."

There was a pause, after which came the congratulations I had been seeking; after that, a chuckled, conspiratorial promise not tell my mother. I left him with my own promise, as always, that I would be home soon. It was March; May would be filled with long weekends. I could find a week if I wanted to—unless this new thing got drawn out. More likely it would be the usual three weeks in August at Belle Île. Then I took some tortellini out of the freezer, put water on to boil, and tried to decide between tomato sauce or pesto.

Later, sitting together on my bed: "So this is the new man in my life, Piaf," I told him, showing him the Wanted poster as I sipped my second glass of beer. Piaf looked through one eye, then rolled over, stretched and yawned. I studied the face—meditated. This was the way it always worked, steeping myself in the available information, coming to terms with what I was up against, sensing where to begin. "And it's always men, these kinds of criminals. Or mostly, I guess I should say," remembering the boss's allusion to Bonnie Parker. "Look at him..."

Checking dates: he was older than me by a dozen years, younger than Louis Moreau by perhaps fifteen. The gap that needed bridging? "But he's supposed to be a hero, Piaf—a real hero, this Jaki Normand." I got up, setting my glass on the dresser as my thoughts probed the mocking grin, the bleary eyes, the three-day growth which made him look so shoddy. "Does he never shave?" I mused.

Now (and often), I still wonder, which Aliette was it who drew her fingers along the base of her white neck, looking away from Jacques Normand and into the mirror? Because this whole thing was about me—not him. And I left my hand where it lay for a precious moment. "He'll shave. For me, he certainly will. And what will I wear when I catch him?"

Smiling, two-beers dreamy, I reached and ran my fingers through the thick knot of hair ribbons slung over my dresser post. Always enjoyable: skin, and the plush of velvet. I asked, "In what colour does Monsieur Normand like his detectives?" and pulled one loose. A blue. A soft sky blue to go with my silvery eyes—for Jaki Normand.

I replaced the ribbon and sipped more beer.

What a wonderful thing beer is! Better than wine, which makes my nose red and my urine burn. The difference between the grain and the grape is the way my mother has always explained it. Just so. Just as a person has to understand her own elements: those parts of the world she is attuned to, which inspire her, which make her dream; natural elements which mix in the imagination and blend with the stuff of style and soul and fun. Like ribbons, textures, beer, cats—and hats.

Oh yes, of course I had a collection. I had berets of all colours, several tams, a topper, a bowler from England, fedoras from my papa's closet, and my prize—an LA Dodgers baseball cap from Los Angeles in America. Dodger blue, they called it. I had sent away for it, to see how it went with my eyes. And it went well; but I could never imagine a baseball player. Not clearly. Not then, not now. I reckoned they probably liked beer though, and I reasoned that Jacques Normand probably—undoubtedly—as a true French hero, drank wine.

Returning to my bed, the Wanted poster was exchanged for the memoir: *Dans les traces marginales.* First, a note from the publisher: "For a generation of French people Jacques Normand and his exploits have become the perfect symbol of freedom." Well sure, everyone has their own way of exploiting a situation. Still, it was vexing to read these words from a supposedly responsible purveyor of cultural materials. Then there was an epigraph: *"Si tu vis dans l'ombre, tu n'accéderas jamais au soleil."* If you live in the shadows, you will never find the sun. These were someone else's words, a bit of sad truth which had gained the status of maxim and could be found in children's school books. To me, the fateful *pensée* did not seem to fit the author's racy, devil-may-care smile.

And there was a dedication:

à Bernadette

Cécile

Lise

Nathalie
Joyce
Francine...
et Annie, *le Maître*.

"Look Piaf, his lawyer made it into the top seven. I wonder what they got up to? ...I bet he had his own private harem, and when push came to shove, he could hide under a hundred different beds."

But still? Ten years later?

And what kind of women were these seven, to spend time with a man who had taken what he wanted as he had lived by spreading fear? Great sex? Or an inability to say "*non*" in the face of wilful force? Usually, after a bit of heart-to-heart when it was all over and done—taking a statement, a visit to their cell or to the posh (but usually tacky) flat they may have inherited, all the ones I've ever dealt with in the line of duty have always intimated it was more than that. That it was love. Or might have been. And this has always bothered me: women who profess to fall in love with these selfish and destructive men.

I cannot agree that these propensities or their lack have to do with "right" neighbourhoods or college degrees. I've met too many who belie those theories. Nor is it about the things your mother taught you. Because not all of us have mothers, and so many of us who do will never believe a word they say. No, to me it rests on the sense God gave us all. Are they really so desperate for affection? So dim they can't see where it has to lead? So deluded when they tell themselves it's only for a bit? Where's their self-respect? What happens to their basic woman's instinct—which is life-oriented, surely? Children or no, mine is; I say that unequivocally. Yes, I'm a critical one. I've learned to live and let live, but I'm always passing judgement. You have to in this business—and all the more so if you're a woman, or you can lose track and humanity becomes a sea of mud. But this judgement is reflexive, all directed toward myself. A survival thing.

That first night I pictured this man—this eastbound man, this hero—I saw him sitting somewhere with blood on his hands, a suitcase full of money or jewellery or drugs, and the thought that the whole country was wondering where he might be. And I tried to see a woman sitting there with him. Some garish prostitute, perhaps, or maybe a crooked lawyer, discredited and cut loose, or more likely, just someone drab the world did not want to see or hear. The woman was trying to be with him but was being ignored and rebuffed because he needed to be alone—had to be alone. To survive. I could not imagine this woman, whoever she might be, putting up with that for very long, not even if Le Grand Jaki opened his suitcase and let her take whatever she might want. What kind of life would it be?

Names...gazing at his seven favourites again as I pondered. A name is a life's indicator. Maybe this list of names at the head of his life's story was just a measure of endurance, like so many marks crossed off on a cold cell wall.

Maybe they fell for his eastbound soul.

I closed the book and compared the two images. Before and after: the myth, illusory, and attractive only for that reason; and the man with the government number across his chest.

"Sorry..." letting the fantasy of ribbons and hats drift away, "the case, my Piaf, just the case. We go straight at him." The Wanted poster won, hands down.

But Piaf was in dreamland.

I rubbed him slowly with my toe and sipped more beer.

3

A PATTERN / A BASIC BODY TYPE

Drug dealers live precarious lives. The abandoned file Louis Moreau had handed me told of one from Switzerland, Alain Bruzi, who had been found behind a local warehouse with a hole through his face, the bullet (not recovered) having been fired from point blank range. The only lead had been a companion, a girlfriend it was assumed, by the name of Anne-Marie, but she had disappeared. Some who had known the victim had known her, but no family name or history was ever established. She could have been French. She could have been Swiss. A pithy quote: "She was just the guy's poodle and she never said a word, not even when he was kicking her."

Two years before, I had looked at it myself, asked around to no avail, then had gone back to more important things: live drug dealers.

In his memoir, Jacques Normand described his first killing as an act of elemental justice—and compassion. Jacques first killed for Joyce, a prostitute he loved, who, as he saw it, suffered unjustly at the hands of her pimp. But he recognized a turning point: "I looked at it and saw it clearly, without emotion, knowing full well that it could cost me a life in prison, or death in the streets. I felt neither remorse nor satisfaction. I had discovered the soul of a killer who could put aside any sentiment or pity for his enemies. I had respect for life, but only the life of those who lived outside my special world. Your basic citizen had nothing to fear from me; we lived in two totally different worlds." Apart from any existential meaning the act may have carried, both the tying of his first victim's hands, right down to the knot he had used, and the business-like, execution-style shot in the face were identical to the circumstances of the unsolved murder of the Swiss.

Apparently, however, no one—save an old cop named Moreau—had been reading Jacques Normand at the time.

As Claude and I compared a stack of unsolved B&E's from the last year or two with the early exploits of a budding Public Enemy, proudly and painstakingly related, it became clear that the long-gone fugitive, or someone, had been following Le Grand Jacques' first moves to the letter. It was all mundane stuff—jewels from the dresser drawer and the like—and had rightly been left downstairs with SU. But it was also tinged with a certain flare.

I summarized aloud, for Claude's benefit, so that we might be in step even if we did not look good together:

"Someone breaks into an apartment. The alarm sounds. Our people are there in a minute and freeze the area. No one moves...except a hairdresser, who comes wandering out of some door with his bag full of hairdressing tools, blasé and unaware. When he's stopped, he shows them his bag and says he has to get to work. They let him pass—he's gone. But no such hairdresser exists. Just like in the book...he went across the roof, came back in through someone else's place, then walked away."

Claude smiled and, opening another file, took the liberty of lowering his bum onto the corner of my desk; he had been doing his homework too. "This one, just a month ago: an apartment is broken into but the owner comes home—a dentist with a pile of diamonds stashed in his bedroom...actually walks right in on the thief. But the thief says he's a cop, that there's been a break-in, and that the dentist is not to touch a thing while he goes for his assistants. And he just walks away again. That job was a replay of his very first."

The entire pile fit the profile: random, small-time, but each a bit quirky. The disguises—no, roles—played to the hilt. Was that a hero's sense of humour or mere arrogance? I would have to go back to the book. "Well," I said, "if it worked once—"

"—why not twice?"

"Unless there's some kid out there with a copy of the guy's book stuffed in his back pocket, acting out each crime..."

Claude's eyes bounced toward the door. He straightened up.

"It's a possibility, Inspector," agreed the Commissaire, stepping in, coffee in hand. "Of course. Always possible. But my own experience with the man tells me there is something of a far greater urgency unfolding here."

I shifted modes, opening my notebook as Louis Moreau crossed the room and gazed out the window, tasting his coffee, forming his words.

"My experience, Inspector, says that if he has got himself back to repeating his first jobs, that means he's running out of space."

"Space?"

"Historical space. Physical space. Personal space. For him they're one and the same. He'll be trapped down there in the streets, acting out his petty crimes but thinking like the legend that he is. That's too much pressure. It will be like a jail for Jacques, and he hates jail. Hates it!" He paused and gestured toward the file. It told of three spectacular escapes followed by desperate flights.

I remained silent in the face of more theory.

Claude helped me out. "So?"

"An explosion! Jacques Normand is going to come bursting back onto the scene, and with a vengeance…" He now settled his posterior in the place Claude had wanted. "This is not just an opportunity, Inspector, it's a responsibility."

I asked, "Whatever happened to the prostitute—that first one, back in Paris?"

He waved his hand in the air, dismissing it. "God knows what happens to someone like that when she loses her appeal. That was years ago… You have to deal with the here and now. You have to be ready for him!"

Well, we were working on it. We also reviewed a videotape, an archival montage of shrill news footage, uncrafted surveillance video, the sound of his voice when it was available, lots of police stills…here was a bullet-riddled getaway car with a dead dog left in the back seat; and the decomposing body of an accomplice who had betrayed him, several close-ups of the mess that is a shattered kneecap, and several more of the cleaner hole in the side of a skull.

"Loyalty was important," commented Claude. "It runs like a river through both his book and all the journalism, don't you find?"

"Like a river, Claude?" I had been noticing that his reactions to these visual highlights of the Normand saga were disappointing to say the least; like canned laughter, they only affirmed the obvious.

"What I mean is you get this sense of a poetic side to him. It wasn't only the money. He was making statements!"

"Or just catering to the crowd."

Claude looked at me as if I'd pinched him. "It's just background," he stammered. "Tell me what you need—I'll get it for you."

I smiled a conciliatory smile. "I don't get a sense of him from this stuff. If it's him, he's down to climbing in people's windows. Who do you think might be loyal to him now…ten or even twenty years after the fact?"

Claude didn't know.

Here was the famous self-portrait of Jacques and his personal arsenal that had ended up on the cover of *Paris-Match*, then a black and white snap of Normand celebrating a successful ransom, grinning as he hugged a blonde and toasted the world from a table at Maxim's. It was followed by several minutes of self-shot, 8-mm film, taken in a nondescript apartment. Same night, apparently: Jaki Normand had loosened his silk tie and popped open a few buttons, but he was still grinning as he spoke into a slightly out-of-sync and muddy-sounding microphone. "*Salut, messieurs les flics.* Tonight we dined à la carte thanks to your careful cooperation in facilitating the transfer of funds from Monsieur Gauthier's savings account to the designated spot. I trust you, in turn, enjoyed meeting Monsieur Gauthier at long last…" At this point the girlfriend entered the frame, now in her slip and a bathrobe, bringing coffee. Smiling for the camera, she made a mawkish gesture of clasping the robe's lapels shut in order to preserve her modesty.

"Unbelievable!" exclaimed Claude, far too in awe of the outlaw's brash display.

I leaned forward and pushed the pause button. "What about her?"

"Joyce Daigrepont."

"Ah…the prostitute from the early years?" Whose dreadful lot had first moved a thief to kill.

"Yes, and she was with him through the last phase—when he really made his mark... She's still in La Santé." A jail in Paris.

"He didn't stop for her on his way out?"

"I guess not."

"I guess loyalty has its limits; I'd like to talk to her."

I re-engaged the tape. Claude made a note. Jacques Normand carried on, stealing property, hurting people, always drawing gasps and raves.

Two others on Normand's dedication list, Bernadette and Francine, were dead. Drugs; both related to misadventure and tough lives. Nathalie, who was never charged, refused to speak about the man except to say that she had been very young at the time. She now lived a respectable life in Dunkerque with three children and a husband who knew nothing about it. She implored me to respect this fact. His Cécile could not be traced. Perhaps she too had married and had children; or maybe she had left the country with the outlaw, and the two now spent their days fishing for supper somewhere warm. Over in cold Canada, Lise had served her time and then returned to waitressing.

When I reached the lawyer, *Maître* Annie Granger, I quickly realized that she was easily my mother's age or more. Truth be told, Inspector Nouvelle of the *Police Judiciaire*, sitting there unseen at her end of the telephone line in a far corner of France, experienced a moment of embarrassment for imagining that *le Maître* and Le Grand Jacques had been involved in anything more than a professional relationship.

"He needed someone to talk to," said the cultivated Parisian voice. "I could listen...he was paying me. *Oui*, you could say passionate...most clients tend to be; but not that deep, if you know what I mean. I would have thought he was dead."

I heartily agreed with *le Maître* that it was real possibility and thanked her very much.

When I called Marisa, the only woman he'd ever legally married and the mother of his only child, I heard anxious surprise—and then resignation. "Please. He's been gone from my life for all these years. I have no idea... No, I don't want to know."

I found I believed her. "What about your child?"

"Wouldn't call her a child any more. She seems to have let him go... I'd like to keep it like that."

"Would you object if I talked to her?"

"Yes. I'd fight it."

An impasse—ended by the other party. "She's just coming up seventeen...it's not a good time. Maybe you can understand."

Maybe I could.

"He wasn't even there when she was born."

"No..." I'd read that bit. "*Madame*, try to forget I ever called. I hope you and your family don't have to hear from me."

"*Merci.*"

As soon as I told Normand's widowed mother I was calling from the police, the line went dead. I decided to leave it that way until there was a real reason to bother the lady. He had probably put her through hell. What's more, Madame Normand was still in the Paris *arrondissement* out of which Le Grand Jacques had come. According to the rules of territorial jurisdiction, if he was back living with his *maman*, he could be no concern of mine.

Bon. I reckoned Louis Moreau's gap was lessened somewhat. Any woman would be a current woman. With some luck, this Anne-Marie, his silent "poodle," would still be somewhere in the here and now.

—   —

We requisitioned a car and went into the streets to look for signs of an ex-Public Enemy.

We showed his face, but, given the likely reaction—panic! wild rumours!—kept his name covered.

Likely reaction? No one so much as blinked when they saw this face. He was gone from their minds. Even the dentist, the latest victim of a dead-on Normand repeat, who had looked into his eyes and believed every word, could only offer the vaguest image: a middle-aged man, mustache, heavy set. "The belly pushing over the belt...you know? ...Yes, most of his hair, I think. But—"

But he just could not be sure.

On the other hand, lots of people had seen lots of Anne-Marie's. Lots of poodles, too.

Too often the beginnings of a case are formless. Our petty thief was someone no one noticed, given to working days as well as nights. I needed a context more clearly defined. Was it studied invisibility—expert, designed to last the balance of a lifetime? Or was it this "explosion" the Commissaire felt was so logical to the nature of the man? Was the ex-Public Enemy living in torment, boiling over with inevitability? Does inevitability show in a man's face the way it does in a flow chart or a situation comedy? Yes, I've seen it: when a man is about to kiss you; beyond that... You want (you need) something to happen. But with no hint of this man's mood or intentions ten years after the infamous fact, all we had were faces—a mid-sized city full of middle-aged men's faces, and this basic body type.

We went to the market. Was that him—spongy belly squishing over one of those huge macho belt buckles, cursing each bump in the pavement as he hauled a pallet of tomatoes? Might he be that portly gentleman there in the American clothes—deck shoes and designer jeans, with the mustache identical to the one in the picture—the Public Enemy at the garden stall, judicious as he tried to choose between the pansies and the petunias? How about that fat man selling melons? Or that soft, pinkish man in the blue blazer, looking clubby, buying strawberries; had the Public Enemy taken up tennis? Could he have been the plumpish egg man who always wore a sailor's cap? Had he been sitting there selling eggs in the market all these years?

And was I hoping to just chance upon him there? Suddenly bump into that soft belly, bounce back a step— "Well, well, well, if it isn't Jaki Normand."

We went downtown. Always lots of overweight middle-aged men out loose downtown. Businessmen. Look... There were two: both fit the description, but one wore his winter mac, the other no mac at all, all set for the summer which had yet to arrive. Which season would the Public Enemy be feeling like today? I wondered. And which tie would our hero choose? The deathly green with silver whorls? Or the crimson, embossed with a cute likeness of Asterix? I spent too many days mesmerized by ugly ties that forced my eyes on drooping bellies. Which was the worst tie in the city, and would that, logically, have to be him?

What about a natty type in a green suede coat that almost hid the belly? Almost. I watched him coughing himself bright red as he moved along in the middle of a clutch of unsuspecting citizens. Would the Public Enemy be out spreading germs like that?

Or was it pinstripes now, to hide a tucked-in gut—his mask a Vandyke and the most expensive mirrored shades? Had the Public Enemy become a well-fed investment banker, off to see another client with all the confidence in the world? Sure, get your prey dreaming of riches before robbing him blind—Jaki's new, more sophisticated strategy?

Could that be him there, by the cathedral, wearing tweed that had grown too tight, down on hands and knees in front of the bronze of the famous priest, scratching around the pavement for something he could not seem to find, his belly falling out of his shirt like an udder?

Was he sitting in the sun in Banker's Square, under the statue of the Emperor? Patting his belly. Thinking of banks.

Had Le Grand Jacques grown a biblical beard over his double chin and taken up a position in a doorstep with his beret on the street in front of him, waiting to receive the money of others rather than take it? A complete change of course for our Public Enemy. An excellent cover.

Had he gone to seed, bilious and dishevelled on the corner, waving a sign telling people they had better repent and soon? When you thought about it, you had to say, Well, who better?

Then again, maybe that was him, a hefty thirty kilos past his hero weight these days, testing out a divan in the store window. Was the former Public Enemy now an overstuffed sybarite, concerned mainly with the finer points of comfort? Very possible. As possible as all the rest.

Was he in the art gallery down by the docks, massaging his bulge while shrewdly assessing the merits of a gouache depicting a sunset in the Vosges? A man of taste now. Or was that him, masquerading as a laborer, working on yet another renovation project farther along the wharf, calmly directing the lowering of a box?—lowering a box! By that point all I could see were the pants slipping below the large stomach, the exposed crack of his bum as he turned to greet the foreman.

Had he come down to the river to read on a bench? What would an ex-hero be reading? His own out-of-print book, over and over? Or something on fitness—how to look thirty-nine again?

Or did he just sleep all day, hogging the next bench, fatness rising...falling?

(Claude drew near and blasted the horn. Our snoozer jumped sky-high. Ha ha. But I laughed too, so bored.)

Moving into the east end... There was a lumpy man who fit the profile, in a canary yellow jersey, talking things over with a bean-pole hooker in grey tights. Mustache checked out too, and the hair. Was he telling her of some weird desire, looking for a fair price to pay for being the only man ever quite like himself? Was she telling him there were a thousand men within screaming distance with a belly like that one and she should get extra for having to see one more? Or was the Public Enemy that poor woman's steel-hearted pimp? Had he taken over from the man he may or may not have killed? Would his "poodle" be waiting on the next corner, still a slave? But on the next corner there was only another man just like that one, sitting in a wicker rocker out in the street, hands folded across his ample tummy. The sign over the door read Bricolage St. Jacques. Who would ever have thought it? A quiet shopkeeper now, here on the poor side of town.

Was the Public Enemy working for the Public Works, riding around on his little conveyance with the vacuum tube: a dumpy gnome, cleaning up after all the city's poodles?

Maybe, like Elvis Presley, Jacques Normand was spending his time with a road crew, picking at his distended navel while waving people through, one lane at a time.

Was that the former Public Enemy running for a bus? Could he still run? A not-unreasonable question when you factored in all that extra weight.

It was worse than frustrating. It was disorienting, each blank shrug and uninterested "*Sais pas.*" I was thinking: Come on people! This is Jacques Normand. You know him! Symbol of freedom! A bona fide gem in France's crown! But although people were more fascinated than ever by extreme forms of expression, it seemed they were no longer wanting to get as close to the actual man. The personable outlaw had been replaced in the popular imagination by those unsmiling killers who "wasted" people (good word, that) like un-thinking machines. The streets were full of action, but heroes and villains were growing abstract.

Where was Carlyle's "great man"? A man cannot affect people where there is no recognition. By the same token, Plutarch suggested that a hero should serve as a "sort of looking glass in which I might see how to adjust and adapt my own life." A mirror? Hardly. The face in the Wanted poster was not even oblique. Middle-aged, paunchy, so typical in his choice of mustache and coiffure; there were no movie stars the likes of him on the cover of *Paris-Match*. If that man were ever cast in a film he would be some bourgeois type, trying to come to terms with the quiet side of love—certainly no ass-kicking hero. The middle-aged softie was no Public Enemy.

And it was not as if there were nothing else I could have been doing. The Republic was losing huge sums to the arms dealers' underground pipeline. There was a file on a woman who was bringing girls in from Manila on bogus student visas to Freiburg, then over the river to our city for sex with the patrons of her husband's dry-cleaning service, and then back out again, always right on time. Just my kind of case. Or drugs: drugs were being sold to ten-year-olds! There was lots of work out there. While I was in the street with Claude, looking for a petty thief—described as a heavy-set, middle-aged man.

4

THE NÉON EFFECT

Claude did most of the driving, fetched coffee quite willingly, and was more than happy to put an official face on things by flashing his medal if he felt the situation called for it. But it was exactly there that the basic sticking point soon showed itself. The situation—and Claude's approach. Chemistry, the smell thing; when he had first come close, I had sensed a disparity. Now he kept getting in my feet, as we say, seeing it all wrong.

When you travel the streets, you see so much that's untoward. Like I say—a sea of mud. We happened to find ourselves watching as a blobbish man brandishing steel snips casually bent, snapped the chain securing a bicycle, and rode away. Claude stepped on the gas, cut him off, threw him up against a wall and started in on him—had his gun up the man's nose, the whole bit. The gendarmes came running, followed by the usual crowd. I sat there with the Wanted poster on my lap and didn't bother getting out. After so many faces on so many streets, it was not going to happen like that. Not with this long-gone Public Enemy.

Another day we were driving along and I saw a paunchy man on a corner laughing out loud to himself—not crazy, just happy, and I commented, "Look at that man, Claude...with nothing to do. He's the brightest face we've seen all week. Are we looking for a man who laughs at his own isolation? Does a man like that go visit with his friends? Or does he just keep walking by himself?"

To which Claude replied, "They say he laughed when a man who betrayed him shit his pants, begging and blubbering for mercy just before he shot his face off."

Or there was the day we stopped to eat our lunch in a square downtown and were sharing the bench with a plump account-executive type who had his nose buried in a biography of Marilyn Monroe. I observed, "People are so endomorphic, aren't they, Claude? They live off the insides of other people. Whoever dreamed up Public Enemy Number One? I think our Jacques Normand would be more likely to run away from the writers, not the law."

All Claude could say was, "Uh-huh. He beat one journalist almost to death and left him out in a cave in the woods to die because he didn't like the man's stories about him."

It was true. Claude had his facts right and he was alert to the ways of the criminal element, but he saw it all in a completely different way.

And my people. Claude had no idea.

We were in a café interviewing Koko Salassian, an Armenian ex-pat who functioned as a sort of talent agent, a man who knew where to phone to find a killer. I held certain liens—an unequivocal photograph of Koko eating lunch with an Italian who was wanted for gunning down six members of a local group who had presumed the city's hashish market was a free one—and so Koko was one of my people. He had been highly useful, and he was fun too. Like me, he had a beloved cat and we could talk around the most sensitive subjects by continuing to make our ongoing plans to bring my Piaf and his Charles together for a meal someday.

"This man, Koko," showing the face, "a proven expert in the field."

"This man is French..." he mused, showing no hint, edging toward it in his usual way.

"Quite so."

Then he suggested, "What about *foie gras*?" in that grave Armenian accent which I did enjoy. "My wife brings this *foie gras* home from her sister's farm up in the Vosges and my petit Charles...well, I have to tell you, Inspector, he adores it. With a bit of champagne in the bowl to loosen it up... Superb!"

I had to tell him, "The champagne would be a nice touch, but Piaf's stomach is too delicate for such a rich treat, I'm afraid."

"Ah. Well then, just a sliver...as an appetizer, before we move on to *la tête de saumon*!"

"Just a sliver, Koko." We clinked our glasses.

"This man liked champagne," said Claude in a voice designed to wreck the magic of the moment.

Koko smiled a bright smile. "And did he have a cat, *monsieur?*"

"No, but he hated slimebags who wasted time."

"Is that a fact?"

Claude leaned across the table and tightened Koko's tie for him. "Yes. That's a fact."

Koko rose from the table. I had to blush as I looked up at him. "Koko…?"

Bewildered, insulted! he shrugged at me and left. I couldn't blame him. My people have come to expect subtlety and manners. Claude was definitely cramping my style. Because our way in could only be through the public. We would have to finesse the public. You always have to. And even Koko was a member of the public. So was a chubby bicycle thief.

Claude was oblivious. Yet all the while he wanted to talk. Get close—partners, right? Sure.

"You live alone?"

"Does it matter?" I knew he already knew.

"More fun by yourself then?"

"Mmm."

"Same with me… Done your test?" To be a Commissaire. Every Inspector with ambitions has to study for it, and on her own time.

"All taken care of. I'm ready whenever they are."

"Same with me."

Soon, to avoid answering his questions, I started asking him about himself.

Out of Paris, 19th Arrondissement: you get off the *périphérique* at either Porte des Lilas or Porte de Bagnolet, somewhere called rue Henri-Poincaré, after a mathematician who developed a non-Euclidian theory of forms. (Claude had looked him up—said he had a face like our Commissaire's: round, and with that same, rather stubborn thing in the mouth and eyes.) I'd never come across it on any of my visits but could see it when he described a two-bedroom apartment on the seventh of twelve floors, a courtyard, women leading dogs along the curb in the mornings, the mother and father with a *tabac* two corners away which they almost never left, a brother, younger, good at computers, who'd found himself a niche in the insurance industry. For fun? Claude reminisced about the bars over in the 17th. I had been there. It's where you're supposed to go and I knew what kind of fun he was talking about. Claude gushed, "I could've sat on the same stool as Jaki Normand. Strange, isn't it? Like he said. Fate…"

Fate courtesy of Louis Moreau—who was not stuck in a car, searching aimlessly.

"I'm starting to think this Anne-Marie is our better bet, Claude."

"Well, he has a history of some pretty wild women," opined my trusty assistant, with that unwaveringly grim awe.

I was growing sick of it—because it wasn't helping us at all. And there is a certain voice that lives close to my heart and reacts when it feels it must. I trust it, so I let it. "What exactly is a wild woman, Claude? That's always been a tricky one for me. Tell me about wild women, then we'll go find one."

He must have heard it—the bite—because he backed away; barely glanced at me with his wobbling eyes by way of response, then looked straight at the road in front of him.

It stuck in my craw. "I'll tell you what," I continued—Mean? Yes, quite probably, but I was having some real trouble with patience—"my friend back home, Désirée, every morning she got up at five o'clock and wrote her poetry before going to see her shrink at seven-thirty, before going to work at nine. And you know what? Désirée could have an orgasm on demand. She just told her lovers to grab her hips before they were going to come and so would she, right on cue, no problem. Oh *oui*, that Désirée was the wildest woman I ever knew. But do you think she would qualify for a place in the life of Jaki Normand? Eh, Claude? Talk to me! This is what we have to figure out!"

"We used to have a dog named Désirée," he mumbled, scratching at his scalp. "Such a stupid thing…she got loose and went to sleep on a warm spot in the middle of the road one night in summer and was killed."

Which sent me away again, inside myself, staring out the window as we turned another corner. When the anger subsided there was guilt. Always that bit of guilt whenever I let loose. True, any cop worth her medal has to have at least a nodding acquaintance with guilt. But Désirée, whom I had not seen for ten years, had been my friend. I had admired Désirée. I had no business telling these things to the likes of Claude. I sighed. "Perhaps poor Myriam will twig to this Anne-Marie."

"Poor Myriam?"

One of my people. She lived in one of the decrepit buildings on the east side, and for drug-related matters she was someone I sometimes went to see.

Walking up the putrid stairs and entering the dilapidated hallway, I cautioned, "Try to be nice, Claude. This place can be a gold mine if you do it right."

Addicts only run if you scare them. There were three grey guys camped in the hall, on the floor in front of a door. They did not appear too worried about the two visitors, but I knew that with one false move, they would literally be crawling up the walls. And through them: escape routes, from room to room, from floor to floor, an amazing labyrinth they had tapped into and now shared with the rats and the roaches. So I silently insisted Claude smile as we carefully stepped around these lolling neighbours, and called quietly as I knocked on her door. "Hello Myriam…it's Aliette. Are you alone?"

"*Oui, oui…entrez!*"

She was in the little kitchenette, blouse hanging loose like a vest. This had happened before. I had walked in on her *flagrant délit* one day when she was with a client, as she liked to call them. Again I could not help being spooked by the sight of her breasts, still young and full, the only part of her that looked like her age—twenty-two—and not like her habit. I had made it my small crusade to always urge Myriam to go for a blood test, and try to get exercise. She was doing her cooking and ignored us till she had finished the operation.

A spoonful of the drug, a drop or two of boiling water, a burning match held under the spoon to cause the reaction; it crystallized into a lump, which she rolled onto the table. Then she cut a smaller chunk from the lump and placed it on the pin-pricked tinfoil covering a coffee cup, lit another match, lifted cup to mouth and breathed in the smoke that would kill her—but not today. Myriam threw her head

back and moved her neck around. Her eyes opened, closed; she sighed.
She cut herself another small piece. "Yes?"

"Anne-Marie—who used to go with a Swiss dealer...Alain?...
who got shot?"

Myriam thought about it. "I'm going to name my baby Anne-
Marie."

I was patient with Myriam. There was no point in not being.
"What about this man?" I showed her Jacques Normand. She seemed
to smile. "Take your time."

Claude took his eyes off her body—began to peruse the place.
Empty matchbooks and cigarette packs were gathered in small piles
around a stained easy chair facing a radio. Small paper bags (Mars Bar
size) lay randomly on the filthy rug. An unfathomable mess of clothes
was clumped on the bedside chair. Her bed was rumpled, the sheets
as grey as her skin. He picked something up by the phone and passed
it to me. A note, written in a schoolgirl's hand on a piece of a cigarette
box: "Call Maman on the 16th."

He glanced at his watch. I glanced at mine. The sixteenth was
today.

"So," he demanded, too suddenly, "did you call your mother?"

"Who are you?" asked Myriam.

Claude flashed his credentials.

"Well, you fuck off about my mother!" And she flung her spoon
at him.

Claude ducked and drew his pistol.

"*Merde!*" she yelled; then twice more, louder, sharper: "*Merde...!
Merde!*"

I tried to intervene. "Myriam...stop it! He's only my assistant...
Put your gun away, Claude, for God's sake!"

But it was too late. Once Myriam was out of control, the whole
place went with her. Footsteps could be heard rushing in the hall, and
hurried dragging sounds in the ceiling above us.

"I'm only your assistant. Thanks! Thanks a lot," he whined as we
drove off. "I'm an Inspector and I really wish you'd treat me like one.
People have certain styles, and where I come from—"

"This is my case, Claude..."

He rolled his eyes, petulant.

"...and I really wish that you would try to get on board and do like I do."

"Like you do? You saw what she was doing and you chatted on like you'd stopped by to borrow a cup of sugar!"

"Do you want me to beat her up for being the way she is? The law can come and get her any time it wants to... We have a man to find. You have to nurture your contacts, Claude. People!—it's all a case ever really is... Sorry if that's not the way you do it against the gangs."

"Only trying to make something happen, Inspector." Surly, asking for a comeback shot.

I obliged. "It's odd...all these years, I never really took you for the tough kind."

His ears went red—didn't like that one. "I want something to happen, all right!"

"Well, so do I."

But it hadn't. Three weeks into the search and we were getting absolutely nowhere.

5

A MODEL MAN

Perhaps there was some fate involved in this case after all. Or luck. Something that kept me from asking that Claude be removed (until it was too late). Because, in a way, I was deflected off Claude— off the wall of his little sensibility and into the heart of the matter. You could even say Claude Néon broke it for me. Wide open? By no means. Only that Claude's way of seeing it finally led me to a first clear glimpse of mine.

During those first futile weeks of the hunt for Jacques Normand, Claude was cloddish, no doubt. Yes, he had learned to be a cop just as I had and was acting on that training. And yes, there are some basic ways of proceeding. But it's the environment, the context of a case, that will shape your actions. It's the same in any job. So you can be angry with a man like Claude. Or (if you're not careful) you can even find yourself feeling sorry for Claude and all the others (still far too many!) like him—the way they get themselves locked into a point of view and just turn away. What you ought to do is learn from their reactions.

We had nothing—except a growing disregard for each other. He was disappointing me at every turn. And I know Inspector Aliette Nouvelle was not the cop he had thought she was. Much less the woman. The blow-up at Myriam's and my lecture really burned Claude's thin-skinned ass. But it didn't stop there. It couldn't stop there.

No, we stopped at a tailor's shop instead. Gilles Vétois, *Vêtements Pour Hommes*. I had decided we should seek out any people within the area whose names corresponded with the outlaw's known aliases. There was lots on this aspect of Le Grand Jacques in the official file. More than one prison psychologist had suggested that because the man his father had been had failed to inform the developing qualities of Jacques the boy, he had never had a true father figure and so had been "outside his body" for the better part of his life. Whatever that was supposed to mean. When it came to the criminal mind, I had learned to take the mental health experts with a grain of salt. Yet the facts bore it out: he'd had fourteen different aliases, stolen, forged and imaginary, attached to his name. He was a natural at costumes and disguises and they had enabled him steal millions of francs.

Jacques Naude, André Baron, Paul Toul, Paul Tourel, Bruno Bondiguel, Jacques Vétois, Gérard Lenoir, Jean-Claude Quémeraye, Bernard Lambert, Robert Blot, André Chabeyre, Jacques Granielit, Roger Dablanc, Henri Vangier. I said, "Names, Claude! So individual, much more so than faces when you think about it, with all the memories and hopes attached to them, all the connections both in the present and back through time… Look at your name Claude Néon. There's meaning there, and it goes far deeper than your face."

He replied, "Right," maybe sensing that I was extending him the benefit of the doubt on that idea.

Thus we stopped at a tailor's in the rue Gambetta.

Claude turned to me. "May I ask what you're thinking about now? The name in the file is Jacques Vétois. My own humble and completely discarded research called up the actual *carte d'identité*. He lived in a different city, he was a fireman by trade, and he looked nothing like that guy!"

A thin and dapper man—who had to be pushing sixty—peered calmly at us from his doorstep.

But the name was there; and, "A name can resonate, Claude. We have to try some different things here. We need some people on our side."

Getting out of the car, he said, "It's your case." Meaning, he was not going to fight it any more. Meaning he would wait till they kicked me off it, then do it his way. In the meantime—like a good assistant—he went around and opened my door.

"*Merci*, Claude." I handed him the Wanted poster. "You lead," I said. "What do I know about buying a suit?"

He nodded. For a while now, Claude Néon had been wondering what I knew about anything. But he took the poster and approached Monsieur Vétois. He flashed his medal and showed the outlaw—face, name, vital statistics—all the information now; why not? "Seen this one?"

Up close, the tailor was tall and gangly, standing half a head taller than myself. Could've been Claude's pa. He rubbed his temple and seemed to study the thing in a way so few had bothered to do. "Well," shaking his head, "it's not the Jacques Normand I used to know."

I admit, my heart skipped a beat.

"You know him?" said Claude. And his eyes were bouncing horribly in their sockets again, the way I'd noticed they tended to do when he was excited. It was an unfortunate tic that made some people defensive and I had mentioned this. Now I tapped an eyelid when Claude glanced my way, prompting him to stay calm. He over-reacted—stood there squinting at the tailor as we waited for an answer to this simple question. Poor Claude: Inspector Nouvelle was making him far too self-conscious about many things.

The tailor remained unperturbed. He handed back the poster and told us, "He used to come in here for his suits. All the way from Paris. Safer, I guess. But that was years ago…before they caught him the first time. He's been in and out twice more I hear," pausing till Claude's terse nod confirmed this. "I wonder how he's keeping? Used to be a real beauty, that Jaki Normand."

Claude perused Jacques Normand's face with a puzzled sigh before letting him curl back up. "Doesn't look like much of a beauty to me."

The tailor agreed. "No. Absolutely. Not according to that…Who would look twice at him?" This was directed at me. I shrugged—not me, *monsieur*; and with a neutral smile deflected the energy back toward my colleague. The tailor took this cue. Leaning closer to Claude's tightened eyes, he said, "But at one time the man really knew how to put himself together. I cut some fine cloth for Jacques Normand…lots of it. And it worked. Some of the most spectacular women you've ever seen." He whistled to punctuate the point. Claude blushed and his Adam's apple dipped in his throat like a turkey's. The tailor deferred to me again, smiling like a man who's proud of his craft and knows exactly what it's meant for. He kept this smile as he ushered us into his shop.

There was another awkward pause as Claude seemed to wait for me to say something. But he was in the lead. I folded my arms and turned my attention to the tailor's selection of ties. Behind me, Claude said—with an odd diffidence I had not yet heard—"So show me something Jacques Normand would have liked."

"Of course," replied the tailor, pulling out his measuring tape as he guided him toward his rack. Presenting a sleeve for Claude's inspection, he said, not indiscreetly although we both knew that I could hear, "This one is pure wool. Jaki once remarked that one particular lady, a Marie-Hélène I believe it was, enjoyed the feeling of a pure wool-covered knee pushing firmly but with a gentle rhythm against the pure wool-covered areas of her body. He said it held its press beautifully under the slightly soggy atmosphere that this activity would induce... You can never go wrong with pure wool, *monsieur*. And this light check is appropriate almost any time of the year."

Which, I felt an urge to add, was something a man at Claude's salary level would do well to keep in mind. But I did not, because this was clearly between Claude and the tailor.

They moved on to the next selection, a stubbly Harris tweed, a foresty russet colour dappled with tiny gold knots and needle points of crimson; sturdy, aristocratic. "Itchy," remarked Claude, upon sampling the texture.

"Oh, we line it with soft silk," assured Monsieur Vétois. "Feel how strong it is, and elemental. Women relate to materials, *monsieur*, always remember that. Jacques Normand once told me how he planned to go on an autumn day to the cliffs above the Meuse with a woman by the name of Marie-Thérèse... How he was going to make love to her on the rocks with only a coat such as this one between the soft bottom of this Marie-Thérèse and the hard stone, with the grey sky overhead and the forests and fields behind. He said it would be perfect for such a day... I wonder if he ever did it?"

I heard Claude ask, "What about the pants?" And yes, as I tested the stretch in a pair of argyle socks, I admit to thinking momentarily of Aliette Nouvelle's own soft bottom. How could I not?

"The pants he would roll up and use for a pillow," said the tailor. It seemed Claude wanted that one. The tailor had to free Claude's hand from this miraculous material before guiding him a bit further down the line to a lightweight Italian silk: beige, with a hint of olive. "For the summer," said the tailor. "For those warm nights. Pure silk. Wear this, and she won't wear anything underneath. You'll wear the silk for both of you... Jacques used to come in here and almost weep as he remembered a certain Marie-Lynne and the silk. You see, Monsieur Inspector, silk creates a mirror effect. Multiple mirrors. This silk is like the inside of a woman's leg. As you caress the inside of her leg, and she caresses your leg or your arm, or anywhere that this wonderful silk happens to cover your body... well, it's as if she feels herself. And she loves that feeling, *monsieur*, believe me. Believe Jaki Normand."

The tailor took a step back. Claude closed his eyes and felt the silk.

I nodded to the tailor and withdrew. Claude did not need further distractions. As I was shutting the door to his shop I overheard the tailor observe, "Nice girl." I did not catch Claude's reply. Whatever it may have been, I'll bet he forgot to mention that I was his boss.

Thirty minutes later he emerged with a cardboard box under one arm and a solid handshake for the tailor. "It was high time," he offered by way of an excuse for extracurricular shopping, tossing it in the back seat, then repositioning himself behind the wheel.

"Shhh..." I was listening to the radio. An open-line phone-in. Some man, his throat caked with nicotine and bile, was advancing the theory that all North Africans are scum. The moderator cut him off and gave it over to the guest, a well-known strategist from the far right who had to agree with the caller but wanted to reinforce the argument with some hard facts. Then a woman came on the line, a woman in a mood to fight. Her boyfriend was from Tunis. All her boyfriends were from Tunis and after considerable experience she had come to the conclusion that the penises of North African men were at least one-and-a-half times the size of the average domestic sample. That, plus the fact that an indigenous bend near the head of the North African cock was an absolute guarantee of ecstasy, so—

She was cut off. Her point was prurient and irrelevant, said the strategic guest.

"Unbelievable!" I declared, shutting off the radio. "Claude, you don't know how lucky you are to be out in the world, working, using your mind. These people who sit at home all day...they get so twisted. It's wrong. There's something terribly wrong infecting so many people..." He merely nodded, lips pursed very tight. "Well," I asked, smiling for the tailor as Claude steered us away, "anything?"

"Well...maybe."

"Well, what?" Gilles Vétois was waving back at me, always happy to help the police and certain I would approve of my colleague's new suit.

"Well, you heard him: he knew him...he really did know him. He used to sell him a lot of suits."

"You really believe Jacques Normand came all the way here for his suits? From him? Claude?"

Claude's head jerked violently, away from his driving—forgetting it completely. No cop likes it when a counterpart calls him a fool. He glared his contempt, his utter loss of faith in the once-cherished idea of working with the likes of me. "He knew all about him!"

I said, "He knew about you, Claude...all about Claude Néon." Trying to be gentle, and neutral—as professional as I could make it, making a real effort this time to control the raw, personal thing in my voice that was poised to lash out; I was beginning to understand it was not Claude's fault.

"Bullshit," spat Claude, slamming the steering wheel, then ripping his notepad from his pocket and flinging it in my lap. "He had a lot of girlfriends!"

"We already know that, Claude..." I smoothed my lap as I studied his notes—a not unselfconscious countermove in response to Claude's agitation. That day it happened to be my yellow-base tartan skirt, pure wool, best quality, brought home by my mother from a trip to the Isle of Skye. And, indeed, the movement of my hand seemed to calm him down, because Claude enjoyed looking at my hands. And my lap. "...But Marie-Claire, Marie-Claude, Marie-Eve, Marie-Lynne, Marie-Thérèse... Claude, none of these names are in any of the files."

"So?"

"Or the memoir."

Claude was calmer now, although still defiant. "So he covered a lot of territory, didn't he?"

"Yes, he did, Claude," handing back his note pad, "he certainly did." I let it rest there. Checking my own notes, I said, "Our next stop will be the rue Sebastian-Franck—a butcher, Bruno Bondiguel."

Claude steered us off in that direction. I stared at the side of his head as he drove. It was much too small for the size of him.

After a few blocks, Claude said, "I told the tailor we'd get back to him."

I said, "Good, Claude. Yes. Maybe we will." Then, "What kind of suit did you get?"

"Oh…" doing an illegal turn and backing us into a spot, "what did he say? Sixty percent wool, twenty percent polyester, twenty percent silk…and a lot more rumple-proof than it feels at first touch. Sort of silvery."

"Sounds nice."

"Yeah," said Claude. "I got lucky…right off the rack. Fits perfect."

We went together into the butcher's. This time I would lead.

Bruno Bondiguel was typical in that he was portly, had huge hands, a bloody apron, a small moustache in the middle of a round and florid face, and thin hair—all of it still jet black—brilliantined straight back with no concern for the more fashionable fluffy, youthful sort of look. And he doesn't need to be, I thought—this is exactly where he belongs. His eyes grew wide when he saw Jacques Normand. And I thought, *bon*, two in a row after a month of nothing. Could there really be something in a list of names? In response to the basic question he shook his head, emphatic. "Never. What would he be doing here?"

I asked, "What does any man do when he comes in here?"

"Oh…some buy a filet, others enjoy paupiette."

"Regularly?"

"Yes, regularly."

"Well then, *monsieur*…buying filet or paupiette: that's what he would be doing here." Holding up the poster once again.

"Him?"

"Why not?"

Bruno Bondiguel paused, clearly experiencing some difficulty with this line of questioning. "Well," he hemmed, "why not, indeed. But who would ever have thought it?" He leaned across his counter and perused the Wanted poster more carefully, just as the tailor had, as if trying to discern something. A missing part? Thick eyelids hooded his expression as he studied the long lost face. Yet this butcher remained a transparent man at a loose end. "You know, I always pictured him...well, not like this."

Now Claude choked on a laugh as we stood there. The butcher drew back, looked askance.

I turned. "Everything OK, Claude?"

"Mmm, fine."

"Getting this down?"

Obedient, embarrassed, he took out his pad. The butcher continued to eye Claude—taking his measure, much like the tailor had done. Men considering other men; given the context of the hero, this was the most intriguing thing.

I proceeded. "It occurs to me that perhaps this man might wear a disguise when he comes to buy his meat."

"Well, yes," concurred the butcher. "In fact it would seem not only possible, but logical."

"*D'accord, monsieur.* We begin to understand each other. So, the next possibility to explore would be whether any of the men who come in to buy their meat ever come in with a friend. Are you starting to see where I'd like to go with this, *monsieur?*"

"Oh absolutely, Inspector. But I have to tell you that in fact most men buy their meat alone."

"Alone? Always?"

"*Ben*, it's a very personal thing...eh, Claude?...*n'est-ce pas?*" Gesturing toward him as he spoke. Friendly enough; encouraging even, the gesture of a compassionate gym teacher toward a boy who's afraid to jump.

Claude's response was to shrug dully and turn away, walking over to the window, stooping to inspect a row of dusty mustard jars. You could see Claude felt caught out again. He knew I knew he went to the butcher's alone. He knew I knew that, like myself, at that particular time of his life he went everywhere alone. I suspected the butcher knew this too. To me, the butcher said, "*Et voilà.*" There it is. Then, continuing on, he told me, "No…the only man who ever enters these doors with a friend, so to speak, is a man with a curly black poodle."

"A curly black poodle?"

"Yes, and very beautiful—if I may say…"

"Yes?"

"Oh yes…" a thoughtful murmur on the part of Monsieur Bondiguel, now suddenly past the point of defensive dancing. "Which is probably why I can't for the life of me remember what this man looks like at all."

"Not like this?" I drew close to the butcher and held the Wanted poster up once more. A cue card. I sensed this man's conception of beauty was somehow cogent—far more so than the sleazy tailor's.

He stared at it, almost, it seemed, with jealous disdain. "I can't remember anything about him… She always wears a ribbon, you see."

On hearing it, I instinctively raised a hand to touch my own ribbon—the sky blue one, the same one I had worn the day we had started out on this thing. And I felt Claude's eyes upon me as I paused to assess the butcher's quiet revelation.

Inspector Néon frowned knowingly, and he asked the butcher, "Does she have a name, by any chance?"

The butcher replied, "I've never heard it, Claude."

Claude told him, "That's Inspector Néon."

"Inspector Néon," correcting himself with snide respect, daring Claude to push the issue.

I came between them. "But what does this man buy?"

"Mmm," mused the butcher, "tournedos…usually. Sometimes a roast of lamb."

"I see. Have you ever lived in Paris, *monsieur?*"

"Never even dreamed of it."

"Have you ever been robbed?"

"There's the odd lady who forgets to pay for a tube of mayonnaise or some such… But they're regulars—I let it go by. Why?"

"What about your home?"

"No—not that I know of."

"Wallet or papers never suddenly disappear?"

He shrugged as largely as he could, having no notion.

"Ever?"

"I don't know...no...can't recall. I'm sorry, but what does that have to do with—"

"What do you think you'd do if you ever saw this man," I asked. Before he could reply, I suddenly added, "—or the real one?"

"I...well, I have no idea. Probably die of fright...if he didn't kill me first." Apparently this last thought was a joke, because Bruno Bondiguel the butcher smiled: a beaming red face against the gleaming white top of his display box.

A most telling interview. We left the butcher's without having spoken the outlaw's name.

— —

It was coming up noon and Anti-Gangs had booked all available cars for the PM. I took the wheel. By that point I was well aware the reason Claude did not mind driving was because, like everything else, he could not handle the way I did it. Which is to say slowly, at a speed that suits my ruminations. Go screeching off after a chat with a man like that butcher, you're very likely to leave anything of use behind. It's one reason why I prefer walking —by myself. So I drove, nudging us through the lunch-hour swell at a measured pace. I ignored Claude's long hands pressed anxiously against the dash as if he were trapped in a decompressed compression chamber, about to burst out of his sickly skin. The Wanted poster lay open on his lap and Claude was staring at it, apparently immersed in the outlaw's face. Perhaps to save himself from exploding.

"That dull face," I ventured, glancing over, "put it out the window, Claude. Just throw it away!"

He looked up from his trance. "What do you mean?"

I said, "It's useless...in fact, it's counterproductive. The butcher put his finger right on it. Your tailor too, for that matter. There's something wrong with that face. That's exactly where our problem lies."

"I don't know about that butcher," mumbled Claude.

"What's wrong with him?" I challenged. "Salt of the earth, just like the tailor. Obviously people just don't see him like that at all—especially after all these years."

Now Claude was watching the side of my head. "How do they see him, then?"

"Well..." I was searching for some right words, gazing out the window at the parade of passing faces. "He's dark and dangerous...and daring. Sexy. Eh, Claude? All those wild women? And a little sad at the end of the day, you'd have to think as well. A very isolated kind of life."

Claude brandished the Wanted poster in his two hands, fully open like a decree or a will, holding it six inches from my eyes as I steered. As if to remind me in his subtle way that the image was both an official police and public record, issued by the Minister of the Interior of the Republic of France. He said, "He may well be sad, Inspector. And there's no doubt he's dangerous. But he's not dark or anything like that. He looks like this."

"Uh-uh..." I muttered, now preoccupied as we came to the *rond-point*, pressing only slightly on the accelerator as we entered the larger flow.

But he wanted an explanation. "What do you mean, uh-uh?"

"I mean, Claude, that the real Jacques Normand...the one we should be looking for at least..."

I left the thought dangling. It was the traffic cop who worked the circle; he was spinning his arm, urging us to hurry up. I remember this moment as major: the opening of the door at long last and so strangely—I felt lost to the world, my eyes fixed on this lovely man, watching him closely, with every aspect of my senses as we passed, and passed again because I went round that circle at least two more times. Then I watched some more in the rear-view mirror as we left it: his body in constant motion, his face etched against the noonday sun like an elemental shape. A traffic cop. My traffic cop, year in, year out, right to this very moment. Now there was a model man.

Beside me, Claude prodded, "...Yes?"

"Yes?" The traffic cop finally receded.

"The real Jacques Normand...you were saying?"

I pushed the hair back from my eyes. "The real Jacques Normand is beautiful. Obviously."

"Obviously? For God's sake. What about objectively?"

I turned. Was Inspector Claude Néon yelling at me?

"What about objectivity? The place where all sound police work begins and ends!"

Yes, very nearly yelling.

I did not reply. I was concentrating on turning us across traffic and into the lot behind our building. As we bumped across the cobblestones, Claude let it out—another chortle, short and full of disdain—as he had in the butcher's. Or better to say, it broke through his frustration.

I guided the car to rest. Set the brake. Asked him, "What's so funny, Claude?"

"Your list of names. The thought of Jacques Normand ending up as that butcher."

"Or vice-versa?"

"Even funnier..." Because Claude came from a family of shop-keepers.

I was not inclined to laugh. "He knows something."

"Like what?"

"That it's him: our Jacques—even if it's not the one he's always wanted to see. And that Anne-Marie...the poodle. She went with him after he killed the drug dealer. And they're still together. Finally, Claude, finally something concrete."

Claude, whose facetious grin was steadily hardening, said, "I think he meant a poodle."

I asked him, "Why?"

"What do you mean, why?"

I said, "Because he's a middle-aged butcher."

"Right...salt of the earth."

"Exactly," I countered, "...his way of seeing it, the kind of words he uses—I've heard much worse from his kind and they think they're being the sweetest guys around. A poodle, indeed."

Joël came out of the garage to collect the car. We got out.

"No," said Claude—and I sensed he felt he needed to win this one. "He meant a poodle... No dogs in the butcher shop. You know?"

"Come on, Claude—you know no one in France obeys that rule."

"Maybe... You have to listen to what people are saying."

"And you have to work with what you've been given, *monsieur*."

Claude held the door for me. Despite everything, Claude always held the door for me. But as I passed under his nose he whispered, "Why are you so arrogant? Why do you have to make something out of nothing? Why are you like that?"

"A poodle makes sense," I stated, and headed up the stairs.

"Forgive me," entreated my partner, his plea echoing in the stairwell, "but what the hell are you talking about?"

"I might not, Claude," I called over my shoulder, and I kept climbing the stairs. "I'm starting to not want to forgive you at all."

"I'm not being unreasonable!"

"No?" Now I stopped, waited as he came slowly up. "Claude, what is it that you want from this case?"

"Movement," he said, very deliberate and reasonable. "What do you think I want?"

I stared into Claude's uncertain eyes for several moments—and I believed him. So I smiled. "Think of it like this: you have to make a leap of faith, out of yourself..."—here I made a motion with joined fingers, undulating, a bird flying, like my mother showed me when I was little—"...like that, Claude: out of yourself and into the case. Do that and the case just might make you a happy man in spite of all your pain. Have you got that?"

He stood there wondering whether he had it.

"It might not," I continued, "but it might. So leap, Claude, leap!" My voice echoed in the stairwell. "Before you get pushed. OK?"

Claude said, "Mmm."

I said, "Sure, Claude, mmm. But all we can do is work with what we've got. Otherwise it's like turning over scattered leaves...no?"

"Mmm," he repeated. But this time it was more to say, yes...so? I'm listening. Beneath the aggravation factor, Claude did want it to work—yes he did.

And I tried again to share. "So try to project a little. Put yourself in his shoes...I mean, how clever...logical, in a negative sort of way.

He has to be with someone. But anyone else would talk. Your wild woman—sooner or later she would talk, to somebody…anybody…like a butcher, and that would ruin his cover. But someone like her—forgotten, silent, mainly loyal…like a poodle. Claude, it fits."

He bowed his wrong-sized head a moment, then confronted me. "There's just no basis—"

"But there is a basis," I said. "His out-of-print story about his sad and heroic life…" I pulled the book out of my valise and showed it to him, just the way we showed a Wanted posted to a butcher or a tailor. "He's with someone, that's certain."

Claude asked, "How do you know?"

"Because he has always been with someone." Flashing the book again, I explained it. "Claude, you give me this parade of fabulous well-tailored women called Marie-Catherine and Marie-Rose… I'm giving you back a kicked-around poodle called Anne-Marie."

He smirked. "And a beautiful man with an ugly face."

I nodded my confirmation straight at Claude's disbelief. "Incredibly beautiful." And I could see it left him sad.

No, Aliette Nouvelle was not at all what he had thought. But something in his inability to connect had touched home, had found my sympathy, and that tough thing, that insistent thing, that relentless and absolutely certain thing in my voice retreated back inside. Suddenly I could be nice again. In fact I felt I had to be; it went against my grain to leave a person feeling bitter. I told him, "Smile, Claude." If I could, he could too. "We're a team, and today I think we might actually be getting somewhere."

Yet here it was again: a man's eyes looking back into mine, saying: right…but where? What is it with you?

Fair question. What was it that made me begin to smile? Was it power? Needing to win—like Claude? What were these things that touched me and gave me direction?

To be honest, at that point in my life I was never sure. Perhaps a little more so now. Perhaps.

Nice? I don't know. But Claude did try to smile as he followed me up the stairs.

6

FACTORING IN LOVE

He had always been with someone. And if I was going to allow for the notion of beauty, I had to reconsider the fact of love. For better or worse, there is a connection—via the soul, no?

The outlaw's memoir may well have been a blueprint for petty thievery; it was also spilling over with overwrought passion. Either he was God's gift or he suffered more than most so-called overachievers from that deep-seated lack of self-esteem we keep hearing about. According to Jacques Normand, each woman in his life loved him magnificently, giving everything for him: their bodies, their souls, and most significantly, their freedom.

In Canada, Jacques and Lise, on the run, in the woods, surrounded:

"'Don't move, Normand, or you're dead!'"

"I started to get up—that instinct to run. There was a shot, and Lise threw herself in front of me, creating a shield with her body, screaming at them. 'No! no! don't shoot!'"

"I tried to push her away, but by then the cops were on us."

…And they were both on their way to jail.

Then Lise's final words before they were separated: "I'm with you to death." As if she were living in a movie.

Maybe that was the simple answer; the majority were waitresses and *putes* and the like, women with limited horizons, and Jacques transported them to another world. Could it be? Could it have been worth it? For the sake of the credibility of my sex, I for one will never be able to agree. "But look at this, Piaf… 'My only thoughts were for

Lise. Her gesture of throwing herself in front of me when she saw that my life was in danger filled me passion and pity…' He wrote seven hundred love letters to his Canadian girlfriend. Seven hundred! Can you imagine?" Passion and pity. But then, he escaped and she did not.

After a run down through America into Venezuela, Jacques came back into France through England, with Nathalie, a cashier in the duty-free on the ferry from Dover to Calais. "She was sincere, but she was living a dream that risked being shattered in the most violent way. Her love for me was like that of a geisha who admires her master. For Nathalie I was the strong one, the dominant one, but also the delicate lover. And her passion was not faint; she loved me for having taught her how to be a woman and to understand pleasure in all its forms…" And she happily cooked his cassoulet while he hit banks throughout Normandy for a year and a half.

When the authorities finally twigged to the identity of the man who had no qualms about doing two banks in a single day within a few blocks of each other, he did the noble thing and cut her loose. "Nathalie loved me with a passionate love, and the Trouville job [a bank manager with two holes in his belly, a wild chase that left three cops in hospital] made me into a sort of Superman in her eyes. It took a lot of patience to bring her back to reality, to tell her what had to happen. 'Listen, my girl, you and I were great together, but if you stay with me your life won't be worth a *sou*. It's certain the cops have been ordered to shoot me on sight. I don't want you to be there the day the bullets start to fly.'"

Then he returned to Paris and became mythological over the course of three and half years, before Louis Moreau used a captured member of one of his gangs (who would die within a week of Jacques' second escape) to locate and finally trap him. The Public Enemy entered La Santé in May of '78 in the company of the same Joyce who had inspired his first killing. Four years later Jacques made a dramatic run from his hearing at the Palace of Justice in Trouville, holding a gendarme's gun to the head of the presiding judge. A year after that, this letter was waiting for him when they put him back in his cell:

"My love… If my eyes stream with tears as I write it is because I have held them back for so long and today they are freed by the joy of knowing you are alive—I, who have trembled with fear for your life and with the sadness that enfolds my life in knowing that you are once more a prisoner of these walls. It is more than four years that my body has been trapped in this place. I pay, and will continue to pay, I know. But if this, more than my own hateful deeds, is the price of loving you, then my punishment is easy. Knowing you were in danger each and every day of our separation has been a cross for me to bear. I live for you and through you. Your dying would have separated me from your destiny and I would not have survived. Each time the radio told of another shoot-out I had to turn it off, so afraid I was of hearing the worst. You could never imagine this suffering. And it was worse knowing you were in the arms of other women. [Included among these would have been Cécile and Francine.] But they had only your body. My love, I know that your heart was reserved for me. For us, nothing will ever change. You have to understand what you did for me. I have suffered with you and I have suffered for you, and when, under a mistral of caresses your lips fill me with the tempest of your passion, you make a permanent spring bloom in all the seasons of my heart. If you were to drink my tears you would receive again, and always, my heart's pardon. You have earned it. You are the only man I will ever love and respect completely. My lips rest on yours. Let them speak. They have so many things to say. Let them conjugate the verb to love in the past, in the present and in the future that will be ours one day."

Incredible! But there it was on page 643. Who could ever imagine writing such a letter? "Piaf, if I ever wrote a letter like that to you or any other object of my affection, you would think I had lost it, *n'est-ce pas*? I mean, there would definitely be something not right with Aliette…"

Even more disconcerting was Jacques' commentary on Joyce's note: "She hadn't changed. Still the force of character. No bullshit— only love. And after all that time. It costs a lot to be the woman of a man like Jacques Normand. The law has a fear of women who really love…" I don't know if you could call it fear, but I did have some trouble sleeping, trying to fathom it.

And none of Jacques Normand's masks or public posturing could stop him from falling into the kind of love that makes a man want to marry. And not with a *pute* from the bars, but a quiet girl he

met on the beach in Spain. Although Marisa did not make it onto
Jacques' dedication list, it was through his brief chapter on this
woman and that passage of his life that I found myself edging into a
corner of the hero's domain that truly intrigued.

That he could write, "She was purity and beauty, the incarnation
of my opposite…" and yet sit by, more amused than amazed at her
credulity as his lawyer (Annie, *le Maître*) convinced her that his secret
life "away" (time in jail!) was really quite a noble one, that her Jacques
in fact worked for the Secret Service "…because it was impossible for
me to tell her the truth and her imagination did the rest. She looked
at me with this admiration. She believed she was the wife of James
Bond. I preferred to leave her with her illusions." This was disturbing.
What kind of man, this hero, to marry—and then to live at such a
drastic remove?

He wrote: "The one and only thing that can change a professional is love. Only the love of my wife could ever change me. But this
love was not strong enough to hold me. I was fooling myself and reality
would have its due. I was in love with action. Against this mistress,
Marisa could do nothing."

And when he grew weary of the charade he told her, "You're
starting to break my balls with all these questions. If you're too stupid
to have figured it out by now, you never will. The money, I go to look
for it…understand? I'm a thief! I live off the harvests of the bourgeois!"
(Yes, Claude, a bit poetic.) "I love the girls and the bistros and I just
don't need all your shit!"

Marisa told him, "Jacques…I'm a poor wretch to love the likes
of you." Indeed.

Jacques analyzed it thus: "I could find only one explanation for
this contradiction between the sensitive lover and the killer: I was
living two parallel lives." (No, *Maître*, not too deep.)

⸺   ⸺

Joyce Daigrepont was transported from Paris, accompanied by
a lawyer and a guard. Joyce was just finishing up a quiet fifteen years
in jail. Her hair was the same platinum tone it had been in Jacques'
home movies but the sparkle was long gone from her eyes.

I asked her, "What was it like working with Jacques Normand?"

"The money was good. Everything else got to be a pain…too serious. No breathing room. I liked him better when I first met him."

"That was?"

"Around Clichy right at the beginning. He was just a boy who wanted to be a man. I showed him a couple of ways of being a man."

"You were a prostitute."

"Jaki never called me that…"

"And you worked with him…"

"Ten years later, when we were together."

"Did you admire him?"

She shrugged. "He helped me and he was nice."

"How?"

"Well, back in Clichy…he helped me get away from an asshole who was trying to run my life."

"He killed that man."

She shrugged again and looked at her lawyer for a moment. "One day the guy was no longer around. I was happy to never see him again. I didn't ask where he went."

"What about Jacques: do you wonder where he went?"

"No…he could've gone anywhere."

"Do you miss him?"

"No, not any more."

"Did you love him?"

"Love," said Joyce, and scratched under her nose. "Sometimes, I think I did… With Jaki, everything like that was only sometimes."

"But you wrote this?" I showed her the letter on page 643.

"Mmm," perusing as if it were physics, "yes, I did. One of the guards helped me. It was in another life…" handing back the book.

"Do you have any idea where he might be?"

"Dead…he has to be dead."

"Why does he have to be dead?"

"I would have heard from him."

"Did he ever speak of coming to these parts? Switzerland?"

"No…he loved Paris…if he got his hands on jewellery there were Swiss he knew who could fence it. But we never went there."

"The way he tells it…" showing Joyce the face on the back of the memoir, "he more or less accepted the inevitability of running full speed into a violent death. Can you tell me more about that part of him?"

"Well," she said with a tired sigh, "…he wasn't selling flowers, was he? But I wouldn't know… I never read this… Yes, far too serious some days… Me, I'm more of a magazine reader."

I left it there, thanked Joyce and sent her away with her guardians and Claude, who was free to continue the interview if he felt like it.

7

REFOCUSING

Over the course of the next two weeks there was a string of petty burglaries perpetrated upon the property of individuals, all with names (*de famille*) conforming to Jacques Normand's recorded aliases. These came up to me via the diligent Commissaire Duque of the Urban Police, whose office was directly below that of my own Commissaire Moreau of the *Police Judiciaire*. He had been requested to send us all B&E's of a certain profile as they came to his attention. It was a favour more than anything, the discrete message being: investigate by all means—business as usual; but we would be interested in copies. "Why" was not Commissaire Duque's concern. Obviously we were on the lookout for someone. Luckily Duque was the kind of career cop who assumes that others in other departments know their business and the limits thereof. He was far too busy to spend time worrying about it. I doubt he knew they were coming to me.

Of course there are dozens of minor break-and-enters in any mid-sized city within any two-week period and it can usually be readily determined that the thief was more interested in cash or fencibles than a name. But those names kept popping up. Getting somewhere? A breakthrough? When some of them began to be repeated…and then again, I had to deduce provocation. It seemed I had pressed a button. Jacques Normand, or someone, was responding to our quiet visits to a butcher, a tailor—and these other very basic citizens.

André Baron
Robert Blot

Bruno Bondiguel
André Chabeyre
Roger Dablanc
Jacques Granielit
Bernard Lambert
Gérard Lenoir
Jacques Naude
Jean-Claude Quémeraye
Paul Toul
Paul Tourel
Henri Vangier
Jacques Vétois

Norbert Naude was a news addict, supine in front of his television for the better part of each night. Jean-Fréderic Lenoir prayed often and fervently in the course of an evening. Lise Baron was a lesbian, and a very popular one. The six possible men called Lambert were all observed in quiet family settings, as were seven Tourel brothers and one David Dablanc. When I wasn't looking, all these people lost small amounts of cash.

Three Quémeraye families suffered losses. But none claimed a waiter—the profession noted on Normand's false papers—nor any other likely candidate for an ex-Public Enemy amongst their ranks. Simple introductions confirmed they were neither the sort nor the body type.

The local Vangiers were an elderly couple who could barely climb the stairs to their apartment, let alone in the sort of window the thief had used in robbing them and the others.

There was no one by the name of Chabeyre in the prefecture. Nor Blot; the closest Robert Blot the computer came up with was a retired mailman living in a trailer down in the Midi.

The lie of the girlfriends sold to Claude prompted me to follow the tailor, Gilles Vétois, one night—to Myriam on a street corner. Sad; but the man had his alibi regarding the two break-ins that same evening—at the Toul residence (Marc-André, a worker at the Peugeot plant) and at the Granielit health food store (its proprietor a tiny hobbit-haired woman called Sylvie).

Claude was placed on a night shift for as many evenings as it took to establish that Bruno Bondiguel, the butcher, the only man in the city whose actual name fit perfectly over the bogus one, went off regularly to some art class in a building on the edge of the business district. (Minor revelation: our Commissaire, Louis Moreau, also attended. But this was not included in either my or Claude's first notes.)

In due course, both the butcher's and tailor's homes were also hit.

It was a minor crime wave. I interviewed each suspect who became in turn, each victim; but none of it—the secrets, obsessions, the material losses—meant much except that it was indeed a game of odds and without the help of reinforcements I was not likely to be anywhere near the right place at the right time. I wrote a formal letter to Gérard Richand, the Instructing Judge assigned to the matter, requesting visual surveillance in the butcher's and a listening post, at least, in the tailor's. What I was really looking for was a polite way around Louis Moreau.

Gérard responded by calling me down to the Palace of Justice for a word.

Time had stained the *Palais* a sort of mildew colour. Each of the thirty stone steps leading up to the door was a smooth wave of foot-sized dents, indicative of the weighty matters people carried with them in and out. The inner quadrangle was still, thankfully, inaccessible to cars, and tranquil, with benches under spreading plane trees and well-tended beds of annuals—a civilized spot for a person to sit and contemplate her testimony in any of the courtrooms on the first and second floors. The third floor, comprising the offices of the court, is called the Parquet. The learned trial judges had the largest, plushest rooms at the north end; the *Procureur* and his team occupied the street side; the Instructing Judges had the south end. Gérard's was the head office. At thirty-six, he was the first amongst my peers to shoot ahead and take over. One could do that in a smaller prefecture like ours. Michel Souviron was just thirty-three, but everyone was watching for him to become *Procureur*—Chief Prosecutor—any time now. And I had been having my own small premonitions of better things to come...

The Judge of Instruction—who will not appear in any subsequent trial or inquest except through a written report—is a balance, a buffer between the so-called "forces of justice" in a system which can get far too complex but which was made to be fair. If the PJ Commissaire (Louis Moreau) personally requests an inquiry, he will deal directly with the *Procureur*, who will assign it to the senior J. of I. That is protocol, unwritten but well observed. The impartial J. of I. literally instructs the police regarding their rights of procedure as they apply to things such as enter-and-search, evidence, the holding and interrogating of a suspected person. The J. of I. may also conduct independent investigations of implicated persons and relevant circumstances. And he (or she) may confer with the Proc's office before making decisions while going about a *reconstitution du crime*, in order to ensure that these decisions will not be wrong ones, which the defence could later use. This structure and its underpinning rules can often become antagonistic—when, for example, a cop begins pushing a certain theory about a crime and the J. of I. believes said cop will need much more if she expects her idea to fly, or when the Proc appears driven by certain political pressures. So the J. of I. can be no one's friend. The relationship is a strictly formal one all round and may never become personal, in terms of, say, sharing a strategy.

Which always made my visits slightly ironic because Gérard had been my first boyfriend in this city. Six months, seven years ago: a young inspector, a new magistrate, both fresh out of their respective academies, strangers together in an uninspiring place and sharing an attitude toward their work. People had called it "serious"—the attitude, that is. And yes: there were some wonderful nights leading to sex during which the inspector would present a case (hypothetical, of course) with a twist or a hole and the grinning magistrate would tell her how to get there. I would always attempt to sneak through the side door or try to land, with a daring leap of my own nascent logic, right in the middle of the perpetration. *Flagrant délit*—gotcha! Then it would be his problem: the skewed legal bits. Mmm, fun for a while, until I became distracted by his fastidious ways in the bathroom, the kitchen and even the bed. (Gérard would always cheerfully admit, after a Suze and soda or two, to being highly rules-oriented.) Of course I had my own tics to worry about. And I had been definite in not wanting a baby at that point in my life. Six months had been plenty. Our careers had continued on and we remained friendly.

All to say that in the instance of Inspector Nouvelle and *le Juge* Richand, it was formal, but not quite.

"So. A bit of a slow beginning."

"A bit, yes. Although it seems I've reached him now. This name thing. I've got him playing. Or maybe I've got him angry." Then I added, "If it's even him."

Two things before I'd even opened my notes:

"You mustn't go anywhere near the family."

"I know. She told me."

"She's sued so many people who've tried to get in on his life, it's become a kind of cottage industry...last thing we need around here."

"I don't want to see her. Has nothing to do with her."

"Glad you see it that way." One done with; over the page to the next. "And there were words from Paris about bringing people all this way—three people, actually...for less than five minutes?"

"Nothing to do with her, either. Sorry..." Five minutes with dreary Joyce? Was that all? Well, how long does it take? When face to face, a cop should never assume she has a lot of time. I wasn't one to abuse the public purse, Gérard knew that. "...I had to find out."

"Perfectly reasonable," holding up the transcript, adjusting his glasses, chin dropping further, "but how do you know?"

"She wasn't interested."

"Not interested." Gérard repeated it in his stolid way, then waited for elaboration.

I looked out Gérard's window. Down in the quad the annuals were just beginning to show their delicate faces. Beyond the boundary of the city skyline the foothills of the Vosges lay solemn beneath fierce April clouds. "Well," turning back to my host, "she was interested, obviously—but she didn't care. She had no idea about the real man. Horrible to say it, but I didn't really expect her to. But you never know from a photo, do you?"

"No, you never do... And who's the real man then?"

I took the memoir out of my case and placed it front of him, trusting he would realize I would not present something so unprofessional in the presence of any other judge. "It seems our Jacques has something of a death wish, but he's not dead... Maybe. There's the hero thing, for sure; he paints himself as an outlaw who hates the system, loves honour and loyalty, and will step into the ring for a woman like our Joyce. Gérard, that Jacques Normand is gone and long forgotten. I've only found two people who even remember him. This man's gone back to the time before all that; or maybe it's the far end of a Public Enemy's learning curve. Lord knows. But this man hides his face. Those roles and disguises. Not at all the kind to come crashing back into style, guns all ablaze... Nowhere near the beautiful hero we once knew."

I paused and glanced again into the sylvan distance. Gérard considered the face of Jacques Normand. With a smile for Gérard, I asked, "What do you think of all this?"

"Well..." hearing my full question—quite out of line, but, "it's unsolved, isn't it?"

"Yes. But do we need to solve it?"

"It would be nice to solve it."

Wouldn't it, though? Come on, Gérard—talk to me!

He read me clearly. He always did. But there was the formal line that lay between us. Yes, and his interests were different now, weren't they?—out of the ranks and into management, you might say. With two children too, exactly as he'd wanted. I had shaken *madame*'s hand once or twice. "He has every right to look into it," he said of Louis Moreau. "It's a huge thing, if it could be accomplished. He's done all the digging and piecing together for you. It's bizarre, but we've all seen it."

"Mmm." Moreau's theory. Moreau's collected facts.

Gérard said, "I don't know if we have a need, but we do have a duty."

"And Michel?" Souviron, Proc-Apparent, he was doing everything now but sign his name.

"Everyone's hoping for you, Inspector."

"I gather it's only a Preliminary if people are worried about train tickets and phone calls...but no one's actually said so, and I would have thought—"

If police aren't sure a crime has been committed and are working to prove so, it's deemed a Preliminary Inquiry. If proof is presented, or someone is caught red-handed (*flagrant délit*), then you are into a Rogatory Commission: more important, bigger budget. Either way, you still have a J. of I. watching your moves, deciding how and if the game will continue.

"Absolutely," said Gérard, "...but not exactly. We have banks and kidnappings, five or possibly six murders, all of it well documented, lots of it left outstanding... Talking Rogatory, to be sure..."

"Then?"

"This one's special."

"Oh, God..."

"There's the time factor. And the fact that none of it occurred in this prefecture. And the fact that these more recent break-in's, as interesting as they may be, are still really only circumstantial at best and, when coupled with the first two reasons, not the kind of thing—"

"What about the drug dealer?"

"Impossible to prove at this point. We don't really want that one."

"You might need it."

"Not if it's him."

"Hmm." The legal background suddenly took on relief. They did not give a damn about the shooting of a Swiss pusher called Alain; that was just a scented shred to set me on the track. Neither did I, but..."it's not even a Preliminary, is it?"

"It's special." Repeated with the kind of studious patience for which his kind were noted.

Which brought us to my request.

"No, nothing electronic. Sorry."

"Come on, Gérard..."

"We need permission. You know that."

"I could get it. That butcher would—"

"A complaint would be the end." Sternly now, laying down the law such as it was in a case that had been deemed to be special. "There is no subtle way we could negotiate it...not with these questions you've been asking."

"What questions am I supposed to be asking?"

"I'm not going to tell you how to do your job," he said, easing back into the friendly ex-lovers' mode—easier to tell me from there that he had no idea how to progress in this thing, "...and I'll trust you to do the same for me, all right?"

"What about a man?"

"You've got a man, Inspector. You want to leave him in front of the butcher's shop for a week, I suppose we could say yes..." Even a *planque*, a stakeout—Claude across the street, leaning against a lamppost in his new suit, hiding behind the sports section—requires the approval of the J. of I. "But if every cop...or even five cops, knew we were looking for him, the press would find out... He'd read it...and he'd leave. You know that."

I considered Gérard. That day, facing him as he sat there growing into his role as a solid pillar—he too had put on some weight and it was almost funny—he looked a lot like the spruced up Jacques Normand on the back of the memoir: with the same dark hair, still growing well, waving softly back; and with his now-sagging cheeks. Could Gérard respond to imagined beauty? The love factor? Might he rewrite an inspector's mandate to somehow accommodate these basic things? "I need some help, *monsieur*. Another way in. I mean...he's not who we think he is."

"Yes," admitted *le Juge* Richand, staring dumbly as he flipped through my notes such as they were: pages of streets covered, a poodle with ribbons, this cluster of echoes that had been his names. "What does your boss say?"

I shrugged and bent my smile in a certain way: Oh, Gérard, don't play games.

"He knows the man," he said, handing back my pad.

"Some men change," I told him.

"Your boss believes in you," he assured me. "Keep going, Inspector. Do what you can."

So, forget crime-fighting technology or another partner; add "special." The ones meant to be on my side were hedging their bets.

Then Commissaire Duque sent me an eyewitness from a break-in at the Lamberts. The Lamberts were number three on my surveillance route; it was the second time they'd been hit. Their home was in the north end, just a few blocks, in fact, from Commissaire Moreau's residence, where both the Gérard Richands and the Michel Souvirons had recently bought. Monsieur Lambert was a notary who had inherited a family concern; Madame had degrees in both business and chemical engineering from our own Haute Étude and was apparently making a name in the local potash industry. So there was lots more to take if a thief had a mind to: a German sound system of highest quality, a set of interesting Louis XV chairs, several small but worthwhile oils. But (again) it was only rings from a drawer, and cash from various purses and pockets—another clean and professional job in all respects. This time they allowed me to talk to their child, who, like the Scottish nanny and two fine German Shepherds, was still recovering from a liberal dose of chloroform.

Seven years old, well cared for, and with the kernel of a story: "It was two Pierrots," he told me, "like in the picture on my wall... They came in like the moon, so quiet... One of them had curly hair under his hat, like Lucy (the lady from the Hebrides) but black." Thank you. I took this small thing back to the car, and at the end of another day, back home. Two Pierrots. I could work with two Pierrots.

What I (still) do is go for a run. Twice around the park, about a 5k. An excellent means of refocusing the mind. Refocus is all you can do when it's "special."

You take the case, such as it exists, and as you run you lay it into your breathing pattern. A hunch. An image. A list of names, say; or a "poodle"; or some few honest words behind the maudlin claptrap that is a forgotten man's memoir. Linked by rhythmic breathing, these elements will bind together like a chain. And like a meditation, they connect with the heartbeat. It's a physical thing. And the endorphins, those chemicals that gather in the brain, are physical as well. More so; their effect exceeds the body. Running is something I believe in. It always serves to bring a word, a fact, a face, a feeling into the realm of soul. A good run helps make soul out of almost nothing. They don't teach you this at the Academy, but you can start from soul if you need to. In fact I would recommend it for anything, from murder right through to love.

(And if you go for a run, you can have a beer.)

As I ran a picture formed:

The one with the curly black hair like Lucy's would be her. His Anne-Marie. They work in silence. She's handing up tools: gloves, a crowbar, cheesecloth, chloroform. But no guns. She tells him... *We don't need the guns any more. Just the hats, the faces, the dreamy suits.* There's no fuss coming back from him on that score. He's thinking, *Good girl. You happy? It has to be better than Bruzi's screaming...his slapping you around. Anything has to be better than that. We have this thing we do together now. We're good. It gets us all we really need. Doesn't it...Anne-Marie?*

And a hand up to the ledge—there!

What's it been—two, three years now? I don't even know. Maybe that's a good sign—for once. You don't remind me of my wife at all. Shhh!...Nice house. Nice kid. Nice dogs...Pew! au-pair here could do with a bath.

They steal.

Then he asks her, before they sleep, *Why would anyone want to come digging me up? What good would it do?*

She doesn't answer. Can't help him. Doesn't really care. That's his question—his problem, ever since she has known him. She's only there because he's beautiful. Difficult but gorgeous. For better or worse, the man behind the mask is her man.

And he holds her for a while, gently playing with her curls until she sleeps. Then he stares at his wall. (So, where could his wall be?)

The dialogue is all his own:

What does anybody need my life for? I'm a thief.

You're Jacques Normand.

No...just a thief.

Yes. Le Grand Jacques; and always will be...Show her!

Show her? What? ...What was that?

Passing the pond, there were distractions to a detective's meditation. People lying in the evening grass, entwined. I tried not to stare as I ran by them, back to Piaf, a beer, my bed—another night by myself with his book.

- 8 -

A GENERIC MADAME

First question: Why the need, at this late date, with all that skill, for the disguises? A clown suit; the need to make it seem like play. For love? For the sake of her affection? To disguise the fact of what he was, after all these years? Or was the clown act, in all its variations, an act of contempt? Even hatred? Had the false names become ironic bullets, a way to wage a bitter fight with what he had been? Was his life still something far beyond her—beyond the simple existence of a loyal Anne-Marie, something that was down on paper, official, part of history?

Bitter history.

If you happen to be a Greek hero, chances are good at least one of your parents will be a god or a goddess. But Jacques Normand was solidly French, and his parents were the perpetually struggling proprietors of a small printing business. "I looked at them, always on the edge with their affairs: business, house, the next vacation; never quite there, never quite happy. It was always later...maybe next year, as if they were still waiting for life to begin. I heard this too many times. And I saw my friends and peers going off to apprenticeships at the post office, the corner garage or with the notaries. None of it had anything to do with my dreams. I decided my life would be different."

Different? He climbed through a neighbour's window one long-weekend, looking for something to steal. Pretty normal. Depressingly normal.

What kind of man was lying in wait for this not-very-original boy? The kind who attracts some not-very-original women, for one thing. And the kind who revels in the romance of it all—when he's winning: "In the heat of the action I was always out in front. My true friends could always count on me. I never missed a rendezvous. I was waging a personal war in a milieu that had its own laws and codes, where pride forbade weakness and guts masked any suffering."

One highlight (the previous reader had marked it well) was described on page 581. Betrayed, surrounded, his (third) capture imminent, Jacques prepares to open the door, cajoling the cop on the other side, telling him to rest easy; his gun is on the floor, all he holds at that fateful moment are wine glasses and a bottle of champagne.

"'What kind of guarantee do I have of that, Jacques?'"

"'My word...nothing but my word.'"

"He came in. Here were two men, face to face: no longer the Public Enemy and the Chief of Anti-Gangs, but two hardened fighters who knew the value a man's word. Moreau had taken a huge risk, but this was a man who understood the importance of such a gesture to a man like myself: I always respected an honest opponent. In the street one of us—the less quick—would have lost his life. But Moreau made this move to secure my arrest: his life against the word of a killer. The ordinary citizen could never comprehend it...I mean the one sitting on his ass and never risking it: would he ever be able to understand this moment between two men?"

Great stuff!

This was also the kind of man who forsakes his code and gives in to pitiful bitterness when he has lost. Jacques spent a total of seven years in French custody, two more in a jail in Canada. He wrote a poem about it, "Le Cachot" (Isolation Cell):

"*Oui, madame*
It turns and turns, with a thousand steps leading nowhere,
In a concrete world where the bars are trees flowering
with despair, inhuman, shrinking, without tomorrows...
its nourishment slid through a grill along the floor
...a bowl of water, so he may drink.
He is alone...without sun
Without even his shadow.
Unfaithful companion...she left,

Refusing to be a slave of the living-dead.
It turns, it turns, and will continue
Until the day when he is beaten for good and falls to the ground
like a wounded animal, and after having made his singular cry
is left to die,
To find his only freedom in death.
Do I see a tear…!
But why be sad?
And you say to me, "poor dog."
That's a mistake.
It is a man, *madame.*
He is imprisoned.
A man whom your peers have condemned so utterly
In the name of your Justice
In the name of Freedom."
Dated, September '83, La Santé— "Where I exist so meagrely
that I am barely a man."
(We pause here to dab our eyes.)

And yet it seemed true that when locked up, Jacques Normand
did indeed look for and perhaps find a grain of life's truth.

No, not in poetry. It was his daughter—La Puce. The little girl,
four or five, had come to visit him in the company of his mother. (Her
own, the woeful Marisa, refused to go.) He wrote: "I was hoping to
become my daughter's friend, someone she could confide in, say
anything and everything to, and trust with her deepest problems. And
I wanted to tell her everything, the truth about myself, so our love
would not be based on any lies or games… I needed that to have a
reason to live. I had run out of space. Locked up, at the far end of all
his suffering, a man cannot bear a lifetime of isolation. A man cannot
accept his own spiritual destruction."

It was in consideration of passages such as this that a detective's
natural antipathy relented somewhat. I believed him. I sat there with
him, waiting for her next visit.

Because sympathy always snagged me. Someone like Claude
would likely say it was my weak spot. I say it helped me feel the man
I was seeking. I was trying to reach him and somewhere there had to

be a connection, if not through his career, all but forgotten on the street, then down deeper, through the heart of the actual man. This problem with love. This enduring need, despite violence, cruelty and ruination.

A daughter's deepest problems: in their own way, they served the same purpose as a *pute*'s turgid passion and a waitress's body flung in the line of fire. It seemed everywhere this man of action had gone *dans les traces marginales* there was a woman, and he had needed everything from her and more. Even the prison, La Santé, was described as "a leprous old woman." Horrible, yet as a frame of reference for a bitter man in an isolation cell, it fit.

Then another door was left open and he went through it, leaving everything, including his reason to live. No words, written or otherwise, since that day. The symbol of freedom had disappeared. I looked again at the publisher's pious hype on the jacket flap. *Freedom*: the major theme. Was freedom more important than love—for his little girl, if not his wife? if not those others, all so emptied of their biggest hopes? How were those two reconciled in this hero's story?

Claude was right: cops are trained professionals, and when face to face with smashed bodies, people grieving, broken property and lost years, professional objectivity is indeed the only thing that will get you through. But we cops are also singular souls and a story is a very private thing. I was starting to hear his words. Not the flamboyant *grande histoire* as presented by my Commissaire; nor the grizzly gangster script Claude Néon seemed to be hearing. History was lighter than the spring air. Violence was nowhere evident. Not in this case. The current case. There was something more subtle happening, and those evenings, alone in my room, I listened in my own way. I was starting to feel close, as if I might know him. *Could* know him. As if I could be the generic *Madame* to whom he'd addressed his mournful verse.

But my Commissaire was less than thrilled with my progress.

"Love? Inspector, love was where he stopped to regroup, to set his sights. No, with Jaki, it's action. *Le beau geste*, that's always been the defining thing. And a bit of a shame," he mused with a dry laugh, "to be wandering around talking to babies and butchers. It's not exactly the way we used to do it."

I knew: word of honour, two happy warriors sipping champagne. I took the memoir from my valise and placed it on his desk. To
show respect. "The names were his hiding place."

"Yes, and the masks too."

"I had to do something and—"

"And maybe it's worked. No one's taking that away from you.
They do talk, don't they, those butchers and tailors?" Chuckling
again: more of a snort this time, exuding a veteran's ironic rue. "A
butcher's shop. Yes, indeed—that could light a fire. Maybe you've
managed to touch on something here."

Hmm...positive reinforcement. We all need it. "I'm having trouble," I told him, flatly—no whining. "That gap you were talking about.
Too much history. It's something I've never had to deal with before."

"Still, I'm surprised it's taken you this long to realize that by-the-
book police work is not enough to draw Jaki Normand out into the
light. You were given this case because you bring something different
to this profession of ours, that instinctual spin which has served you
so well. I think you're not working to your strength."

"I've nothing to draw him out with," I said. We both knew that
wherever there is instinct, there is solid evidence to give it form:
human flesh and/or other tangible materials. "And he's watching. He
must be. It's as if he were right around the corner."

"He always was. It was to his advantage."

"If you could help me push Gérard Richand for the camera...or
leak something to the press...a small thing, to get his attention. It
could be oblique. History...an anniversary. Maybe there's a bit of that
spark left. The one that used to love to tease the press?"

Louis Moreau gazed past me as he shook his head. "No cameras,
no leaks. An anniversary... I like that one... But no, Gérard's right.
It's a fine line we're treading here."

I thought, *une petite annonce* then, from the inspector in charge
of the case—a one-line want ad: Dear Jacques, could we meet
(privately) and talk about this? I said, "More men?"

"Maybe. When the time comes."

"But how can I anticipate? It's too wide open. He's baiting
me...some kind of game. I don't know. But it's obvious. A team of
gendarmes to cover my list?"

"Too delicate for an army, Inspector. We miss once and he's gone. Worse...he'll go, but the matter is bound to come out. I won't let you ruin my reputation on a bungled dragnet." Always frank about it; it was one of the things one admired about him. "This has to be tight. One-on-one...and Claude Néon for protection," now shrugging as if apologising, "simply because of the physical fact which, as we know, is also an historical one."

The physical fact. Louis Moreau was committed to this lethal Enemy. I looked away, uncomfortable in a way I had never been before in his presence. OK, he's your man, I thought, help me!

I was feeling an itch. Suddenly I was longing to be home in my bath

The Commissaire perused my notes yet again. Then, "How's he doing, by the way? Néon."

"Has trouble with patience."

"Yes..." Nodding back down into the file.

Patience: so important, what with the way time works in this business. Good police work means connecting moments of emotion and revelation with logic and fact; it can be a long process. That would be the nut of his speech. I knew he knew I didn't want or need to hear it. I blurted, "But how did he know? The names? He picked it right out and came straight back at me."

My Commissaire shrugged. "I don't know...the butcher or the tailor chatting in the street like you suggest. Or," with a thoughtful tilt of the head, "...maybe he's been checking on me."

"Would he?"

"Wouldn't put it past him... Revenge played a big part."

"I thought you had this...this relationship."

"Oh...well, for one hour, one day. It's not as if we were bosom friends. The rest of the time I was chasing him down, and for all I was worth I might say. In the end, he got past me...but I took his life away. Yes, it is possible he has heard and come straight to sources looking to make sure. Putting on a gendarme's hat, walking in as bold as Mata Hari, peeking in my desk...Jacques would do something like that."

And the possibility was making Louis Moreau gaze into space again, smiling like a boy at the back of the class.

"So?" I enquired after a polite interval. It brought him back to earth.

"So, now bear with it," he said. "He's the one who has something to prove. If you're right, Jaki Normand will keep pushing. It'll get big, I guarantee it. Far bigger than this name game, if that's what it is. Then we'll have the kind of context we need in order to do what needs to be done. It's not as if we don't have bait as well..." The phone rang. He picked it up, "...*Oui*," and listening, made a note. "*Merci*." He rang off. "Our friend Commissaire Duque is being very attentive in support of our cause."

"Could he know what it is?"

"Not from me he couldn't."

He handed me an address—downtown, the boutiques.

– 9 –

AN ARTFUL PLAY

Not exactly a break-and-enter. And not a boutique either, but a chic bistro where shoppers could go when they ran out of steam. Wanda. Hefty prices belied the nifty name. Nice inside though: muted afternoon light from a wall-sized window at the back looking over a tiny square with a willow and a bench. I had never had the pleasure.

After a cursory inspection of the scene we were standing on the front steps, trying to obtain useful information. We had an angry woman (whom I vaguely knew) in the company of her boyfriend. Sadly, although good-looking to the point of distraction, he was too full of wine to be much help... And we had a large maître d', arrogance incarnate and sorely aggrieved. The woman gave us a story about a ruined meal, ill-mannered staff, the worst service! and a wallet which had ended up in the maître d's pocket. (Nothing missing from inside it.) The maître d' snarled bitterly about a pair of unruly guests—but especially her, shrieking, weeping, distracting everyone; what was worse, his prized corkscrew, normally occupying the place where the hysterical woman's wallet was found, had gone missing. Wanda's man (whose name did not fit my list) swore he was the object of a cruel joke, clearly designed to ruin his good name. A waiter—unknown, planted by his rival across the square, surely!—had taken advantage of the busy afternoon trade to slip in, provoke the woman and create a chaotic scene during which the corkscrew was stolen and the wallet planted on himself.

"Describe this chaotic scene."

An accomplice. Just when the woman seemed to be regaining her self-control, this poodlish creature, done up like a buttermaid, suddenly emerged from under their table. The whole place erupted as she dashed for the door. Before leaving she'd lifted a medium-rare steak straight from the plate of one his most loyal clients, alas, obviously no longer. A complete disaster.

A poodlish creature for an accomplice. I asked the obvious question.

"No—of course not. Not allowed. What do think I'm running here?"

"People ever want to?"

"Some people try, with their wretched little Fifi or Lulu tucked under their arms. I send them away. We have standards."

"And it's against the law," mentioned Claude, but whether for the benefit of this man or myself was left unclear.

The maître d' curled his thick lip: thanks, cretin.

Claude, demonstrating poise, let it go by.

I asked, "Anyone try today?"

He realized something. "Yes."

"Recognize them?"

"No...looked like a shoe salesman on his day off."

"What did you do?"

"Sent them packing."

"Angry?"

"I really couldn't be bothered to look."

The unknown waiter had been noted by Commissaire Duque's gendarme. Thus I waved a photo under the victim's nose, a police file shot of a handcuffed man in waiter's livery, slightly mussed at that point, being led away from a smashed up room. "Could this be the waiter, *monsieur*? Think carefully, please..."

The maître d' barely glanced, dismissing it as he would a dealer of less than magnificent vegetables. "He looked like a waiter. They all look the same to me. Leave me alone. I've told you everything I know. I'm innocent. Ask her. Nobody has asked her anything..."

Our other victim. The woman in question was at the foot of the steps, wrapped in the arms of her lover, kissing him, languorous as she moved her fingers through his falling hair. She was whispering that she forgave him, that she loved him—she really did. In fact we had asked her as much as the situation called for; it was not the most serious of crimes. But complex was another matter. Complexity of a more personal, semi-literary kind intimated by Jacques Normand. Tapping the lucky lady on the shoulder, I told her politely, "I have one more question."

Lucky? Oh yes: from her cherry red patent slingbacks to the ivory comb in the back of her hennaed hair, she was absolutely right, blending as perfectly with the hard new architecture as with the softening four o'clock sky.

One Charlotte Barthès. Around my age. I knew her from a distance, from the gym in the *Centre Communautaire du Quartier* at the top of the park, a place to run in January. She wrote articles for *Le Soir*'s Sunday edition, always about the most interesting people, and had recently published a book about taking control of one's life. *Du sexe au salaire; comment bien faire.* I had read the excerpted chapter: how oral sex is the bottom line, and money is a simple matter of always having an option to go with your smile. The things she was saying were not wrong, but still, it was the kind of book a certain kind of person feels she'd better buy, and this Charlotte was the kind of woman who seems born to service that sort of feeling. She was one of those who just knew how to do it all, including having a lovely—and certainly rich—man like this one, fawning, who might even be the father of her absolutely beautiful child. (And a hell of a smoocher! Claude gaped at the sight and I stared a little too. It had been a long time.) In fact it was a wonder Charlotte was still here on the edge of the world and not in Paris. But here she was, and somehow she had ended up spilling tears over her stylish lunch.

"Was this the man who served you?" Proffering the photo.

She untangled herself from their embrace and looked at it. On to other things now, but this had to be cleared up; she would be no one's fool. "If you could call it that," she sniffed.

"Yes?"

"More or less."

"Do you know him?"

A well-practised sort of smile asked, Are you kidding?

"Ever seen him before?"

"No." The same kind of eyes said, Please go do your work.

Mine said, I will, *madame*—but first I'll just run it by your bleary boyfriend here.

Eric was his name and he nodded carefully. I could see he was a man in the process of trying to smooth a serious breach. He obediently confirmed everything, and added, "…He said to call him J.-C." Then, an incautious afterthought: "I still think he was too nice to do something like that." Charlotte Barthès did not like to hear that at all; poor Eric had stepped right back into it.

"Thanks." I smiled. "We'll do our best to sort this out." Then we left them—on the verge of another fight.

Walking north, back to the quarter and the Commissariat (there had been no chance of a car on such short notice), I tried to see it:

"Why would he steal a simple wallet and then try to frame an equally simple maître d' like that one?" The clownish game-player we'd been presented with? Or someone else, from the darker reaches? Angry. Deeply angry. "Work with me here, Claude… We have to try to get a clearer sense of the overall picture."

"He wouldn't let him in his precious *resto*."

"That's all? What would he have against that woman?"

"Maybe he's in love with her."

"She doesn't know him from a hole in the ground."

"Doesn't matter…only adds fuel, doesn't it?"

True enough. But I said, before I'd even thought it, "I don't think he'd fall in love with her. Not his type. Too flashy…too risky."

Claude accepted that and moved on. "Maybe he's in love with him."

"With the maître d'…?"

"Thinking more along the lines of that fish, Eric."

"Doesn't fit." Uh-uh…not at all. Not Jacques.

Claude's next question could only be, "Who the hell really knows anything about love?"

"Mmm."

We walked. A good pace; the endorphins came. We passed people—people together, in the streets, in doorways, and in the cafés, all types, and all of them were immersed in each other. Even the ones who were being ignored or doing the ignoring had this thing they could call a relationship. As my eyes travelled past them, I was thinking hard about the Jacques Normand I was coming to know, off hiding somewhere, *emmerdé*...bothered? no, more than that: pissed off—at love.

But he has this Anne-Marie who is nothing if not faithful and he wants to make something out of it. He wants to rejoin the world, if not for his sake, then hers. So they approach the fine bistro. Not looking for trouble, just some fun. A change from hiding.

A shoe salesman on his day off? Sure—a certain Henri Vangier, on my list of fourteen names: an artisan from Toulouse who did piecework for the footwear industry, whose papers had come into Jacques' possession on one of his many flights into Spain. Not quite a salesman; I gave him slicked-down hair, a frumpy business suit; the glasses guarantee no one will detect the fire in his eyes. They check Wanda's menu on the wall. It's not Maxim's, but it looks all right.

The maître d', glistening silver corkscrew dangling from a fob chain which he twirls like a happy barker, stands in their way. "Sorry...not like that, I'm afraid—it's highly inappropriate. Your friend, I mean."

Who doesn't even have a frumpy suit to wear. Why would she? They never go anywhere—except through windows. Ah. Well, she can live without lunch at Wanda's.

But Jacques is piqued by this rejection. And the more so as Charlotte Barthès comes striding up with her handsome man in tow and breezes past them without a glance—not even a look!—to be ushered inside with a bow and seated at a table by the celebrated window.

Once was a time when Jacques Normand would have thought nothing of uncorking that fat man's head and forcing this selectively blind woman to look at him and remember him for the rest of her life! Now? He has come this far out into the daylight—and been hurt by it already, when all he wanted to do was eat. What to do? He has to do something. It's in his nature to hit back.

They go away. They return and enter Wanda's, this time by the employees' entrance.

Charlotte Barthès is sipping wine, watching her Eric. Pure brown eyes with silky lashes, but worried: *You keep looking around*, she notes. An accusation.

Enjoying the surroundings, muses Eric, defences dangerously down. *I like to watch the birds fly by.* Because although the man's features are as cleanly drawn as the lines on the highway, there is a haze clouding his demeanour. It's as if he has been built to blend. But can he really be blamed for being comfortable? Apparently…

Why won't you look at me? she demands.

But I have been. You're lovely.

Not good enough. *Everybody compliments me…everybody!* And who could doubt her? *Except you…who sits there staring off into space. Why is it I never get the things I need from you?* Her voice has a lofty quality. She knows what is good, and what is less than. I had heard it, in no uncertain terms; Jacques Normand would hear it too.

Eric wonders: *Why do you have to be so difficult?*

I'm not being difficult. I'm buying you lunch.

Then why don't you enjoy it? Gently. There's nothing wrong with this guy but the soft spot behind his rock solid jaw line. *And me as well?* he asks. *I love you.*

Not the way she wants. *I think we should talk about this relationship of ours…*

He sighs with resignation, stares down into his empty glass.

This is Jacques' cue. He steps forward, trim and correct, the hair still slicked down but now at a racy angle, the furtive insecurity and clerkish glasses of Henri Vangier having been replaced by the brash professionalism and pencil-thin mustache of one Jean-Claude Quémeraye, *garçon. More wine, cher monsieur?*

Thank you, says Eric.

Jacques pours, whispers something like: *Got yourself a real one there, mon ami…* The tone is just right. Friendly, from the heart for Eric, while carrying just enough for a hypersensitive woman to hear.

Eric shrugs, *Merci.* He's glad to have found a friend.

Now Jacques turns to her, offering the bottle. *And for madame?* Her response is pure ice. It's not that she's too worried about being called a "real one"; it has more to do with the idea of a conspiracy.

But Jacques is in no way cowed. Big smile: *Oh, come—it was just a simple compliment. Santé!*

She waves him off with a scowl. He goes. But the boyfriend thinks it's funny. Laughs; big mistake. From there it builds—or better to say, deteriorates. Jacques plies wine and emotional support of a sort to Eric with one hand, serves up small but telling blows to Charlotte with the other. Not too difficult to set that kind of woman going.

But what happens? I could see Charlotte, so self-contained like a perfect jar; she knows exactly who she is, but she needs flowers—no: demands them!—for the place inside. And the ex-Public Enemy—he was coming clearer: playful, angry, weirdly balanced between the two—who sees where no one else can that the splendid Charlotte might ever be so poor in spirit. But how does her wallet get from her purse to the maître d's belt? And what on earth is Anne-Marie doing under the couple's table?

I stopped. Where were we?

Inside the quarter now, in the rue Bernard Délicieux. One of the darker ones. I thought I'd been down it before, must have been. But I was feeling tired; feeling a slippery sensation inside me that was not conducive to work. If I couldn't have my bath, I wanted a beer. "I'm not getting anywhere with this, Claude… Let's sit down somewhere for a minute, all right?"

No argument. He scanned the street. In fact there was a sign overhead: Café Rembrandt.

—   —

One passed first through a small vestibule where there was a brief notice, written on paper, faded, framed under dust-caked glass. It read,

"To ornament a single piece most dearly,
'Tis best by sundry means to improvise
Accessories that deck its gist unclearly:
An artful play on art that doth surprise."

Signed, S. van Hoogstraten. It was good solid advice for detectives, low-lying Public Enemies, almost anybody.

Inside, the Rembrandt was cavernous. Not big, but spacious, with shadowy nooks where anonymous patrons could take their refreshment, and smoke and read as if sequestered in an ancient library. The low murmur could almost be seen, weaving like a pulse through shafts of afternoon sunlight that splayed down in medieval angles from a row of slot-like windows in the vaulted street-side space above the cross-beams. In and out of brightness passed a waiter, quiet and intent in the transport of his wares. The light would frame his hand for a moment, or refract through the liquids on his passing tray. Peaceful. A good place to have landed in. Claude and I each had a glass of beer.

Relaxed somewhat, I spread the file photos across the table and pressed on. "But what does he come away with, Claude? A corkscrew. A weeping woman. Mayhem...some trouble for a man who probably deserves it... Somebody's lunch. He didn't even take the money. Traded it for a corkscrew."

"If it's the truth."

"Let's say it is. That maître d' steals from the likes of her the minute she walks through his door. He doesn't need her wallet."

"Then to prove a point."

"What point?"

"That he can do it."

"Do what—put on an act, pick a pocket, do a bit of sleight of hand? Is that what he needs to keep him going?"

"No. That he can still do it: be Jacques Normand."

"Ruin things?"

"Shape things."

"Hmm." Claude was following me, even adding to the idea. That was encouraging. But a smarmy fat man selling overpriced food? Would Le Grand Jacques be bothered? I couldn't see it. No, it was her, *la belle* Charlotte, an ideal woman by current standards, a prize you might say, who had pushed him into acting. That was the challenge: the co-opting of her glory, the subversion of her discontent. It had to be something like that—the odd game that I had allowed myself to start to imagine, but which I could not quite complete.

Our present waiter—and proprietor, as it turned out—was Willem van Hoogstraten, a wiry man of indeterminate age on account of a delicate complexion, milk white till he smiled, at which point his cheeks turned a raspberry colour. His sharp nose flattening to the slightest of bulbs at its tip, golden grey eyes, skeptical lips and wavy straw blond hair placed him north of here; but he spoke only rudimentary Dutch and was twelve generations removed from any connection to the one who had lent his intriguing verse to the entrance way.

"Nice place," I said, as he served our second beer.

"Might as well be. It's my world. Live right up stairs in back…" gesturing with chin raised up into the light, the colour rising around the corners of his mouth again.

I liked him—he was everything the maître d' at Wanda's wasn't. "This man ever pass through, working or otherwise?" Turning the shot to face him.

Willem bent over it. "Can't say he has. The outfit hasn't been around for years. But look at him: whoever he is, he's not really a waiter."

"No…" I agreed, sipping, aware once more of the slippery feeling inside me and accepting the sense of suspension that was coming on. The walk, the beer, this atmosphere; it did not take much.

"This one—he's in all the time." His finger tapped the face of a younger Louis Moreau, in the background of the bullet-spattered tableau, but clearly there, overseeing the (temporary) arrest of Jacques Normand. Then, looking up with the kind of jolt most people registered when it finally occurred, it was natural for Willem van Hoogstraten to ask, "Who are you, anyway?"

Claude wordlessly flashed his medal for the benefit of our host.

I, believing in the value of public relations, offered my hand. "Inspector Aliette Nouvelle, *Police Judiciaire*… A regular, you say?"

"Here this morning."

"Who with?" None of my business, but impossible not to ask.

"Just Georgette."

"Georgette?"

"The artist's model." Withdrawing.

"I see." I had never heard of any Georgette. Louis Moreau had always seemed the prototypical bachelor-for-life, the kind who claimed to be married to his work. But he was a healthy one, and with a certain look in his eye when he thought he wasn't being observed. "The Commissaire and an artist's model—imagine that."

"Maybe I saw her," offered Claude, "up at the front of that room—the art class he goes to with that butcher."

"Maybe… What's she like?"

"Oh, you know—old, kind of silvery…"

"How old?"

"Don't know…about as old as the Commissaire, I'd guess."

"Yes…what else? Was he there…our bogus waiter?"

"Didn't get too close. She's standing there without clothes on. One just doesn't go walking in."

"No, one wouldn't."

"Everybody has a lover except me," he muttered, unthrilled by the wonder of our discovery.

I could have said, Well neither do I, but I suspected it was something else he already knew about me and I had to continue to be careful on that front. Admittedly, Claude's initial ardour had cooled; sitting in a car the way we'd been is a marriage of sorts. But at that quiet moment I suppose I was feeling sympathetic, among other things. "Don't worry, Claude," giving him a pat on the shoulder as I poured down the rest of my beer, "one day you'll start to shine. Come on," standing, leaving money—my treat; "we'd better go."

For a moment Claude seemed to soften. It must have been the place. I knew he wanted to stay right there and have another. But he stood, perfunctory, and followed me back out into the street.

10

CROSS-PURPOSES

For me, the Billings Method of Natural Family Planning was two things. Practically speaking, it was a way of keeping track and keeping safe without pills, foams, plastic devices, invasive examination or surgical procedures. On a deeper level, it was a barometer of hope. Thus it was later that evening, as I sat on the toilet and meditated, the way people do, on the nature of the things inside myself, that I had to confront the loneliness in my life. For as I now saw in the tiny glob of stringy, stretchy stuff between my fingers, the slippery sensation I had been experiencing since the afternoon had been a portent of the "S" mucus, designated by Doctors J. and L. Billings and their collaborator Professor Odeblad as essential for the survival and transport of sperm. I was fertile again—perhaps only for a day. If I could be with someone that night, I might conceive.

It was more than loneliness. It was the cross-purposes which my life presented.

No, I had no lover, but my commitment usually cushioned it. I mean my commitment to my work. Instead of someone's touch, I had my instincts, that combination of sense and imagination, and I believed they were on track, guiding me, however slowly, on this frustrating investigation.

Yet here was my body, also operating just as it was meant to.

The Billings Method is not about science or mechanics; it is about communication, for people who are responsible to and for each other, for those who know each other well. I liked to think that the way I lived my life was a way of communicating, that there was always someone who was affected, and who affected me. I believed it was the only way to live, and all the more so when one lived alone.

Alone with a job to do.

And so I believed I was communicating.

But with whom—reading, studying, intuiting and reconstructing as I moved to bridge the gap that was the case?

With Claude Néon? Barely.

Gérard Richand? Yes, but officially, dryly.

Louis Moreau, then? Yes and no. There was an emotional conflict of interest occurring on both our parts, and why pretend otherwise?

I had to believe it was the man on the other side of the gap. And admit that I was imagining sitting down with Jacques Normand at the kitchen table. I could hear myself going through the Billings Method material with him. I saw myself sharing a glass of beer, explaining the slippery sensation. Of course it is dangerous—often fatal—for a cop to fall in love with a theory. But this was no theory. It was an image, bonding with the physical part of me. Not despite myself, but because that was the way I was. Committed. And because I could not ignore my body.

As I shuffled out of the bathroom, there was a yowl from outside. The porch door was open, the curtain was jumping with each gust of April wind. I looked out. "Piaf...?"

Another plaintive yowl, directly above me.

April evenings, in our part of the world, it's still quite chilly. The northeastern breeze caused the hem of my nightgown to play on the tops of my feet as I stepped outside. I looked up to find him hunkered in the eavestrough, stuck there and scared, a full moon, white and patient, observing. I reached up. "*Viens*...jump! Jump into my arms! Come on..."

No.

I had to climb onto the railing and hold the eave with one hand as I stretched for him. He backed away. We stared at each other. "Piaf...*viens ici, mon petit*. It's all right." I got a good grip, stretched still further and with just a little bit more of a long, long reach, I had him tucked under my arm like a loaf of bread as I jumped back down to the balcony. Stepping back inside I tossed him on my bed, pulled the door shut and climbed in under the covers.

As he crawled into my arms I asked, "But how did you get up there? I bet the moon got into your old blood, my Piaf... Or did you dream there was food on the roof? Such a romantic cat... Oh yes, you are!" A scratch and a hug, then I threw him on the floor.

Then I pulled the blanket to my chin and stared at my notes, casting my thoughts back to the scene of that afternoon's odd performance at the *resto* called Wanda, but too soon found myself drifting, so inevitable, back to awareness of my own transitory condition and the itch that was its calling card. I could not stop wondering: what does he feel like? What kind of face does he show in the dark? To his Anne-Marie? Her face was a problem too, because it was getting in the way of the thing that was developing between myself and the outlaw: our communication. Cross-purposes were making concentration difficult and the respite of fantasy impossible. That night I fell asleep with my hand between my legs and dreamed a likely ending to the strange affair downtown:

There is that fabulous Charlotte woman. A soft haze obscures the face of Eric, her beautiful man. Mmm...*le beau* Eric looks a little like a certain traffic cop; while the lady is putting her hands across the table, wanting to be touched. But her lover does not reach back. And why would he? Look! Under the table—

A poodlish buttermaid is hiding there, reclining against the lover's knee, nuzzling his thigh like a dream girl, a real pet, while he caresses her soft mane. A buttermaid between the legs...now there's a fantasy come true.

Up on the surface, poor Charlotte reaches a little further, with a sense that she is being left out. *Here, Eric...*

(Here, Eric! Here on the edge of France...)

While the smooth cool nose below glides along his flannel leg.

Charlotte Barthès seizes on a movement, flings the tablecloth up with the spontaneous rhythm of rage. A buttermaid!

But now with straw-blonde hair and ice-blue eyes? *Can't I get in on this?*

Sorry, Aliette—it's Anne-Marie! springing out like a champion and racing with her apron flapping, the little white buttermaid's cap jumping wildly on her raven curls like a telltale on a sprint through an afternoon squall. She helps herself to an unguarded lunch and leaves. The patrons are all struck dumb.

Hear poor Charlotte weeping.

Want to see that again, Inspector?

Mmm. Please. Chaos. Over and over. Sad. Sad...

And so full of hands: thief hands, stealing a wallet from behind the sound of despair...deft hands, doing another bit of master finger-work on the bamboozled maître d'...practised hands, opening wine somewhere with a silver corkscrew, splayed fingers working burnished metal, then lifting a glass: *Here's to your eyes!*

And here was my chance to intercede...

His voice is romantic but undefined. She is leaning forward, reaching to catch some defining thing. How to hear him? How to make him hear me?

But it's unresolved. She is still reaching—now alone, under the moonlight, wind swirling, her whole body stretching, shining and clear. Here's to your eyes...

He: somewhere near. She: so aware of moonlight illuminating her entire life!

What about that part, Inspector? Shall we see that again?

Oh, yes. Roll it back. If I can't hear him, maybe I can at least see his eyes... Straining to catch a glimpse; a sense of rolling, struggling, not with a man but a question: do your dreams mean anything at all?

They shouldn't, but they must. They do, but they can't.

Keep listening!

I will.

But his eyes, his face: this remained at the heart of it. One face, his "Wanted" face, forgotten, shabby and old; and the other face, dark and fitting perfectly against my own. It was a question of attraction. Somewhere between his life and his reputation, between the situation with Claude and the expectations back at the Commissariat, between my desire for success and this impulse surfacing through the distilling wonder of my own slow concentration, was his face: a permanent thing (if I could only see it), a portal to look through, into eternity, into the place where all fates are dreamed up and cobbled together, for as long as it takes to see.

Cross-purposes. You have to live with them. Sleep with them, too—and carry on.

— —

I confess I never did get back to Charlotte Barthès. She could only ever be a minor victim and a vague dream figure in a mystery such as this one. (Although I still do see her on occasion in the low-impact aerobics group at the gym.) Instead, I went back to my list of J. Normand aliases and for more ten days and nights played a game that I could never win, spending hours waiting in front of one place and then another, watching.

It was my case and I felt Jacques Normand was talking to me. But how?

A problem of tone. Bemused? Come, let's play a while here—it's been a long time.

Or was he spitting it out? Just who the hell are you to come looking for the likes of me?

All I could feel as I ran here, then there, inevitably too late, was: unclear Jacques, connection's fading, never find you like this. Stop the game.

And he did. The break-ins stopped.

We waited. Five days, five nights. No movement. (And, oddly, no B&E's anywhere in our town; as if he'd commanded all thieves to take a rest.) Now near the end of April: a bit rainy, but mild, even sultry of an evening. And the beginning of another cycle for me.

Then he did the bank. Things happened quickly after that.

11

RESPOND. RÉPONDRE. PONDRE.
PONDÉRER. PONDER. POND...

The gendarmes had roped off a large area and a crowd stood in the morning sun, buzzing. The main city branch of a national bank had been hit. The attraction was the hole in the wall. One great block had been removed from its place along the foundation. Blown away, you'd have to think. But there were no signs of an explosion. There were no signs of any work at all. Without even bending, a person could walk through this hole and straight into the vault. Indeed, cops and bankers and members of the press were walking in and out of the hole again and again, as if testing and confirming its existence. The Anti-Gangs group was deep in consultation with Louis Moreau. Our IJ squad (*Identité Judiciaire*)— clue finders Jean-Marc Pouliot and Charles Léger—was hard at work trying to interpret the dust.

I did not interrupt. I hung back. I acted like a guest. My investigation was "special."

I could see Claude wanted to get in on it. He was wearing his new suit and he knew all the reporters. This was his kind of situation. But Claude was on a "special assignment" with Inspector Nouvelle and it would have been out of place to try to suddenly step back onto centre stage. No one likes that and I knew (because he'd told me) that when his assignment was over, Claude wanted the boys to welcome him back to the land of the living. So he did his best to remain in the background. After testing the hole to our own satisfaction, I stayed in the vault, listening to a bank official's dry excuses: How could he know what was taken? These were safety deposit boxes that had been emptied—the most private of private property. Claude quietly followed up on the name in the band of the dusty *ouvrier*'s cap which had been found on the floor of the vault: R. Blot.

"The old guy who swept the floor," he reported, stepping back into the vault, "close to pension." Now reading from his notes, "A bulky man, but bent over, palsied, prone to hacking up the tar in the lungs. By all accounts, not at all the type to have much knowledge of bank vaults or the electronics which keep them intact... Been here for years."

When I reminded him that R. Blot was another of Jacques' old names, Claude immediately went into his devil's advocate mode. "But how could anyone wear a disguise that long? Just a doorman for the thieves is more likely. Easy to scare an old man like that and keep him on a string. Then again, who would trust a share to the likes of him? Too slow to disappear, the kind who would talk about it in his sleep. More likely conned into opening it. A hostage? I'd say in the river by now—certain."

I listened, but with half an ear. I was staring through this magnificent hole in the wall. There was something happening in the crowd.

Claude was saying, "...IJ say they're going to keep this," meaning the hat. "What do you want to do?"

Pointing, I said, "Claude, there she is..."

"Who?"

"Her." She was retreating casually from the door of a police car that had been left wide open, slipping back under the barrier and in amongst the onlookers. What did she have clamped in her jaws? It looked like a sandwich. Sleek in the obligatory black of the streets, straight and graceful under the exploding mop of black curls, she went trotting off in the direction of a side street. "You see? Down that street!"

Claude saw. And the red ribbon bouncing lightly behind her. Of course he saw. "Yes?"

I don't remember being overly dramatic about it. "After her," I commanded softly, "...quick!"

I do recall a split second of astonishment (or it may well have been defiance) as Claude looked into my eyes. Afterward —I mean after the end of everything—we agreed to put it down to his double-checking the order. Not only permitted, but prudent. But after he was certain that I meant it, he certainly did run.

The crowd noticed immediately. Something was happening. They pointed and hushed, and fell back as the detective in the spiffy suit streaked past them. They looked, but most could not see the poodle at the top of the block glance back with vague surprise as she chewed on a crusty baguette, then dart away—so quick. Faced with this amazing acceleration, Inspector Néon almost tripped over his own feet. But all eyes were on him and he knew it; he thrust out his chest and sprinted off in pursuit.

I lost sight as she ran directly north, then east, back into the heart of the quarter via the park. It did not look like Claude had much of a chance.

Then I went out into the square and pushed my way through the throng until we were face to face. She had been watching me come toward her, waiting with this cold impatience, as if I were late. "You!" I barked, pointing a finger in the manner they teach in the Psychology of Engagement elective at the Academy. Although there was no need.

"Yes, it's me," she replied. Unafraid. Certainly not about to turn and run.

"You were standing with her when I got here...I saw you."

"With who?"

"Her...!" I pointed down the street—at nothing, by that point. The woman only shrugged, the contemptuous one French people often extend to overly earnest officers of the law.

"What are you doing here?"

"Watching the fun."

That kind of answer has always irritated me. "What's fun about it?" I demanded, harsh; again, using a basic technique meant to isolate and subdue.

Another blasé shrug on her part: the fun was obvious. She changed the subject. "I like your ribbon."

I was caught off-guard. That morning I had put on a thin butterscotch-coloured strand. I had to feel it, to confirm this woman's observation. And I did so, letting my fingers trail down the nape of my neck, then around, along the line of my jaw as I tried to readjust. "Thank you," I allowed, and contemplated this woman, close up: Equine, the jaw set defiantly and had been so for many years; she appeared to be of the same vintage as Louis Moreau, but age was belied by silver hair which fell richly past her shoulders, and by a body that was still proud, trim and strong. A big woman—a good three inches taller than my five-seven. A broadness in her bearing exuded work, authority. Her complexion not too sunny, but hardy, with traces of wine along the upper cheeks. The long Bruegel-ish nose with the slightly bent turn leaving one nostril more round than the other was between patrician and peasant. Likewise, the green eyes, coolly judging, seemed to look out from some unfathomable place behind the veil of time. She wore a denim shirt and high-waisted slacks of faded army green. Chic but not rich, a democratic combination. Yet her ribbon was a most elegant morning grey.

I had no greys. "And I like yours," I said.

The woman acknowledged this with only the slightest of nods. "Who are you?"

"Georgette Duguay." Reaching into her bag for the obligatory papers.

"The artist's model?"

"*Oui, c'est moi.*"

A hard kind of voice, one which, based on our first brief words, I guessed was easily bothered by bothersome people. A gesture on my part said forget the papers.

"Inspector Nouvelle…!" The Commissaire beckoned me from inside the hole in the wall.

I looked briefly but forgot to respond. "You were with her." I was searching this Georgette's face.

"Who?"

"Inspector Nouvelle…we are waiting!"

As we both looked toward the hole in the bank I thought of the waiter in that Rembrandt Café, and Monsieur le Commissaire having his coffee there on a quieter morning. "Is he your boyfriend?"

Georgette Duguay shook her head, as if to say don't even think about asking such a question.

"Look," I said, "I know you give a drawing class…"

"*Oui*. At the Institute…upstairs. Every night at eight-thirty."

"I'm interested." Businesslike; I could be as cool as this woman.

"You're free to come along…the same as anyone."

Le Commissaire continued to wave, calling me in, my impatient master. I responded with my own wave: I would be there. But the bank was not important. Nor the money. Just the hole, and the worker's hat: this little entertainment he had left. "And how are you connected to Jacques Normand?" I asked, inquisitive, very unprofessional—truly confused.

"Who is Jacques Normand?" Blanker than the toughest tart.

So I left Georgette Duguay, the artist's model, and returned to the scene of the crime. After fascination's initial sweetness, I found myself resenting her. Here was someone else having some kind of game with me. I did not want games. I was a serious person, acting in good faith. And I knew she had been waiting to meet me.

Later, after the audience had departed, Moreau and I stood by his car, conferring. In fact it was turning into an argument.

"…But she was seen with your Georgette," I repeated.

"She's not *my* Georgette, Inspector… Have you been following me?"

"Of course not. But it's a small world, *n'est-ce pas?* Out here in this tiny corner."

"Very small indeed." He sipped his coffee, obviously perturbed.

"It came up in an interview," I offered, straightforward, absolutely no insinuation intended.

"Where?"

"A café. She seems like an interesting woman."

"Georgette?" He shrugged. "Just an artist's model."

"You draw her then?"

"That's what she's there for."

"I never knew…"

"Why would you?"

"No reason… It's just a…a surprise." I smiled a bit.

And he smiled a bit as well, as if to say no harm done. But that was all. It was none of my business. Stick to the case, Inspector.

I intended to. "But you've been seen with her, and they were seen together—watching from the barrier. And the suspect has been seen with him. Or someone a lot like her…"

"I don't know who Georgette knows. I don't see any connection or reason to—"

"For one thing, we have to consider the possibility of revenge. Like you said."

"I'm not worried."

"Even so. It's my job."

Louis Moreau agreed; that stolid nod. He finished off his coffee. He gazed into the empty cup. "This morning we have a hole in the wall of our biggest bank," he said. "I look at this hole and feel sure that it's the break we've been waiting for, that we've got to him, that he has left behind any game he may have been playing and responded at last… I look at that hole and I think this is surely the best of all possible points of re-entry upon the public stage for Le Grand Jacques Normand, barring, perhaps, a spectacular murder—although obviously no one wants to see anyone murdered… Inspector Nouvelle, I feel excited about this development. Stimulated, you might say. But here I find my investigating officer, my star inspector, fretting about some two-bit sandwich thief. Could we not perhaps at least consider the bank in passing?"

I got the message. I told him what I felt. "Anyone could walk through that hole Commissaire, absolutely anyone."

"Apparently."

"I'll be surprised if they find anything they can use in a court, or that the press can take to make a grand discovery. Even that filthy hat…" Our two IJ men and a cluster of gendarmes were still picking away, dusting, taking measurements and pictures. "Amazing bit of work, though. No argument there. I can't imagine who he did it with."

"Alone," he murmured, "…all alone."

"Yes, quite so." In the appropriate tone. I did feel the weight of what he had said. The man was my mentor. He had singled me out as if by instinct, like a mother seal locating her pup amongst a seething mass of fur, and I had no intention of undermining the professional bond. "It's a strange thought," I added, "working all night, all alone in there, finishing it so perfectly. No?"

"Mmm."

"But it's just another gesture... He's calling. It's clear we have to go to him. Maybe you could say something to the press... Maybe now?"

"No." His eyes were tightening, saying don't push this angle.

"But why?" I asked him. I had to.

"It's your case."

"Then it's me," I said. "That hole was for me. And with all respect, Commissaire, I'll deal with it."

Le Commissaire did not reply. I hung there, polite, attentive, giving him every chance to say more, but he did not appear to have any more to add. The professional gap is always disturbing, but so is it inevitable. Divergence of experience, differing methodology, and in this business, the personal element: one hunch versus another. When you are given the responsibility of the lead position, all you can do is assume respect will be accorded. The whole system depends on it. Louis Moreau's privacy and Louis Moreau's displeasure; I would take these into account.

Thinking quite specifically of respect at that moment, I peered to the end of the street and complained, "Oh...where is that Claude?"

We ended up going back to the Commissariat without him. When I got to my desk, something was not right. But what?

Reaching—my pencils were gone from their jar. Every last one.

My pencils. How could I stay organized without my pencils? The question played straight to the notion of respect. Because if I was not organized, then where was I going? Progress. It's what they want to see. One keeps track in one's own way. But without pencils to map it out for them, it can begin to collapse.

Of course I could get another pencil—that was not the point.

It was the violation of an inspector's system.

Who would do that? Claude, getting his little revenge? It was definitely possible. I had observed his look upon receiving my order to chase down the poodle. And I knew well that if he weren't allowed to love me, he could easily hate me; the more so if he thought I was discarding his ideas, walking past his little parries of form and logic, and giving him orders he could not abide. It would not be the first time that had happened.

Pathological was the only word for it, and the grim evidence was mounting. A man had killed fourteen women in an engineering school in Canada—had just mowed them down on an insanely cool walk through the halls and classrooms one frozen night, then killed himself. His goodbye letter claimed their presence meant his exclusion, humiliation, sorrow. In New York, a gang of boys out "wilding" fell upon a woman jogging in a park, raped and almost tore her apart. During their trial they complained that they were being discriminated against. Or one could leave the headlines and look at Jane Goodall's chimps: the males wilfully wasted away through sheer melancholy and self-neglect while in the throes of despondency over losses of power and the female affection that apparently goes with it. Regression, revenge and self-destruction; it was like an ongoing battle against the dawning of civilized day. With these facts in mind, I could easily see Claude Néon, feeling maligned, grabbing my pencils and breaking them in one angry snap.

But—walking the length of the hall to double-check—Claude was not yet back from his chase.

Returning to my chair, I opened my drawer and there was a ribbon. A blue, sky blue, lying there. As I contemplated it I felt an increasingly rocky jostling in the region of my heart. This ribbon belonged in my room. It had no right or reason to be where it was at that moment. Its context was an aberration. Forbidden. And irresistible. I concentrated on breathing evenly. With the edge of my finger I wiped away the dampness that was spreading across my brow. I remember I tamped the edge of my finger with my thumb. When I picked the ribbon up, I held it away from me. It lay across my hand like a dead bird as I went wandering down the stairs and back out into the street.

— —

Just a ribbon. The simplest of adornments. Timeless. As old as colour. Designed to enhance, to allude; the flag that signals beauty, a metaphor for the things non-apparent, the knowledge that cannot be known or shared, except in privacy.

Running home, thinking pure pornography (which I'm not averse to, but it's usually according to my own schedule)—licking,

sucking, biting, hands full, hands crawling, rolling, engulfed by heat
and breathless from penetration from every angle. I felt I would run
my legs right off, as if they were not serving me well and so should be
left behind. Then, standing in the doorway of my room: I had been
so dry and focused when I'd walked out of it that morning; now, here
I was, soaked and bewildered as I walked back through.

I saw my ribbons, all of them hanging there by the mirror. All
of them but one. The colours seemed animated, a kaleidoscope of hues
and I felt the exhausting pounding in my chest transmuted to
exhilarating panic, thrilling me with expectation as it went flooding
through my heart. Sitting on my bed, I began to sort, to organize, to
put them all into their proper place. Not thinking and no longer
worried; I was savouring every nuance of his presence, making it last.

When all my ribbons were arranged across the bedspread—all
but one—like an army in divisions, I got up and stepped back from
the display. Only then did I take the blue from my pocket. Before
placing it, I felt it between my fingers, rubbed it against my cheek…and
I breathed in the atmosphere of my room. Because it was still partly
his atmosphere, partly his room. Then I placed it, between the royal
and the robin's egg. That was its place, it belonged right there; it had
left its home and now it was back. Gathering all the ribbons into my
hands—scooping them up indiscriminately, I lay down, holding
them clumped together on my belly. I closed my eyes. Now I could
allow myself to wonder.

It's an exchange: while Aliette Nouvelle puzzles over his night's
work at the bank, Jacques looks at the line of empty beer bottles beside
the fridge, at the underwear hung to dry on the hooks and taps in the
bathroom, at the note "Garlic Press—Red" on the pad by the phone,
at her shoes, her hats and ribbons. He does not go through her
drawers—he's not the type to cry into a pair of panties or dote on the
scent of a scarf. In fact he does not touch a thing. Although he has been
tempted to read more about the Billings Method, he refuses to allow
himself to even turn over the page. He respects her. And he must be
wary. He only wants to see where she lives, feel out her environment.
In one way, it is quite routine, like staking out the bank; in another,
it is as if he were exploring for the first wonder-filled time the new
home where his spirit can come to rest.

And this cat is a good old cat. He wants to give him a second helping of breakfast, but he can't risk that either. A good scratch is as much as he can offer. But it seems to suffice. The creature lies back in his arms, luxuriating, and willingly extends its chin at the touch of his finger. Jacques wonders if the cat's mistress might have the same predilection. She will! And he'll make her boil, but first she must simmer gently.

The old cat farts.

Oooh, disgusting! He drops him back on the bed and snaps out of his reverie, aware now that he too must reek. It's the first thing a woman would notice, particularly one so finely tuned as her. Yes—taking the measure of his own secretions—it has been a long and hard night's work at the bank; he is indeed quite rank. And there is the briefest chill of panic. How ironic: he has just emptied the vault of a major bank without so much as a blink. Now here he is in a detective's bedroom, realizing he needs a bath and that she would know he had been there.

Perhaps that's good. "Hint of Jacques." He ought to patent it before someone else thinks of it, to give to Catherine Deneuve.

But he has stayed long enough in his dirty clothes. He should go. What to leave? Something more than a whiff. Ahh…a ribbon. Yes. Travel lightly. Steal a ribbon.

Selecting, touching every colour that she loves; and he finally becomes aware of his face on the old Wanted poster now tacked to her wall. Tired. Exactly as if he has been up all night.

Or for ten years.

Jacques tries to fathom it, can't stand the sight, so disappears.

I roused myself, slightly lost there in my own room with the scent of a man, and the tangy redolence of Aliette blending, infusing, enfolding it, enfolding him—still touching, tentative, dreamy, at my overheated lap. Then lifting my skirt and pawing with abandon until the tension was released. And then twice more. Then sitting there. One feels silly. One just doesn't care. Piaf watched me, alert, his senses brimming, front knees tight together, toes at the ready, enjoying each moment, I could tell. I knew he thought I was another cat.

I was having to wonder (one last time): are detectives supposed to respond this way?

It's a hard question. But basically, they are trained to size up the situation, and enter it. No?

Yes.

And the conditions will form the response.

This must be true as well.

What about heroes?

Heroes don't respond. They react. There is a difference.

Respond. *Répondre. Pondre. Pondérer. Ponder.* Pond...a face reflected, and a voice refracted.

Or: Act!

I took the rest of the day off. I went for a run through the park (by the pond). And had three beers that night with no qualms at all.

12

TRANSPOSING TO THE SINGULAR

The Commissaire sent me back for a second look at the hole in the wall and the plundered vault.

"I've been thinking about your problem—the recognition factor. Now is our moment, Inspector... But it cannot be us who breaks the news. There has to be something physical sitting in that vault—or even stolen from that vault—that is undeniably him. Something we can show the press—that they'll have to recognize. They'll start splashing his name around and he'll come out to wallow..." As he spoke he was rubbing his cheek in a compulsive way I had never seen. Worried? Or merely frustrated? In any case, not at all the cool, bold authority who had passed me the Normand file nine weeks prior. "...And please don't offer me that stupid hat."

It would not have crossed my mind to do so.

"There has to be something. There always is...there always was. A good detective can find it."

Certainly he could challenge me. And I could try to tell him again we shouldn't waste valuable time on the bank. "It's too clean, too perfect. There's nothing there. We'll never find the one who made that hole unless we get a full confession. All we can do is find him—Jacques Normand."

"Where?"

"Her." Offered straightforward and humbly, in no way wishing to antagonize.

And he could dismiss it again. "We can't afford to have good men chasing poodles, Inspector." Turning away from me then, perfunctory, to other matters. "...Bad for morale. Makes us look bad. All of us." With a quick glance back, to make sure I'd understood.

Stress: it looks worse on faces where it has never appeared before. He bent to a pile of paper work. He did not look up when I asked, "Any word of my assistant?"

"Inspector Néon has been injured—fractured his nose. We should let him rest a day."

"By all means." More than happy to let Claude rest. "Chasing the poodle?"

Now Louis Moreau looked up from his pile of papers. "On a car window."

"How horrible. Which car?"

The Commissaire's eyes dropped away once more. No comment.

The upshot, with all that had been happening, including this feeling that the delicacy of our rapport was unravelling, was a stated "yes, sir" followed by a walk to the bank. It was all I could do under the circumstances. Free of Claude, though: absent, with a fractured nose, poor man. A car window? Dubious; although later I could hear true pain through the phone line. But would I bring him soup and flowers? Not likely. I had a feeling Claude Néon's morale had a direct bearing on Louis Moreau's stress. It didn't matter; it was a relief to be on my own.

Jean-Guy Marcotte from Anti-Gangs was also back at the scene cross-referencing staff members' stories. He informed me that they had definitely used Robert Blot (or a reasonable facsimile) to gain entry to the bank. It looked like the floor-sweep had been wined and dined, then punched. (Or had he simply inserted a finger in his throat?) Vomiting on the doorstep, he had then lain in the mess caressing an empty bottle of three-franc *gros rouge*. Upon seeing this pathetic sight, the night security man's natural sympathy had overridden his professional prudence. His act of charity had left him lying under the manager's desk with a brain full of chloroform—their rather dated, but still effective, anaesthetic of choice.

Jean-Marc Pouliot from *Identité Judiciaire* was there to guide me through the technical aspects. "Once inside they put a chair on top of a desk, climb up and split some wires in the surveillance to freeze the image of an empty bank. Secure in their privacy, they walk into the open vault. And they could have walked back out in half an hour with enough wealth to disappear forever, but it seems money is not the only thing they're here for. There's this notion of a hole…"

"They." Like Jean-Guy, Jean-Marc was locked into the idea of a gang and I did not dispute it. Part of the exercise was to see if anyone might discern a single-handed Jacques Normand in the mix. But the forensics man clearly believed only "they" could have accomplished such a thing in the course of a single night. As he talked on I simply filtered it, transposing to the singular:

There are layers to work through before reaching the concrete blocks which connect to the street. He starts slowly, carefully, tracing lines in the plaster with his hammer and chisel, then cutting solid sections, placing them like artifacts in green garbage bags (all found neatly stacked outside for the city to collect). Dust is unavoidable. And the inner guts of the wall, diagonal slats of lathing supporting a rougher, pebbly plaster, are worse. Impossible to work efficiently. A mess. But he cleans it all up, meticulously.

This was the hardest part for me to see clearly. His tidying up. Was it driving him crazy, making him hate himself for attempting such a grandiose display? Or was he completely organized? One of your modern wizards: cool, compulsively neat, and knows exactly just how to do it—for his audience?

But his audience no longer exists.

No. *Ergo*, this job must have almost ripped him apart, a lot like the electric saw Jean-Marc was saying "they" used. Mists of crap wafting into his nostrils and eyes, skin caked and parched with the dead air of century-old debris. Were we seeing something of a masochist here? Not fun: smashing, ripping, then cleaning it all; tears running down his cheeks (most likely), spitting dust.

Until he finally strikes stone, half a metre in. One big block, nearly two metres square.

"Here it gets interesting," said Jean-Marc.

Guiding an extended diamond bit with the finest of coordination, he drills to the centre from as many corners as can be exposed, creating a star-shaped grouping of converging lines. He uses teaspoons to measure a blend of ammonia, corn syrup and plastique onto swabs of cotton batting. These are carefully packed into pencil-thin tubes of soft rubber and inserted gently into the fissures, to the heart of the rock. Then he cuts more rubber into plugs and gently tamps them in behind.

Yes, interesting, with close-ups all the way of a veteran putting a lifetime of experience into his job. I listened politely. Technology, I thought; not too original, but people do love to see the knowing hands at work. Is that exciting? As entrancing as the smell of a ribbon? The technical co-opting the erotic—personally, I find it sad.

Maybe Jean-Marc noticed something in my eyes. "Nothing very state-of-the-art," he commented, as if suddenly needing to distance himself from his own narrative; "...But they knew what they were doing."

"So, then: boom...?" I asked, sensing the approach of dawn.

"Not quite. Have to soundproof it."

"Of course."

"*Un tapis de pneus*...found it round the back."

"Ah." A quilt of rubber patches fashioned from old tires.

"Two of them, actually—they were quite particular about keeping it clean in here."

"That take long to make?"

"More than five minutes...probably brought it along, and a couple of them would have had to go back out to the street to lay it."

"Yes..." Now I was prepared to allow his Anne-Marie a part in it. A support role: I could see a slender figure out in the streets breaking into the trunks of cars, stealing tires, bringing them home (wherever that was), watching him cut them into patches and nail them together. But not happy about it: angry eyes demanding, *Why the hell are you doing this? You don't need to do this...it's not worth it. It's just not important any more!*

If you don't want to help me with my life, just leave it.

So she helps him, naturally; and when it's time, she is there in the alley with the things in the back of their vehicle, and she helps him set it up. The cover of hard rubber will muffle the blast, reduce it to another bump in the night. But I was quite certain he sent her away again, poor Anne-Marie, before setting it off. The climax—leaving through the hole; this has to be his and his alone. "And then?"

"After they've been through the boxes—a little push on a button and the stone implodes—a pile of rubble."

"Which he cleans up before going."

"He?"

"They," correcting myself. "I tend to think in terms of the one calling the shots..."

"It's amazing how clean," concurred Jean-Marc. "Might well be someone's signature...you might cross-ref that."

Clean holes. "Yes, I might...*merci, monsieur.*"

"Always a pleasure."

I joined Gérard Richaud, who had come in and begun picking through the wall of opened safety deposit boxes. It is common practice for the Instructing Judge to make a personal inspection of a crime site, bodies, weapons, et cetera.

"So does this mean the hunt for Jacques Normand is now officially on the books?" I mused aloud, but with professional discretion.

"We have a case, obviously."

"Obviously. But what are you supposed to find?" This with a tone of irony only an old friend would appreciate.

"A likely target," said Gérard, with no irony at all.

I considered my old boyfriend's perplexed expression as he dipped into a box and removed an early but by no means valuable copy of *Les Fleurs du mal*, flipped through and replaced it. He was a boss now too and perhaps Louis Moreau's sense of reputation and rising urgency was not affecting him in the same way it once might have. Perhaps he now felt the same pressures as that man did. "But what are you going to say to the lady from the evening news, Gérard?" I knew he was not the type to lie. The system was remarkably adept at attracting the right kind.

"I'll say I don't know."

I stayed with him, gazing over his shoulder as he stared blankly at a recipe for *moutarde forte* tied to a bundle of financial papers; gawked nervously at several back issues of a publication called *Shaved Quarterly*, certain of its bizarre pages marked with bond certificates; tilted his head, sentimental, at pictures of a man in uniform; then blinked stupidly at a threadbare old sock containing five gold Napoleonic francs.

"How can I know?" he finally asked, rhetorical and typically lawyer-like. And worried. Yep, pressure on Gérard now too.

It was not an inspector's place to know how or what he knew.

"Look at all this stuff!" he complained, "all these personal little things. Just things! With love and shame written all over them. Wealth, too, of course—this is a bank, isn't it? But it speaks much more of lives than numbers, wouldn't you say?"

I had never actually had a safety deposit box.

"All of it's so specific and private...and too particular to mean anything!"

"Gérard, that's not the point—"

"Yes it is!" Dam bursting... "Moreau says find the target and we'll all know who shot the bullet. Sure, that works with how: show me how he was killed and I'll show you who did it...The point is, Public Enemy Number One could fit into any of these little boxes...these little lives! He took the money and some jewels. A thief, pure and simple. There's only the hole."

"Well, that's what I think."

But he was not in a mood for commiserating. "Do you think I'm going to stand up and make pronouncements on a hole in a wall?"

"You'd have to pick your words carefully," I mused. Biting on a smile.

"Absolutely not." Gérard was categorical.

"Might be irresponsible, yes..."

"The hole is a big zero."

"But a statement nonetheless."

"Inspector, a ghost has never yet said anything useful in a court of law."

"Trust your instincts, Gérard."

And trust the facts, I thought, somehow glad to realize he held the same fear as the Commissaire; i.e., nothing to hold onto.

"No," he muttered, going back to the rows of boxes, "I have no particular suspect marked at this point in the inquiry." Flat and disinterested. Would the media people detect the rue behind the new Chief Magistrate's statement? Probably not; Gérard was too much of a professional.

Now his dour face twisted in involuntary reaction as he unwrapped a linen hanky found folded in a velvet jewellery box and tried to make sense of the need to keep the shrivelled remains of a nipple from a human breast. How right he was, *le Juge* Gérard: strange people, and as likely to be your own sweet mother as the weird man at the corner with the shades always drawn. Little boxes full of secrets. Private property. As if everyone were a thief. No heroes evident here.

I left. I did not want to interfere with his thoughts. As it stood, they might mean protection—some support from the Chief Magistrate should Inspector Nouvelle happen to fail. Nor did I want to be in the feet of the rest of Anti-Gangs boys, just now arriving for *their* "second look." The presence of Inspector Nouvelle would only start them second-guessing all that might be said from higher up. Poor Gérard. Louis Moreau had him starting to chase his legal tail.

And in his own way, a ghost had them both by the balls.

But that (and the analogy) was their context, not mine.

13

A Heart Beating in Real Time

The Institute was built according to the same dowdy neo-classical scheme as the Palace of Justice, but without the large steps to the door. Of what, and when it had been an "institute" I had no idea. It waited there, with its name and its silence in a small square just inside the boundary of the business district, attended by two statues: a war hero on his horse, and a cube of modern stainless steel falsely balanced on one sharp corner. I climbed seven steps to the plaza and crossed, pausing in the shadow of the portico to look back at the city, softened by dusk. My city; my career. Then I pulled open the heavy door and stepped inside. I felt my way in near darkness, along the hall and up the stairway. At the top I turned and saw the room at the end of the upper hall. The door was wide open and the light inside fell starkly on the woman posing at the front.

Eyes are seen differently, in many ways more clearly, when observed in the profile. Georgette Duguay was statuesque as she profiled the stride of a runner. Regardless of the heightened effect induced by the small riser upon which she had positioned herself, the presence of her body was more compelling than I had imagined. She was obviously an expert, running through a timeless sector, the figure she cut recognizable to anyone as essential. But it was her remarkable green eyes which drew me into the room: they watched without a trace of the woman, the model, the person on the street. They were the eyes of the moment. Of running.

There were maybe thirty of them in attendance, of whom Louis Moreau was most familiar. He was at an easel in the second ring of places, in a more casual, tie-less weekend garb, but focused in a manner I had often seen and considered most professional—and he did not acknowledge my entrance. No one did; not the butcher or the tailor or that Willem from the Rembrandt Café.

And definitely not Georgette. I was given to understood that silence was the rule.

I soft-footed it to the back and began to set up my things. A large sketch pad; and to work with—what? charcoal, Conté, a simple pencil? The man beside me, a paunchy teacher type in tweeds and horn-rims, dusty hair brushed back and wavy, seemed to have all three on the go in deft hands that had already blocked in the defining lines of the figure. It had been ages since I had pursued anything "artistic"; these things, and a large leather portfolio case, had been purchased just that day, after the visit to the bank: a leisurely shop, in and out of an afternoon rain—nice without Claude.

So I was tentative as I tried to begin. The Conté felt too metallic in my fingers. The man beside was now busy shading with his charcoal. I took a piece of my own, but it was so messy; it seemed to smudge the white paper at the slightest touch. The pencil mark I made was too thread-like, almost invisible. I went back to the Conté crayon.

Could an inspector remember how to do this? It was not like riding a bicycle. Making a line—that would be Georgette's leg. But once you get to her belly she'll be off the page. So, smudging it out, then ripping away the page and trying again. Block in the basic proportions first. Don't worry about perfecting the shape of the baby finger. The hands should be about the size of the head. Even if they don't appear that way to the mind's eye, they are—so see them right, and do it. Running. Feel the action to get the tension. There's nothing there you've never felt yourself.

I worked away at it for two hours during which Georgette broke her position twice to take a few steps and stretch— but only that, and then resumed it again. There was no break. The man beside me finished his work within the first hour, and, without a word or any other kind of acknowledgement, left. Louis Moreau was next to leave (and without a glance back at me). Several others were not far behind him, but their leaving in no way disturbed the ambience created by the model's stone-like stillness. There was nothing at all social about this gathering. No talking occurred between any members of the class. The woman at the front offered no instruction of any kind.

I would make a few marks then lose my concentration—find my eyes wandering from face to face. The butcher, the tailor, the waiter; all of these people looked familiar. Too familiar.

But what else did I expect?

I believed I would know it when I saw it.

Watching the Commissaire: he seemed to draw well but his refusal to acknowledge my presence was another distraction and I digressed further, trying to remember if I had told him I was planning on attending. Or had I only implied it? Could he really think I was following him?

No. It was this Georgette. A link.

A link to the poodle.

Not a poodle—stop it! A woman! But a thief. Louis Moreau could wave her off with his very special brand of disdain, but it was a fact: the two women had been there together, watching the aftermath of the crime at the bank. They had looked comfortable, elbows touching, sharing a smile, obviously known to each other. Friends. An artist's model and a thief. Why not? Neither of them nine-to-five. I could see them out together, trying on hats and eating cake.

As my hand tried to obey my eye, the voice I trusted ruminated on this abiding hunch.

Because—now contemplating a shock of silver hair where it lay settled in the nape of the model's extended neck; making a tentative flicking motion with my wrist in trying to render it—Jacques Normand had been inside my place again that day. Nothing taken this time, but I had known it in a minute—had gone straight to an actual piece of the physical evidence Louis Moreau had insisted on as he'd steered me back to the bank: a strand of silver hair (not mine, not yet), found snagged in the band of an LA Dodgers baseball hat. The surprise of this discovery had been somehow mitigated by the thought that my visitor had felt at ease enough to bring a friend along. A strange man, this ghost of a Public Enemy. But growing familiar.

Only question: was I supposed to worry?

In the end Aliette, the newcomer, made a horrible mess. When the model broke the pose and stepped back into her corduroy slacks, I was alone but for Monsieur Bondiguel, the butcher—whom I had observed to be, with his gigantic hands, the most meticulous of detail renderers. He was serene, and the first one to make eye contact as he packed away his things.

I stepped back from my work with a feeling of re-entering the local time zone. It was absorbing, this drawing. I had never experienced it that way in school. My image of the running woman was a chimera of lines laid upon lines in a futile attempt to nail her down.

The butcher shuffled out.

And I could feel I blushed as I faced Georgette across the space of the empty room. "Aren't you going to look at my work, Georgette?" This was blurted in a coquettish tone I regretted even as I heard it pass my lips. It was nowhere near the right way to approach this woman.

"I don't want to see your work."

"But why not?"

"Not interested."

"Not interested? But I want to learn...why would I even show up?"

"I wouldn't know."

Just like that, the woman was getting the better of me again, as she had in the street. Resist it. But I could not; I felt twelve years old, demanding, "How will I learn if you don't teach me?"

"Teach yourself."

"I hardly know how to begin." Looking with increasing woe at the scratches I had produced.

Georgette was blasé. "Don't think about it too much, *chère madame.* Look, then start. What we do here is purely physical, after all."

Non-advice. "But how can you—?"

"You begin by beginning to see what the thing is. Only deal with what is in front of you. If you can do that, then it will show itself to you. It will guide you. It's a lot like love, you know...?"

Love? "I need help." Blushing again; saying it in a way I would never have to any Commissaire or colleague; or, for that matter, to anyone I could think of at that point in my life.

Georgette Duguay only nodded like some isolated queen, and then, picking up her bag, walked out of the room, leaving me to gather my things together, turn off the light and find my way out of that rather spooky building, guided only by the slightest hint of a moonbeam that had found its way in from I knew not where.

— —

I remember feeling distinctly glum as I followed the heavy man into the quarter. It was a feeling born of the fact that I did not want it to be him. He walked leaning forward, plodding, seeming to create his own momentum through his very bulk. And he walked fast; I thought he might hear the scuffing of my shoes as I hurried after. If so, he could stop, turn and pump a bullet or two into my stomach, then keep on walking into the night. As far I knew he had never killed a cop, but the thought crossed my mind.

Around another corner and we were heading for the Commissariat. Local, walking distance, just as my Commissaire had suggested. He had been watching me for years. He had been coming to my room and my dreams for longer than I would ever know. How romantic. But why me?

We passed *la Brigade* and turned where I turned, every morning and every night. The *brasseries*. I had always ignored them—while he had been inside with his secret, drinking beer. He likes beer. Well, good. But he passed the bars and the darkened windows of the shops in between. Then he was trudging across the *rond-point*, straight for my place!

He veered right and entered the park instead.

I approached, crossing the dark lawn toward the pond where my man reposed on a bench, alone under the stars. There was no question of taking him by force. My gun was stowed in plastic at the back of my underwear drawer. Although my skills with elbow and knee were available, they were not exactly "at the ready." Because mine had always been the more civilized way of doing it: directly stated, appealing to the subject's sense of humanity and his chances in front of a judge.

His hat, a threadbare homburg, was pulled low against the brisk night air, and he methodically poured shots from a metal flask into the cap, and then down his throat: one...two...three, like a machine. Replacing the cap, he laid the flask aside, laboriously bent double and began to massage his lower legs and ankles. When he sat back up he sensed me there at his shoulder. Turning, with a heavy person's slow expression of surprise: "Huh…? Madame Inspector…!" Then, with basic courtesy, "Sit down. Have a drink with me."

"Sore legs, *monsieur*?"

"On my feet all day."

"And all night…Monsieur Normand?"

With the smile of the innocent, he proffered the flask. "No, just the butcher…all I ever was and will be."

I tried to look inside the flask as I considered this. Noticing the butcher watching in a funny way, I threw caution to the wind and gulped. Scotch whisky. Not my favourite beverage, but warm in my stomach on a brisk spring night; a drop in temperature after the rain, the last one I hoped, before May offered summer up in earnest. I took another hit, then handed it back. "*Merci*. But you could be, couldn't you?"

"*Madame*…this notion of Jacques Normand you seem to have…I don't know what to tell you. I've honestly never met the man." He swigged, squeezing his eyes tight for a moment as he gulped it back. "But I suppose, yes, I could be. Anybody could be, couldn't they?"

He handed back the flask. I accepted, drank twice, then offered it back again. He put up his large hand—you keep it for a bit—and recommended rubbing his shins.

I sat down on the bench beside the butcher. Sipped once more. "Does that mean there's nothing special about him?"

"Of course there's something special about him. His career. The papers. We all know him…or we used to." Now he straightened up, reached and gently lifted the flask out of my fingers.

"No—just him," I said, "the man: does he stand out in a crowd?"

"I never thought of it." A swig. "He must…" The butcher seemed to meditate on the silver sheen of the flask.

The Inspector felt like she wanted another drink.

"Getting a stone out of the wall of the bank like that," mused the butcher, "…that would take some doing."

"What makes you think it was him?"

"Who else could it have been—after all these years?" The burly man shrugged as if it were the most obvious thing in the world, and handed me the flask.

"But the papers haven't said a word," I countered, "nor the television…"

"The papers and the television don't run small shops in quiet streets, *madame*. They don't push prams in the park or sit in cafés or drive around all day in a bus or a cab or a truck, waiting, hoping—"

"Hoping for something to happen?"

"*C'est ça*…The newspapers and the television, they plow ahead. They have to, I suppose."

"Were you waiting?"

"Not on the edge of my seat…"

"But…"

"…But he's a hero, isn't he?"

Again—to him—logical. The logic of the heart beating in real time. The logic of memory coloured by the sweetest moments.

The scotch warmed me. The butcher warmed me. I saw the big face bowed over the barrel chest, his eyes steady, at peace. What would it have been like if it had been him? He was fatherly or perhaps avuncular was the word. Whichever, how would we have dealt with the teasing, the scent of him on my pillow? Because that had to be dealt with. But it was not him. It had been only his fingers: the facility with a piece of charcoal and a detail that had made an inspector think it possible after all. A thief's hands. A hero's hands—and his.

Sorry, wrong man.

But there was no need to say it because he wasn't wishing he were someone else. Not at all.

Past the butcher, the city lights reflected off the surface of the pond, shimmering and, as always, more beautiful, more romantic in a watery aspect than in the stark clear air.

"How long have you been in Georgette's group?" I asked.

"Oh…long time. Years. It's like she has always been here. Good for the soul, drawing."

"Is she always so unfriendly?"

"It's not that…not really."

"What is it?"

"I don't know…I'm so used to her. I'd call it…hmm?—neutral, say. And absolutely serious. Always."

"Neutral?"

"It's what she does…her poses. She has always been very careful about that. As if she doesn't want to get in the way."

"Your friend?"

"Nobody's friend, I shouldn't think. Just our model."

"Mmm. Here…" Scotch. Not so bad.

"Thank you."

Thank *you*.

Returning home, I went directly to the refrigerator and something sweet I had been keeping there. I came into my room eating the remains of a cake in messy mouthfuls, straight from my fingers. There was something I had to try.

Piaf appeared from under the bed to round up the crumbs which fell in a steady stream.

"*Salut*, Piaf…God, I love cake!"

I managed to undress myself with one hand, passing the treat back and forth from left to right to left as I unbuttoned, unhooked, untied and removed. Then I stood naked, watching myself in the mirror as I made to devour the last chocolaty bite. "Look at this, my Piaf. I'm a model, all right?" The cake touched my lips; I froze. "…And this face is more memorable…watch now!" Into my mouth it went, where it was savoured and swallowed as I held my position. "…than this one." The face opposite my now empty fingers. "What d'you think of that, Piaf? We all need a prop I guess—except maybe someone like Georgette Duguay." Looking down at him, standing there waiting for more cake. "But what do you think it's like to be a hero without a face? Just the props. Poor man, he must be smashing his head against a wall. Scared, too—he won't even send a smile to his beloved. He's really stuck."

With that, I licked my thumb, switched off the light and climbed into my bed. Piaf jumped up.

"No…! good night," throwing him back down again.

Then I lay there waiting for Jacques Normand, calm, totally unrealistic in my willingness, until I fell asleep.

14

LIKE AN OLD ELEPHANT

That morning I chose a plain white shirt, plain white ribbon, and a plain (but expensive) navy blue suit. I fed Piaf and let him out on the balcony, then left at my usual time. Crossing the *rond-point*, my traffic cop greeted me with a morning smile—bright, and coloured with a dopey adolescent blush, as if he somehow knew he'd been working double duty in my dream, lending aspects of a lovely face to the outlaw lover I'd been conjuring. Certain aspects of a lean and rhythmic body too. I smiled back...*bonjour*, then, reaching the far side of the circle, entered the quarter and made my way to work. I took the long way on a pleasant morning, stopping at Erly's Boulangerie for a chocolatine. I bought an extra, hoping Claude might be enticed to share a pot of coffee and tell me about the flight of the poodle (and, if he wanted, the injury to his nose). I was mounting the steps to the Commissariat when Georgette Duguay, at the wheel of a quite decrepit VW Westfalia camper van, pulled up and lurched to a dramatic stop, rolling down the window.

"Good morning," said the artist's model.

"Good morning to you."

"You look nice today."

What a strange woman. It was no problem being a polite inspector, but I instinctively remained on my guard. "I feel nice today, Georgette... What do you want?"

"I want to be friends."

"Friends? But why?"

Georgette smiled—first time I had seen it. "I'm interested in you. In fact, I think I like you. That makes you unusual."

I took a step down, toward the van. "There are lots like me…"

"Not everyone attracts the attention of Jacques Normand."

"What do you mean by that?" I demanded, sidling up to the van and, it must be said, beginning to shake some. "You're going to have to explain that one to me, *madame*…and friends too, for that matter."

"Tell me what happened in your room last night."

"You mean yesterday morning. You should know—you were there." I had proof.

"I mean last night. You and Jacques Normand…you must tell me."

On a reflex, I flashed my medal. "*You* must tell *me*."

Wrong move. Friends melted, replaced by stone. "Don't insult me," muttered the silver-haired woman in a voice fairly dripping with scorn.

"No insult. Just a fact."

"It's not your silly little medal, Aliette Nouvelle…it's your heart. I'm interested in your love life."

"My love life… What in the world are you talking about?"

But Georgette was clearly disgusted. She rolled up her window and summarily pulled away into the morning traffic.

Leaving me flummoxed. I found myself calling down the street after her, "Georgette…wait! What are you talking about?"—but was left standing there, utterly confused. The uncertainty was not helped by two gendarmes, then four more, all giving me the oddest look as they came out the Commissariat door.

I climbed the stairs, hung my coat and took my pastries down the hall to Claude's. Monique, our collective secretary, saw me pass and called, "He's down in the lock-up with the boss." I had no treat for the boss. I put Erly's delights back on my desk and went down.

Where I beheld the fugitive poodle, lying on a cot in a cell, listless and sad.

Who wouldn't be? The small cot was dingy and musty. One could almost taste the gritty rust on the metal frame. The stone wall, washed lime-green, rose to a small window with three bars: two to hold onto while you smashed your head against the third. Seeing her so suddenly like that, I could not hide the fact that I felt more sympathy than elation. The Commissaire and Claude were hovering close by as I gazed at the prisoner. I turned to my boss: "How...? Where did you find her?"

"Claude found her."

"With the Commissaire's help of course," rejoined Claude, distracted, dishevelled and racoonish today on account of broken vessels spreading under his eyes from the region of his bandaged snoot.

Louis Moreau casually added, "And with the help of that traffic cop who works the circle outside your apartment."

"But how...? I mean, I thought she'd got away."

"That was yesterday," mumbled our chief, watching me.

Claude kept gingerly tapping the bridge of his nose.

The prisoner remained slouched there, bleak.

"Then when?...and why wasn't I told? I..." But my thoughts trailed away. Disorientation was starting to swirl, quicker and deeper at the centre of me.

"Just this morning. We...Claude, that is, also saw Jacques Normand climbing down from your balcony."

And I was aware that I blinked a few times, but I could not help it. "Jacques Normand on my balcony...this morning? What are you telling me?"

"Only that he's obviously quite pleased with you. It appears he was following you to work."

I turned to the woman in the cell, in need of...what? Her confirmation? Or her support in the face of this outrageous thing? She stared at me—right through me. Turning—Claude Néon's bandaged face would not hold its shape. There was great distance in every dimension of the cell block. The Commissaire's words—I could not get a fix on where they were coming from. Only that I knew they were wrong. Absolutely wrong. It seemed I hung there weightless, waiting, until, as certain things came clear, an energy, something essential that boiled in my heart, took hold and transported me. "I...this is absurd! What were you doing outside my apartment? Shame on you. Shame on you!" I turned to the other man. And now I asked. Now I demanded! "Monsieur Commissaire, I want to request a new assistant. This Claude here is acting far beyond the bounds of his duty. He is creating a malicious fantasy out of this case. He is trying to undermine my work and my reputation!" But it was far too late for such a request and I knew it, even as I saw myself moving with no clear intention toward Claude Néon. "What are you trying to do to me...?"

The Commissaire intervened. Broad chest, strong arm. "We're not trying to do anything to you. We're trying to catch Jacques Normand."

"Well so am I!" I screamed it at him. Then, deflating, I turned away. I let my forehead touch the steel bars. "But to spy on me...and accuse me of hiding him in my apartment. Why would I hide him? I don't even know him. I was alone last night. I don't understand this at all..."

But the ribbon. He had been there, and more than once.

And hadn't I been expecting that he would be there again?

This accusation. This innuendo. Georgette—my love life. It was as if it were in the air, like the scent of nearby water in the middle of some impenetrable forest. Everyone could feel it—not just me.

That I was the one he was coming to.

That Jacques Normand wanted Aliette Nouvelle.

I felt an arm on mine. It was a gentle arm, looking for my trust. Or was it only looking to dissuade me from moving away from them, toward something *they* could not trust? It was Claude: solicitous, sympathetic and unreal. "Inspector Nouvelle...Aliette, I was only doing my job. Only reporting exactly what I saw."

I turned away from them. "Leave me alone."

No, Inspector Nouvelle wanted nothing more from them. Why? Because she knew she didn't need them any more. Standing there in that depressing room, I realized I was a woman separated by a chasm much wider than credibility. Why would he want anything to do with them when I was in the picture? It was my case. All I had to do was be strong, and hold on. The outlaw would be mine. The matter of France versus Normand would be settled.

The Commissaire tried again. "Just tell us what happened last night. We're all on the same side, remember."

"I was alone." Quiet. Direct. The voice of Aliette Nouvelle. He could not hurt me. It did not matter what he thought. I repeated it. "I was alone..." while staring at the prisoner: at her pale, porcelain-like skin, dark eyes and heavy brows. And the doll's nose, the feral, thin-lipped mouth. A poodle? Why not? The sharp features under extravagant black curls, the angular body, the black jeans and top— again this morning, the basic uniform of the streets.

The Commissaire noticed. "You seem to know each other."

"Yes, we seem to, don't we? What's her name?"

"She won't say."

"Anne-Marie?"

A blank stare. Too bad. But I knew this sad, silent poodle did not believe me either. Not a word. I straightened up and headed for the cell block door.

"Where are you going?"

"To my desk. Have Claude follow me if you like." I left the door swinging as I walked out.

⸺   ⸺

I felt like an old elephant cut loose from the fold. Not fired, but marooned. (A cop is usually cooked before she's fired.) What could I do—wait for Jacques Normand to save me? My hero!

Gérard Richand accepted Erly's other chocolatine but could offer little in return.

"Get out of it...withdraw."

What you are obliged to do when you find you have an "emotional" interest in a case. It happens all the time and the people in charge are not unrealistic. Aren't we all just human, for heaven's sake? You just have to be realistic about it too. Get out of it. Withdraw. There are plenty of other cases. A rest is also something that might be useful, given the circumstances.

He refused to even take my deposition on Claude's "sighting."

"Can't...sorry. Too bad your place isn't over the bank."

"Oh for the love of— Gérard, Moreau's using me!"

"For what?"

"I don't know!"

A pause. A kind of a scattered look. "Welcome to the club."

"It's not right."

"You took the case."

"Yes… Apparently he's taking it back."

"He's your boss. It's his prerogative."

"Why doesn't he just ask?"

"Would you give it to him?"

I couldn't answer that one—not honestly. "We used to trust each other," I sighed. "He taught me so much… I'm…I'm really lost. You have to put this down on the record."

"It won't mean anything."

"But Claude—following me. It's all a big—"

"Others saw him. That traffic cop was practically kissing him…some people in their cars…"

"Does the traffic cop even know what he looks like?"

"I don't know. He must, I mean—"

"Nobody else does. Maybe two men in this city know that face and the traffic cop's not one of them! …I've got pages of notes to attest."

"Then you're covered, aren't you?"

"I won't withdraw!" I stated. Or perhaps hissed.

"It's up to you," he replied. "Sorry, but it really is. Legally, you're still at zero. As for your standing with Moreau…" Here he offered an abrupt, quite unjudge-like shrug: your problem; your call, Inspector. Then Gérard, former lover, now almost friend, resurfaced. "I'd withdraw. Whatever he's doing, it's dangerous."

"Did he ever kill a cop?"

"Moreau?"

"Normand."

"No…not as far as we know."

"He never fucked one, either…at least as far as we know." I couldn't help myself—the frustration was spilling out.

And, of course, this was not language appropriate to the setting. He blinked and rose. The meeting was over.

"But why, Gérard?"

He paused, looking at me with different eyes now.

"…Why would he want to? Why me?"

"This is neither the time nor the place for me to attempt an answer, Inspector. But," quiet, shrewd, "if you're so concerned, then maybe you can imagine why others might be…" while politely (and officially) showing me out.

And adding guilt to my sense of isolation.

Yes, very wrong to throw it at him like that. Gérard couldn't know what I wouldn't tell. And if I told—well, there was nothing "legal" there at all. Up to me. I did not feel like returning to the office and so walked without looking where, but presently found myself wandering across the plaza in front of the Institute.

Inside, it was dust-ridden but not so foreboding as at night. And not as empty either. An AA session. A Tai Chi class. Old ladies doing watercolours. People sitting in a circle, all of them weeping. Sounds of medieval singing from a far-off corner. But no Georgette. Only rows of easels, waiting for half-past eight.

Back down on the main floor, shuffling into the large room off the main hallway: a central chamber, or what used to be, with a cathedral ceiling and vaulted windows—now the sculpture room. The place was strewn with shapes. They were strong but not very finished; some were blockish, like a cliff side; others were lumpy, like a hill. Even those pieces meant to represent the human form were still vague, still trying to become what they were meant to be. There was a gap between the idea and the physical thing—the same as there was between me and Jacques Normand.

I sat down on a pedestal, under one towering chunk of alabaster.

There was danger. There was this completely unsatisfactory quality of the unseen, the undisclosed. There was also a sense that I could only go forward, follow it, till I caught the next and better glimpse.

Because there was relationship.

I was involved with this man. It was out of context, yet, somehow, deeply bred.

2ND PART

15

FREEDOM'S MIRROR

He had been trying to write—and to read. He had been struggling to see it: Whatever came next, it had to begin with clear-eyed assessment: Public Enemy? Apparently. But a hero? Bunk! A big mistake.

One American philosopher, a certain C. Peacemaker, whose book *Lead Solo* had been translated by the local French psychologist J.-P. Blismes, had taken some basic precepts from the Age of Enlightenment and said the hero is the man who accepts responsibility for his life—*point final*. In those terms, Jacques could suppose he may have been a hero. He had chosen his course and followed it. He was always prepared to accept the consequences. But only for himself. This was key. Could a hero exist alone?

Every other writer he admired, from the Greek to the modern, Taoist to Talmudic, and a few poets in between, had put it squarely in the context of man as social animal. And how peace is a precondition to man's flourishing in this state of social existence. They spoke about overcoming baser instinct and ambition. They said that, ideally, every man is a hero and the city, with its walls built to repel the Hun and thwart the thief, is the environment wherein civilized souls can thrive only if they communicate. Through words, through actions. Because the power of communication is the thing that creates civilization. He was fascinated by the notion that civilization, walled in as it may be, uses its powers of communication to expand its limits, to break the boundaries of time itself. His life had made him acutely aware of time and he found this notion inspiring, if not daunting. The past: how to smash it so it may never be reconfigured, all links to those *bourgeois* expectations untraceable. And the future: how to break through when it has become literally a concrete wall with a barred window?

Well, he was a communicator, was he not? A writer. His memoir had sold well enough—for a while. Yet Jacques now had to admit that his writings had come from a distinctly less than civilized perspective. Clearly, his own (frequently Hun-like) actions had been those of a thief.

Therefore: No hero in this picture. Just a prisoner with a lot of time and anger, some paper, a pen, a publisher who knew exactly what to do. (Jacques never did understand why his publisher, a man with some strong ideas on how to sell books, had backed away from the offer of Jacques' collected poems and letters.)

What about a warrior? He was a member of a class of men with a code which set them apart. It was all very clear to any man who chose to join. They bonded, they trusted (or not), and they employed warrior ways to settle points of business. Bold, aggressive—in a word, physical. The field of battle was the urban street. Yes, he could live with warrior. He didn't mind warrior at all. *Noble* warrior, if simplicity is to be esteemed. Or: ignoble and barbaric, if human progress depends on the socializing factor.

The more he studied it, the farther the glamour receded. He came to agree that peace and quiet is a useful thing.

So: a thief—plain and simple. Jacques Normand had originally set out to steal money and things of value—*c'est tout*; and Thief was the vocation. But since he (very deliberately) sought out a certain degree of action to colour the thief's activities, he had required a feasible persona. *Alors*, the Warrior was only a role; sure—a way of accommodating the thief's inclinations and ensuring the thief would survive.

But Public Enemy? That role implied enmity, hatred.

He never disliked any particular member of the Public. Never hurt any of them unless they got in his way. He thought only of the objects or the cash. If he ever had an enemy it was someone actual; they knew each other and they fought it out. He never knew the Public at all—except in the sense that he did learn how to use it.

Beyond that, Jacques Normand didn't need or want to know the Public.

Question: how, then, could the Public ever "know" a man like him?

But it did (or thought it did). It loved him.

Could he ever love the Public back? Hardly. If you use people, it's impossible to love them.

Jacques knew why the Public loved its Enemy. Freedom. And especially here in France. *Liberté, Egalité, Fraternité.* He always knew they felt they were missing something—in all three, if they thought about it too much; the modern soul was too savvy to truly embrace each of these grand abstractions as anything more than a slogan. But the inclination toward an actual freedom, a visceral gut-borne feeling—that was something to be craved even as *egalité* became a traffic jam, *fraternité* a social security number. People could still sense *liberté* somewhere; and so they turned to a man who was *of them* but not one of them. Why? A symbol and a vicarious thrill.

What he did was never for them. It was for his benefit, his own freedom. That was the extent of it. Very selfish, this thief. And he made no bones about that.

But, stories. Words. Pictures most all. Other types of men and women, needing to gratify a different sense of worth, made the people believe this thief Normand had something they did not. Poor Public. Poor France! Poor Jacques. Because it is hard not to respond to love—even when you're as mean as he was. The thief was still a man.

Hero? It got twisted because of Freedom.

It was bigger than him. It was always bigger than him, and he bought into it—and could never buy (or steal) his way out. So it was true: freedom was everything. He declared it in his book because he'd lived it, from those first small heists, going through back doors and unlikely windows in the dull back streets of the 17th *Arrondissement,* all the way to the banks and supper at Maxim's. Jacques' life became a concept. An idea. And many of the other books he turned to held that happiness is nothing if not absorption in an idea—especially an idea everyone loves. He was the man: Freedom incarnate. And the career was a manic rush devoted to the bittersweet cultivation of the myth of himself.

His first real taste of it came after the army. He had returned from his tour in Algeria, bubbling over with the romance of action. He was back on the street and supposedly in search of a career. He wanted nothing to do with it. In fact, energy and imagination gave a demobbed twenty-one-year-old to believe he had been permanently removed from the ranks of the socially contracted. Look: page 175. "Even then, there was that fatal sense, that inkling of darkness; it had always been part of it. And it came with a sense of story. I had fallen into the habit of observing the people around me, in the street, in the *métro*, in the little corner *resto* where I took my midday meal. What did I see? Sad faces. Tired eyes. People worn down by poorly paid work, never making any more than the minimum wage—but tied to it: to survive. I saw people condemned to perpetual mediocrity, incapable of satisfying their smallest wish, stuck forever gazing into the windows of *de luxe* boutiques, *restos* and travel agencies, their guts hooked to the daily meal and a tasteless glass of *gros rouge*…people who knew their future before it was lived: robots, exploited and slotted away, slaves to the alarm clock. All the expressions that people used… 'no time to do it!…be on time!…saving time!…wasting time!' As for me, I would live outside of time. I would have the time to live."

Lately Jacques had been going back to that page, rereading, trying to see between the lines, to see how they might apply to his present situation. But in the here and now of that beautiful time—that timeless past where myths are best left to stand or fall—he only knew that Jacques Normand had tasted action, seen death, had learned to understand this thing about honour among men; and that he enjoyed the feel of a gun in his hand. And, loose again in the streets of Paris, he'd returned straight away to the lies and deception that had served to separate him from his parents from the day of his first ejaculation. He returned to the back doors, the risk, and the quick and large rewards.

That day—the first in the life of a nascent Public Enemy— Jacques had found himself caught *flagrant délit* in a dentist's parlour. Before the fear could flood his brain, there was a voice: an impulse, a stroke of sweet genius, whatever it was—something prompting him to "Pretend! Dream it up!" An act. A cop! He pretended he was a cop and walked away, leaving the dentist feeling things were well in hand.

The ease and simplicity of it opened a door in his mind. A parade of faces came marching through. When the newspapers had first given him the mantle "Public Enemy Number One" he'd liked it—it seemed to fit well, and proudly.

"Fervent. Playful. Violent? Oh, *oui*: that pisshead journalist who had to mock me, a scummy coward of a partner who turned under pressure; each act of violence pushed me forward, further into it. Even in jail it was a kind of role to be upheld. Freedom. There's integrity there...there really is!"

Anne-Marie shrugged. She'd heard it a thousand times.

Then, escape again. The final run from Paris. And a change.

The fatalistic impulse, the certainty that he would die charging through a storm of lead with the eyes of all France glued to his every twitch—it had been easy to write these things while sitting in a jail cell. Necessary, too. Out here in the hinterland, in a van that was never parked in the same place twice, the romance of death had faded. Without it, life began to take a long time. He was aware of something coming full circle, the notion of Time once again confronting Freedom for status as the defining thing. Some days it could be a new sort of prison.

Back there, in the heat of it and then in jail, lost memories had been easily filled by the fact of his infamy, a larger-than-life Grand Jacques. Out here, he was learning that trying to recover a life can be painful, not to say confusing.

Depending on the day, Anne-Marie's silence on these matters could be either comfort or curse. Her perpetual silence—self-imposed the night they started living together, after leaving a drug dealer dead in their wake. ("A vile man. Not a man at all. He knows nothing of love.") Jacques sensed it was her way of giving in to a higher power. Or at least to a life she had never wanted but was made for. He had been getting to know that feeling as well: the feeling of coming to terms.

The challenge was to live without the headlines, and those revivifying jolts of gaudy romance. He needed to do that and yet remain the man he had created. Jacques Normand. Not in style; not overtly. And not in deed; at least not so crudely. Only essentially: master thief, and master of his own fate. Because, out here, he had been living with a sense that he was not, and maybe never had been, in control of this thing called his "life." And that went against his notion of Freedom.

But there was hope. Hope waited, eternal, fear's quiet sister. Georgette Duguay seemed to have been waiting for him, at the far end of his flight, like a new mother. Which was impossible, he knew; but she knew who he was and still accepted him into her sphere.

Jacques had been thinking of one of those men's groups—you know? Where you confess, where you share. But drawing was better. Singular. Like that heroic man out being responsible for his own life; yet with drawing the man was always looking in the same direction, so as not to lose his orientation. Always looking at her. Drawing was as close to confession—and to the society he imagined lay on the other side of confession—as his thief instincts would allow him to get. So, evenings, there was Georgette's group and Jacques had never missed. It was an odd point of re-entry, to be sure, but once he found that room of hers, he needed to be there every night, doing it with the rest of them.

"I can be like the rest of them. I can fit in."

Anne-Marie (not artistically inclined) doubted it. If she could never fit in, how could he?

And there was hope in the fact that Georgette and Anne-Marie seemed to have found something in each other. While he brooded, wrote and read, off they went, wandering the streets, to window shop and drink tea. Two friends: such a basic thing. The sight of them together was another small connection to the world and it made him smile—even if to smile at the thought of a friend felt like a splinter, long covered over and nestled beside a nerve.

No, no more *de luxe*, no more Maxim's. Window shopping was the extent of it. He always swore that had they been more settled, he would have bought Anne-Marie whatever she might have wanted. But there was not much room in a van for gowns and shoes and things, not after the room Jacques needed for his stuff—a couple of hefty trunks filled with the materials and accoutrements of the personages he had assembled. She never complained. She seemed to understand. Anne-Marie could enjoy lunch as much with a rumpled Henri Vangier as with a skittish Jacques Normand. Probably more so.

"You see? We're partners."

Yes, she stuck by him. And he held her hand as they climbed through windows, dressed in motley. It was easy. It was by the book. His own book. What else was he supposed to do—open up a *steak-frites*? Everyone has a talent. Everyone has to earn a living. Everyone has to have a life. His was a quiet life, in a van, in a dreary border city.

But free, more or less.

Georgette was the one who complained. "Why do you persist?" Referring to his collection of clothes, his ability to disappear behind matte, rouge and talcum powder.

"I'm taking great chances coming here, exposing myself like this." It could be anywhere: downtown for a lunch, for example.

"Great chances? No one's forcing you. And no one recognizes you anyway, Jacques. You don't have to be a clown any more."

"A clown?" It hurt and baffled him. Georgette knew him, but not as well as she thought she did. He was being responsible. Making sure no one got hurt. Whatever else, Le Grand Jacques was still dangerous. You did not want to meet him. You did not want to cross him. But Georgette said things like that—wounding him, reducing him. He lived with it because he needed her. Arriving in this place, at this juncture, Jacques knew he had one foot in and one foot out of life. He was looking for the other side of himself; he knew he needed this other guiding voice.

A new mother? Something like it.

It had been Georgette who brought the news about the butcher. One quiet afternoon (they were all quiet afternoons), he was sitting in a corner of the Rembrandt with a *pastis* and the paper when Georgette and Anne-Marie returned from a midday expedition, sat down with him, ordered their usual from that ghostly waiter—so much like every other day.

"Some inspector—Aliette Nouvelle—she's been looking for you in the butcher's shop."

"Who told you that?"

"The butcher."

"The butcher?" Even as he posed it, Jacques felt the query floating vague and light toward the fragile place inside himself.

"Don't worry," assured the artist's model, "he has no idea. You have about as much in common with the Jacques Normand he imagines as one of his sides of beef. He's just in love with Anne-Marie."

A debate ensued. He sipped his drink and pondered it. What the butcher imagines...

A butcher called Bruno Bondiguel. A man whose name he had stolen and used as his own.

His names. Jacques had to grant, it was an interesting place for her to begin.

Because being Le Grand Jacques is like being the Queen of England. Or the richest man in the world. Who are your friends? Who could possibly be your real friend? You have almost everyone to choose from and that is where the problem lies. When he'd started out, a kid practising the art of ugliness to win respect in his chosen world, he had two friends: Daniel, and Richard. Ricky—older, a man who knew this new kid was the real thing. They were partners. They were a gang. They were friends.

But, *c'est vrai, il est spécial, le petit Jaki*; and soon—watch out!— here comes Public Enemy Number One! Amazing! No one can touch him!

Right. In the underworld, the biggest name is the biggest liability, the biggest target. Natural friends began to shy away. They weren't stupid. New ones presented themselves. No, never any problem attracting new friends in those days; but they came too close too quickly and Jacques found he could never really know them.

Public Enemy. When such a creature runs out of men to trust (and it happens quickly), his community expands in different directions: Pick a pocket. Steal an old man's papers. He'd actually hunted out these types—watched them, studied them in the same way he perfected his waiter or his hairdresser, his dreamy Pierrot. They were fat and fond of Sunday. They had wives they would regret each day but never leave. He usually chose someone below the professions— they were safer, and Jacques was no snob. The salt of the earth. They were only names but they were soon included amongst his most effective partners. Later, alone in the van on the edge of life, they had been his only friends. His targets too. The ones he saw in Freedom's mirror.

And now? Could an inspector—an Aliette Nouvelle—ever stand a chance of pulling the right name out of a hat? He decided it could be a game. Yes—a diversion. No harm. What possible harm?

It built from there.

- 16 -

LOVE AS A VICTIM OF FREEDOM

The romantic elements of an outlaw's myth vis-à-vis *l'Amour* were problematic when applied to his current situation. Despite Anne-Marie—her beauty, support and trust—love, in the aftermath of his career as the symbol of Freedom, was a constant source of deep uncertainty. He was frequently, and easily, tripped up on this unresolved "issue"—as Georgette always called it. It could happen too suddenly: that anger, erupting, pushing him.

The day they went down to the boutiques for lunch. An outing. A bit of fun under the cover of his Henri Vangier; well-deserved after so many busy nights in a row. In the maître d' Jacques immediately recognized a supercilious ass. An arbitrary man with a niche in the market but not a shred of soul—a lot like a warden he'd once known and hated. And so blithe as he spurned them. "Sorry…not like that, I'm afraid—it's highly inappropriate." He meant Anne-Marie; the way she liked to dress. And then, in the next obsequious breath the man was welcoming that woman and her pretty man as if they were royalty. "*Salut*! of course I've got a table…I've got *your* table!"

That Charlotte Barthès. Jacques knew her; he'd seen her in the paper and Georgette had given Anne-Marie a copy of her little tome on how a woman should live right. Sex and money, that was Charlotte's simple recipe. He'd had a look at it, but couldn't get past the first chapter: "There is no need to fake your orgasm any more; if it is not there, so be it—soon, neither will he be. And there is no excuse for the woman who does not insist on stock options, always with that second, delirious suitor falling at her heels. Play it smart, play it natural, play according to the lay of the land. The game is yours to win and you know they know it..."

He'd seen the tops of Anne-Marie's cheeks turning red as she tried to plow through this tripe. She wouldn't talk about it, but he sensed that it confused her, and a lot more than the guys on the streets ever had. He was sure she saw how facile it was. The problem was all the adulation surrounding the one who spewed it out. He tried to tell her: "Drop your guard for a second and that kind of woman will have you believing she knows all these things that you don't and never will unless you buy her book. Worst kind of charlatan." But Anne-Marie was vulnerable.

And what could a little man like Henri Vangier do about it? Not a lot.

A smooth waiter, however, who went by the name of J.-C.—J.-C. Quémeraye—now that could be a different story. Especially with the help of a dancing buttermaid! Ha! Jacques retreated to the van, did a quick change, gave the regular *garçon* enough cash to cover his next three shifts, straightened his bow tie, and placed himself in the service of Charlotte Barthès.

Charlotte—whom everyone was supposed to worship: J.-C. Quémeraye listened to her carping at her beau as he refilled their glasses. "You don't love me enough... Eric? Are you listening to me?"

Because I need more of you. Because I need more love!

Well, who doesn't! Poor Eric. J.C. felt for him. No one deserves that kind of crap. It was as if this pretty man, this wealthy man (could the likes of her even dream of consorting with a poor one?), had been beaten into submission by his own good luck. So J.C. poured the wine and made small but artful mistakes in what should have been a perfect lunch, taking a bead on this perfect Charlotte while remembering the *psychologues* in those quiet rooms in the annex at La Santé:

I'm sensing this demand for unconditional love.

Really. How much do they pay you for that? Who the hell doesn't want unconditional love? A dog, maybe?

Well, yes...

And when a buttermaid, discovered under the table, nestled between Eric's legs, rose and fled in a whoosh of spectacular speed— stealing a steak right off a plate on the way out!—that fat maître d' was flabbergasted. His guests were mortified. The only sound to be heard in that chic atmosphere was the weeping of the lady who had been wronged, and the drunken chuckle of her companion as he tried to coax her out of her despair. "Well now, this is what my therapist calls a liminal experience," Eric told her. "He says it's when nothing seems real and you just can't get any control. He says all you can do is flow with it...like Ulysses, sailing through the mists of hell. I think he's on to something, I really do. I could get you an appointment if you like... Have some more wine?"

"Shut up, Eric...please shut up!" As if she were truly afraid of something.

So Eric helped himself to another glass and Jacques was glad to supply it. He often felt he could have been a therapist. He knew people—Jacques knew the things they hid.

When the maître d' approached, shrugging his huge apology, there was Charlotte's wallet, stuck snugly in his belly.

She screamed. Screamed for the police.

While Eric swayed and grinned and scratched his head.

And the maître d's red face appeared about to pop.

Then J.-C. Quémeraye disappeared.

Spiteful? Damn right. But that day he got his own back. Highly satisfying, seeing her cry; and seeing that stuffed-up poseur sweat. Necessary too. He explained it to his Anne-Marie "It was love that sparked that one, *ma belle*—the level of love I cannot provide you out of the fear that anyone with half an eye will recognize the real Jacques Normand. It's the expression of love I'm not allowed to show...that I'm forced to swallow in the face of the likes of *monsieur* Wanda. It's that gross display by someone like her—who has far more than her fair share!"

Mmm. Love, and the limits the world imposes.

"...Because Jacques Normand knows how to love. Didn't he write seven hundred letters from his cell in the Canadian jail to the object of his passion? Poor Lise... But seven hundred! When it was right, it was big. And didn't he dedicate his story to seven women, the shapers of his very life? Did he not tell all of France of a father's love for a daughter? And La Puce, isn't she there in his mind forever? No one can ever say she isn't!"

And isn't love such a bitch when you're in hiding?

It was from the headiest heights of this post-job vituperation that he first saw her—Aliette Nouvelle. She was outside *chez* Wanda. He found himself watching from the van as she questioned the baffled objects of a thief's bitter joke. And didn't this inspector look just like one more prim social worker with no idea. Ha! Watching. Still tingling with his anger.

Jacques sniffed a laugh and shrugged a smile for a busily chomping Anne-Marie. "Enjoy it—you did well." Then he went back to his own lunch: cold steak, fresh bread and a big, solid Roussillon—in honour of the large man whose corkscrew he had used to open it. Yes, a corkscrew was the prize that day. That, and a series of sly pinpricks to the flank of a woman's grotesque discontent. Of course it was a joke!

Anne-Marie put the dishes aside and stretched out in the back with *Du sexe au salaire.* At least now, if she must, she could read it with some critical distance. Jacques was feeling better; he thought coffee would be nice as he started up the van.

And so he followed her, the inspector, as she strolled along with her gangly helper. No, she was not much to look at: those eyes—she turned and looked right at him before crossing at a corner—they were a limpid, almost transparent blue. Without help from the solid blue of her beret and coat, they would not have been there at all. You could see through them to the empty sky before you were aware of their intensity. Jacques had seen his own child studying her *Monde de Mickey* with eyes just like that, but she'd been only five at the time. Her skin was not as white as Anne-Marie's. She would tan on a beach. He was thinking that her ordinary body would get brown, or maybe golden, but her thinnish lips would still have that pursed, not quite satisfied quality, regardless of the sun. Straw-blonde hair, straight to her collar, did not excite him; pretty hard to beat Anne-Marie's dark hurricane of demon curls. Shoes and accessories were simply worka-day. Yes, a career girl, working on a problem. It had been fun watching her sizing up that vainglorious Charlotte Barthès.

Jacques watched Inspector Aliette Nouvelle walk straight from Wanda's to the Rembrandt. Well! He could have been sitting there when she walked in! He usually was. He realized she had come to the

scene of the crime to see about J.-C. Quémeraye, that the plight of
Charlotte Barthès, much less a fat maître d', meant little to this earnest
woman. Somehow she had Jacques Normand on her wavelength.

In his mind, the thing moved up a level.

That same night he found Nouvelle, A. in the phone book.
Number 1 F.-A.-Bartholdi, a street on the edge of the park named
after the Colmar man who designed that statue for the harbour in New
York. Jacques had been up it. Jacques had been lots of places. She lived
by the park: he steered in that direction and pulled over across from
her window. He was watching as she went climbing on her railing
trying to rescue her cat, and was half-hypnotized for several moments
by the sight of seemingly limitless moonlight streaming through her
nightgown and into his eyes. It formed around her—around her very
ordinary body, and transformed it. And it was the way she reached out
for the cat: balanced on the railing, precarious; but focused on the
thing—the job at hand.

Then Anne-Marie nuzzled his neck and gave him a look: come
to bed. When he asked himself what the hell he thought he was doing,
he thought, well, it's a game, isn't it? A diversion.

No—not a diversion! No game here! The outlaw was at odds
with himself for the next several days. Because a game, like an art,
requires quality. Lacking quality, it is nothing. The way she was going
about it—asking in butcher shops and knocking on suburban doors;
Jacques began to think it certainly lacked this fundamental thing. She
was courting a butcher. His butcher. And the butcher, if Georgette
had it right, had left a lot to be desired in his description of the actual
man. She could follow a trail of names; but that trail kept doubling
back to a past that was gone. None of those characters were him. Not
Jacques Normand. And, for his part, he could play the cat burglar,
always, and so easily, one step ahead, leading her on—but leading
nowhere.

Jacques thought, if a detective wants to fool around with history,
at least let her get it right.

He had been casing the city's central bank practically since the
day he arrived. It was two things for a new man in town searching for
a new life: a kind of therapeutic test, like a recovered alcoholic trying
out his social legs at a party; and something to do when it got bad, that

is to say, when he felt lost. Because it was second nature to assume the face of a shuffling sweeper while taking the measure of the place. Robert Blot: one of his "friends." This bank was nothing compared to Paris, of course, but it was the richest around. So he'd been checking it out. Preparing. Planning. Jacques was always comfortable in that.

Later on, he'd grown less so, what with Georgette harping the way she did, always urging him to forget the big and the spectacular: "Just a thief, Jacques. Quiet. Subtle. God likes the odd thief... A thief is good to keep things in balance. A Public Enemy...that's nothing. Can't possibly be any more. Nothing human, anyway. Please! Do yourself a favour: no more banks..." He heard this. And he found himself wanting to keep Anne-Marie's life steady, if not safe: "At least we're together. It's all we really need, n'est-ce pas?" while pulling her up by the wrist—she was so light!—onto yet another window sill, then creeping inside. But they were creeping inside together. At that late date, it was something worth cherishing. Where would he, closing in on a chubby fifty, ever find anyone else like her?

With these things in his mind, Jacques had been feeling less and less like he needed the bank.

Then why do it?

A question of character. Scale. Quality. Like this problem with love he was experiencing. A star detective wanted Jacques Normand but it appeared she had the wrong idea as to who he was. He would do the bank so Inspector Aliette Nouvelle would know who she was dealing with.

And he did—all of it alone, except the two tire quilts. Anne-Marie helped with those. It was a stupid thing to attempt, all the more so for someone so out of shape. More than painful! Nine hours of hard labour. He wept his way through half of it, like some overwrought penitent. He came close to popping a gut. But Jacques left no trace, apart from the fact that it was a masterpiece.

Yes. She would know him.

17

CLAUDE'S APPOINTMENT

Jean-Paul Blismes was a local psychologist whose practice was focused on young offenders, but he was also under contract to the Minister of the Interior to serve any member of the *Police Judiciaire* who might feel the need. When one Claude Néon appeared in his office, Monsieur Blismes immediately sensed a need. "Ah…Inspector Néon. Come in."

"Look, I know I've been edgy lately, but really, if anyone has to come to something like this, it's her."

"And who would that be?"

"Inspector Nouvelle."

"Hmm. Well, it seems your Commissaire thinks otherwise."

"I mean—"

"It's all right, Inspector. All we're going to do is talk."

"Better be. You start flashing those stupid ink-blotch things or try to hypnotize me and I'm gone."

"Please. Just relax. Tell me about it. We'll see how it goes."

"Sure… That's exactly what she said."

———

Inspector Nouvelle was difficult to work with and not at all what I had dreamed. I'd always been attracted to her, but she'd completely quashed my hopes. I could accept that. But she had to screw with my confidence as well. I just wanted to get back with the boys.

And then, that morning at the bank, she gave the order to chase that poodle. "After her. Quick!" I heard it, couldn't believe it, and paused a prudent moment to let her reconsider. Perhaps I was considering defying it. Refusal to obey—very major, the greatest of risks, I know. But eight weeks of her whims had left my instincts shattered, my judgement in a knot. Those ice-blue eyes were wide, obsessed. She made a curt gesture with her forearm: the all-powerful circus trainer imposing her will; the hard-nosed cop saying get to it! I was powerless. I jumped through the hole in the bank and ran.

In the space of two steps I knew I had jumped too far.

The woman ran as if enchanted, the purloined sandwich gripped delicately in her jaws, her feet never seeming to touch the ground. At first I was not so far behind that I could not appreciate the beauty of her movement. She leaned into the corners with this ultra-feminine precision. It made my senses ache to see it. She looked back at me more than once and I thought I could feel the most purposeful focus beaming from her dark eyes. Running: it was her *raison d'être*.

And for a part of it I had no care at all for any impressions our chase might have left behind us as we passed. I forgot the catching The thought occurred to me that I would have liked to run alongside her; that if I could, everything in my life might have been different. Running and nothing else, as if toward an inner silence that was like a door. I felt the wind and observed the world as it came to me, whipping through the park, past the courts where springtime players practised their strokes, around the change house where promiscuous men gathered at midnight, past the swans in the lake, an illicit love affair being discussed on a bench. I was briefly in tune and I saw it all.

Then it faded, changed to grey as my heart pounded and my unfit lungs searched in vain for breath. She pulled away and the only clarity was the fact that Inspector Claude Néon held no hope in hell of catching this...this poodle?

And I was starting to hate her for it. The Inspector. For subjecting me to this.

But I struggled on, of course—one's sense of duty remains entrenched. What I felt now was my tie as it flapped in my face. It was like the proverbial glove in the hand of fate, smacking me, challenging me: *Catch that poodle or don't bother to come back!* I felt the sweat soaking through my shirt, enveloping me. Charging through a puddle, I visualized the muddy splatter down the back of my new, partially silk legs. Whoever she was, she was ruining my suit with mud and my day with embarrassment. My sense of Claude was on the line.

The poodle came to the *rond-point* and wove her way through traffic before disappearing into the smaller streets on the far side. As I approached the traffic cop, he was wide-eyed, suspended in a dangerous way. The man looked like he had seen an angel go motoring by. An angel, then me, this bedraggled soul, who came huffing and puffing after, and who, for his efforts, was almost flattened by a milk truck as he made his frantic dash across the circle.

I wished I could give up, but I could not. And as I staggered on, up and down the streets of the quarter, looking through the sweat and tears mixing in my eyes, I broke through another barrier of sorts; surely I must have gone "past the wall" as the runners say. For I became immune to the pounding in my chest, even lost sight again, in my mind's eye, of my mission. I felt my soul shift gears. I imagined we were one-on-one, the Inspector and me—that I was grappling with Aliette Nouvelle.

It was on a grey blanket with a weave of forest green running through it. We were locked together, desperately: me, clutching at her unknown body; she, pounding my head and kicking at me. No words on either side. Silently and brutally she went about getting rid of me. Dumbly, I pawed at her thighs, her knees, and went sliding down the hard edge of femur underneath her shin. I stopped there, as did she, sighing and drawing breath. In my vision I kissed her foot. And then her ankle. I crawled slowly back, tracing my lips along her calf, then her thigh, white and lean. But when I reached the border of her rumpled skirt I was disoriented to be so close. I hesitated, then dared—dared to look up at her face. Without a word, without an expression, she wound up and socked me; incredibly, like no man in any gang. My whole being shuddered, and I fell away.

It was the endorphins that made this grim dream. Aliette Nouvelle had told me nothing much, but she had talked about her own runs in the park, and the endorphins. Now here they were: scattered, erotic, crazy. Yet as they went about removing me from myself, these endorphins gave notice that the propulsion they created was inexorable, meant to give anyone, even someone like me, a glimpse of the eternal. Well, I saw it:

That Claude Néon had two strikes against him: Out of shape. And lacking in hope.

That without these two essentials he could possess no hero-mode, that natural sense of personal sanctity, the feeling of being a hero, vivid, in one's own mind.

That as he ran past his limits, Claude was bound to go plunging into the heart of his life and stumble badly in front of the gods.

And that the gods, who have always enjoyed a hero, passed their judgement. Unanimous, they called Claude's vision—his failed rape of Aliette Nouvelle—obscene. An abuse. This man, so wretched in spirit, had wasted the elixir that is the endorphins. They asked: *What shall we do with such a man as that?* I could hear their voices in the ether, debating. Was it only because I could not catch up with a poodle? The effect of one small defeat? Or was it a pervading point of view?

And could I hear the voice of Aliette Nouvelle behind the voices I was hearing, telling them what to think? *Ha, ha, Claude…you can run but you can't hide.*

I slowed, the vision fizzled. Finally there was nothing left. Drenched in sweat, confused, despondent to the point of blindness, I stopped and sat on a step in a doorway and breathed.

But those gods are remorseless, the way they like to push these things. Before I had regained any semblance of control, I found myself sitting on the other side of that same door—in the Rembrandt Café, staring into a glass of beer. That waiter, Willem, stood at a polite remove, arms folded, sympathetic but professional as he engaged a messed-up cop. "It's all in a day's work, my friend."

"Chasing a poodle? No, it's not…it's not in a day's work. It's not what I do. I'm an inspector."

"It's all right to feel sad. As long as you really feel it." Willem blinked, and with this tiny gesture he urged me to cry.

I held tight. A poodle, and now this *homme rose. Mon Dieu!*

"Let it open your heart, even if hurts," my host insisted, but so gently.

"No. No!…it's because my boss says Claude, quick! and I just jump, yes sir, yes ma'am, and there's no rhyme or reason there at all, but I just do it. I'm the damn poodle…!"

The waiter placed a bright new glass of beer in front of me. "Sadness can give the world a deep and wonderful colour, my friend."

I nodded, blank, empty. I gulped eagerly—and choked. With that, the tears gushed out and spread across my burning face. "And who's my boss?" I know I shouted it.

"Who's your boss?" responded Willem, not exactly shouting back; but his hand was clenched in a fist, arm half-cocked, pumping, empathizing to the limits of professional decorum, urging me—cry, man! Let it out! Go for it!

"Inspector Aliette Nouvelle!" I gasped.

Tell me! You can tell me!

"The pride of the brigade...oh God! with this untouched face and this mind like...I don't know..."

I did know, but I couldn't say it. Willem hovered there, waiting for the answer. I gazed into his patient eyes and sipped. It calmed me. My tears calmed me—the release. I started to see what was in front of me, and feel the thing I had felt the first time, when she had touched my shoulder and told me everything would be fine. The ambience of this place: dark, rich. "...Like a dream," I said, looking around and seeing in a way I never had.

"Incredible!" whispered the waiter.

"Fantastic! She doesn't work. She dreams. It's impossible. And now I chase..." I let myself drift off, sipping, sobbing gently, privately. "I don't belong here," I confessed, after some moments.

"Of course you do."

"No...I should be back out there, back on her trail. Follow those leads, those clues to Jacques Normand!" But I knew I was stuck there, for a while at least, as biblical dust spun slowly in the quiet space. Newspapers were lowering, faces were looking up from meandering conversations, others surfacing from deep inside warm solitude. Then their glasses were raised in unison and the light beatified wherever it fell.

Someone raised a glass in my direction. Greetings.

I managed a smile and shyly responded in kind.

Willem smiled too. "Jacques Normand," he wondered. "Now wasn't he Public Enemy Number One?"

I bit down hard on a thumbnail, nodding yes—yes, he certainly was.

Monsieur Blismes stopped it for a moment. "Could I ask a question here?"

"Yes..."

"Why do you keep referring to yourself in the third person?"

"Which third person?"

"Claude Néon thought this. Claude Néon did that."

"Well, because I felt like I was in the third person at the time."

"And you don't normally refer to yourself in the third person."

"Of course not. Why would I? But she does it all the time. The Inspector—when we're driving around. Like I'm not there, talking to herself about Inspector Nouvelle like it was someone in the back seat. Maybe I got it from her."

"That's interesting. But, leaving aside the Inspector for the moment, what about the gods? I'd like to know how you feel about the gods."

"I told you—it was a vision. From running."

"I see. And so..."

I asked for a breakfast meeting with the Commissaire and was surprised and a little embarrassed to find myself back in the Rembrandt Café.

"A good little place," declared the boss.

That waiter was nothing if not discreet, however, and the regulars, with whom I had communed so wholeheartedly the day before, seemed not only uninterested in my presence, but also unreal. Quite unreal. For I was determined to change the thing before it got out of control. Over coffee and a sweet croissant I reminded Louis Moreau that it was not in my job description to do the things she was making me do, or, more to the point, follow the vague line which seemed to obsess her.

The Commissaire was inclined to agree. "It's odd... I've never seen her go off on such a tangent before."

"No."

Then the old cop reconsidered. "Or perhaps I have. Maybe it's just that I've never seen her make a mistake."

"No one has."

"Mmm. Might be that a woman like her gets it absolutely right, or absolutely wrong."

"Inevitable then," I said. "No one's perfect."

"Bad time to break her streak. I was counting on her."

"So was I." I meant professionally and he heard this.

"Still…" He was musing, staring darkly in that way which was bound to impress and intimidate. "We have to give her the benefit of the doubt."

"Have to?"

"She's earned it."

I held my ground. That is to say I remained politely—read silently—skeptical, effectively appealing to the man's better judgement. The simple question at this point was: why?

"Because she's onto something. It's written all over her face."

"But what?"

He shrugged at me, and for a moment we were equals. I looked at Louis Moreau sharing a younger man's incomprehension, and I knew that creeping doubt had become the bond between us. "Dunno," he finally sputtered. "…Would love to know… You're the one who's working with her."

I nodded—yes, I'm her partner.

Et voilà: two men, one agreement.

I sipped my coffee, feeling the warmth of it in my face; while close on, *tête à tête* with the likes of the Commissaire, the Rembrandt changed and was no longer anything of what it had been. I realized I had indeed succeeded in changing the case. The approach, as it were. Just like that.

Afterward, we sat wordless in the back as the Commissaire's car travelled through traffic and entered the circle by the park. I showed him the traffic cop. "This man…she took us to look at this man. Just to look at him…we went around three times."

As the gendarme in the middle did the dance with his hands, I observed the Commissaire, watching the man as if in a spell—the way Inspector Nouvelle had done. They did share this tendency to mull, to get lost inside themselves in the midst of anything. In many basic ways she could have been his daughter. As I beheld this, I reckoned that although Louis Moreau would submit to reason, he would always defend her. And so I hoped I hadn't made a big mistake in exposing her methods—hurt his feelings, perhaps; made him doubt his choice of stars.

But, too late; it was done. One has to live with one's decisions. And their consequences.

As we left the circle I glanced back, past the traffic cop, at her place. The mystery apartment. Who got to stay there with her— her and that cat she was always talking about? I had heard about Gérard Richand. (No, of course not from her.) But now the man was both married and promoted, and there was scant possibility that the Chief J. of I. and I would ever end up at a table together with a drink and some time to kill: *alors*, Gérard, what's the story on the Inspector? Tell, please, for the sake of every one of us who has ever wished. No— such a scenario was pure fantasy. It hadn't worked and I had to accept the fact that poor Claude Néon would never know the better parts of Inspector Nouvelle's life.

Hmm. Last thoughts, a last look from the back window of the official car.

Then someone came out the Inspector's balcony door. That black mane crowned with a scarlet bow, resplendent under the blue sky. She was unmistakable, even from three hundred meters and receding—

The car turned a corner. The vision disappeared.

I spun and smashed my nose against the pane. "Ow...*ah merde!* Stop the car!"

It stopped. Both the Commissaire and the driver turned to me. "Claude...what's the matter? What happened to your nose?"

I was sitting there with one hot stream of blood surging through my brain, another trickling down from my nostril onto the plateau of my upper lip. I had to say something or drown in a pool of blood and paranoia. This was my punishment for betrayal. So soon. So direct! The bitter fruit of a momentary need to cry about it.

The Commissaire's hands were soft as they pulled away my fingers and gently tested the throbbing membrane for signs of fracture. Then he laughed. "…But this is bullet-proof glass! You could never put your head through that. You couldn't even dent it. What were you doing? Did you see something?"

I too tried to muster a laugh, but it hurt too much. "It was her!"

"Who?"

"The poodle… She was there…on her balcony…." gasping it out. Nothing more sore than a fractured nose; the slightest motion…"Ah!"

"Whose balcony…Claude—whose balcony?"

"Inspector Nouvelle's…"

"Inspector Nouvelle's balcony… What was she doing?"

"Nothing. Just—ah!—standing there!"

The Commissaire was perplexed. "Driver, take us round the block."

I braced myself as the car found its way back. There was the traffic circle, and the traffic cop, and her building, the balcony three floors above the garden and a white cat sitting in the morning sun. We all saw it. Then the driver and the Commissaire were looking at me. There was little I could say apart from blurting out a request to search her domicile. But that would have been too many words in a row—excruciating in my present condition. And internal affairs were the most complicated of all. A request like that could take weeks to effect.

—　　—

Monsieur Blismes asked, "Can you admit that your interest in the Inspector has spilled over into areas beyond the professional?"

"But she lives beyond the professional!"

"You know what I mean, Inspector Néon, there's no point in doing this if you won't face facts."

"Yeah, yeah."

"I think we should schedule a follow-up session… Is it sore, your nose?"

"Very sore."

18

TIME COLLAPSING

Before it was even done Jacques knew the bank was not important. More profound than the agony brought on by dust in the nose and the exertion of muscles gone to fat was an abiding sense, an image that persisted—and which remained as the dawn spread and he was safely away with a new fortune, exhausted but exhilarated, crawling in beside Anne-Marie, holding her, nuzzling, needing. Her eyes stayed closed as he caressed her. Her nipples responded to his soft bites and she moved herself against him, opening to him without fuss or passion, as if she were bidding him enter her sleep, not her body. So they made love, and Jacques knew it wasn't fair pitting her against the image of a detective's eyes. Not fair at all, as he arched and pushed and fucked her hard.

And making love could not chase the thought of a detective from his mind.

It was Aliette Nouvelle who had pushed him through that night. Her serious face had appeared to confront the chaos of his life's complaints—the noise of his anger toward authority, the futile years, the mothering chides of Georgette Duguay, the renewed dream of the Public Enemy.

He and Anne-Marie had decorated the ceiling at the back end of the van with a collage of clippings from his glory days. It was always there in the night, like a blanket. Now, in the mornings, it was always there like flood-stained wallpaper. That morning, as police and press and citizens swarmed around another violated bank, Jacques rolled away from Anne-Marie and lay there staring at the man he used to be.

Unable to close his eyes, he left the van and went to her place.

As he investigated the inspector's home, Jacques was thinking that for a few—people like the author of *Du sexe au salaire,* for example—seduction is a skill, something to be carried in one's pocket. For the rest, seduction is pure mystery. Uncanny: instincts meeting, the sense of the other, a sense which may not know itself that well at all but which knows exactly how to spark and control the other's senses, the other's need to know. This was a woman with a bundle of ribbons, some quaint hats and an old white cat, beer bottles lined up by the fridge and a book on birth control beside her bed—who happened to be a cop. She was the last thing in the world he needed. Apart from the fact of the thing she did to earn her daily bread, did he even know her at all? The things in her home led him to believe he did.

She was good, he was bad. With the Public Enemy rising from the dead, with time seeming to collapse in all directions, it was the only context Jacques could bring to mind.

So stop right there, *mon ami!* Because this has happened before.

To wit: He had fallen in love on a beach in Spain, with no less than Innocence incarnate, and gone happily into the tunnel called marriage with a woman who had no idea who he was. The whole thing was built on lies and games.

"*Salut, ma chérie!* I'm home..." Home from his probationary apprenticeship as an architectural renderer, but not before stopping off along the way at his probation officer's and then the bar where the little jobs got cooked up in the corner, his hands all over the laughing girls who knew what it was all about. She had no idea. She couldn't sense it. But this was marriage and she was his wife, so home Jacques went with the pittance they gave him, to Sunday with the parents and visits with the in-laws, but mainly to this person who believed he was good and gave him a child to prove it. La Puce, he called her—a common endearment: a tiny thing, a flea. Six pounds of pure love for Jacques Normand.

He actually did have a talent for drawing, and, in truth, did not mind doing cross-views and floor plans. There was space there and one could look into it. Concentrate like hell and the day would be over. There were days and weeks when he'd felt at home with the situation. But luck, or the system, or maybe that thing called Fate conspired to end it. The firm went under, the apprentice was freed. The search for the next position always seemed to end in a bar or a car—and trouble; which was fun, but trouble nonetheless.

And she never knew and she never wavered. The wife.

When it looked like he might be away for some jail time (just before the baby arrived), Jacques and his lawyer cooked up the story about the job in the Secret Service. *Maître* Annie G. He always considered her one of the better women he had known; a shame she was old enough to be his *maman* (who didn't know either). His wife listened and believed it.

A great story! The charade went on and on.

Unable to tell the truth and with no flicker of respect, let alone love, for such naiveté, while seeing his little girl, bound to grow up sensing a ghost where her father stood, it was too much. All it did was break his balls. He finally told her so. He had used those very words: "You're starting to break my balls.... I just don't need all your shit!" Then he walked away. To raise hell, go to jail, break out, raise more hell, then disappear forever to the freedom he felt he needed to be the man he believed he was.

These memories swirled in the clean and airy domain of a woman called Aliette Nouvelle. Jacques looked, sensed, and paired them up; "good" brought wife and cop together in his mind like bookends.

Thus the spiriting of a ribbon into her desk at the Commissariat. It was not possible for man such as himself to love the likes of her. It could only ever be a game.

A game of quality. Nuance. Expert moves. Like the bank job.

For all Jacques' effort, however, the bank had fallen short. Lots of noise, but no inspector on the front page announcing she was hot on the trail of France's most notorious hero. He let it go by. No, the bank was not important. He still had the money, after all. And he still had the game.

But he was needing someone to bear witness, to appreciate his expertise. He thought, I'll bring the women in *my* life to play it with me, Anne-Marie and Georgette, to make sure everyone understands what is happening. Simple. As simple as it had been with the wife: watch the cop walk away to her work, get into her place, play.

A big mistake bringing Georgette.

They were trying on some of Aliette Nouvelle's hats. The American baseball cap seemed to fit Georgette; her silver hair looked good against that shade of blue. Anne-Marie wandered out onto the balcony to have a look at the white cat. As soon as she was out of earshot, Georgette demanded, in her pointed way, "What about Anne-Marie? Surely this woman is just a passing fancy."

"Yes, exactly."

"She's police...she's supposed to look for you. To find you and put you away. Don't be foolish, Jacques."

"What are you talking about?"

"You know what I'm talking about."

"No..." But he could hear himself, circumspect and uncertain; and he knew Georgette was seeing his heart. So he admitted, casually, "There's something about her."

"Like what?"

"Don't know... You tell me?" Trying to make a joke of it. First time she had ever played marriage counsellor with him.

Georgette wasn't laughing. "It's not a good time to lose track, *monsieur.*"

"Don't worry. I know what I'm doing...everything's fine."

To that, she said nothing; she sat on the bed and read the inspector's birth control material.

He took the women away, dropped them at the Rembrandt and kept on driving. Bloody Georgette! She could give him such a headache. He drove around in a fog of uncertainty all through a drizzly Alsace afternoon and into the evening; what exactly did he feel about this woman? Oh *merde...merde, merde!* The way one thing grows out of another, out of sight and out of control. Like freedom? Like love?

The guilt did not make it any easier. Supper uneaten, he sat in front of his mirror preparing the puffy face of Paul Toul, Professor of Dental Hygiene, the best one to put beside a detective at the group, while behind him Anne-Marie presented the same basic picture. That remote quality which marked her exotic eyes. Anne-Marie would never ask what was on his mind. And Jacques could not tell her that he felt himself moving past their life together. Nor could he tell her to what.

Then at the group he watched Inspector Nouvelle struggling away with Georgette's pose. She was right beside Jacques Normand now, and completely unwary. Yes! Those shades of the ingenuous wife. But as he watched, it occurred to him that if the mask was too subtle for her to be worried, for her to begin to feel him, that if there was no effect, then why, why on earth, was he bothering? And then he asked himself: what is the effect meant to be? Did he want her to be uneasy? Or scared? What was he supposed to gain from that?

His soul whispered: *This is where it begins to come apart, mon gars. Are you ready for it?*

They had quoted him on the back of his book. "*C'est l'homme qui tient l'arme qui a de l'importance, pas l'arme elle-même.*" It's not the gun itself that is important, but the man holding it. Short, sweet, socially relevant—this idea of the man being responsible for his actions. The hero. Jacques always supposed a quotation like that helped sell a few copies. Mmm Combine the notion of fear unto death with the spectre of a man who knows exactly what he's doing.

Or did. Oh, beloved spectre! That quotation was just another cheap bit of jail cell philosophy and nothing more—the sentiments of a man at a dead end, his identity sitting there in front of him like a bowl of cold onion soup. It had nothing to say about a man on the loose, dangling from a loose end, who had given up guns. (It was Anne-Marie's only real demand on Jacques and he had honoured it.)

Alors, there he was, watching this woman trying so awkwardly to capture Georgette on paper. This lovely woman, because anyone so intent radiates an essential beauty. This accomplished woman (drawing notwithstanding), who led the men because she was better at the job than they were. This deadly serious woman whose purpose was a man who was the Public Enemy in a time when she was still a girl; a time before she knew what a man is actually for. This solitary woman who conceived of a man in a way—in a way that Jacques just did not know!

Without the gun to announce himself, would such a woman remain unknown to him forever? Time to live was the only thing he ever really wanted. Freedom. Standing there in his drawing class, the site of his small link to the world beyond his myth, he watched her and understood that even if you have all the days and years you ever dreamed of, time still occurs. It occurs in generations. This woman from the next generation left Jacques lost in time. That night he finished his work and walked out, increasingly distracted by this feeling.

He drove back to the apartment beside the park. He left Anne-Marie with the van. "I don't really understand. Do you?"

A slow shake of her drooping curls. "No." Looking out of her silence for an explanation he could not give. She received a kiss instead, and, moving over, sat stoic behind the wheel. To wait. To be there. It broke his heart.

But: Anne-Marie will be all right, he thought. Anne-Marie will survive. He fixed his sights on the window above. The white cat was out on the dark balcony, standing guard by the painted rail. He was inside her bedroom in no time flat, with the white cat in his arms.

Ambient light. Eyes adjusted. The perfect setting for the likes of Jacques Normand. Yet, gazing again at that old Wanted poster tacked to her wall, he could not believe, again, that he looked that way. Shabby and common. Her mirror confirmed it though—feeling the stubble of growth covering his chin and cheeks, unbuttoning his shirt and pressing a palm against the sagging flab. Dropping the cat, he took her brush and began to work on his hair, brushing away the last traces of the talcum powder he'd used to construct the last disguise, then brushing still more, manic, harder, in search of a semblance of his former style; while with his free hand he kept pulling on that ruddy jowl, kneading it—needing to make it new.

When Jacques finally got himself into a more presentable state he sat on her bed, and, using the light from the clear sky outside to help him see, began to read more about this Billings Method: "How effective is the ovulation method? The Billings Ovulation Method provides an extremely effective way of planning a family. With proper instruction and motivation, this method in actual practice is 98-99% effective when used to avoid pregnancy. Success depends on a couple's mutual motivation and loving co-operation..." Jacques' daughter had been born out of a night of passionate dancing, and then love with a stranger in a tent on the beach at Marbella. He saw her for a moment—La Puce, four, five years into her life, talking so dearly to him through the glass in the visitor's room in the prison. She had come week after week, insisting that Jacques' own mother take her even if his bitter wife would not. La Puce. To see her face now, growing toward womanhood. Sitting there, he dreamed of it. He could see the two of them, Papa and la Puce out on the street, two people who only wanted to share the years together. And he realized he was wanting to cry. Or laugh! Here in this Aliette Nouvelle's apartment Jacques Normand felt like a boy, just starting out again.

Instead, he froze. There were footsteps on the stairs, and immediately following, the key was working in the latch. He flung himself under the bed and huddled there as she came into the kitchen, flipped on a light and opened the refrigerator door. The cat watched without interest as he lay amidst balls of dust, clutching her Billings Method in his fist. She entered exclaiming about cake and dropping bits of it in a trail which led almost to his nose.

The bedside lamp came on. He saw her clothes falling next and wanted desperately to see her, but couldn't bring himself to move. What was she saying? That she was a model? No, she was a cop! Jacques was too scared to move or think.

Then she said, "But what do you think it's like to be a hero without a face? Just the props. Poor man, he must be smashing his head against a wall. Scared, too—he won't even send a smile to his beloved. He's really stuck."

So he finally heard the voice of Aliette Nouvelle. He believed he heard sympathy there, but she was laughing at him too, he was sure.

Yes. The next moment she was laughing and her feet were suddenly gone from the floor. She almost crushed him as she landed on her bed, bounced down and snapped off the light.

The cat jumped up. The cat landed back down again.

Jacques stared into darkness, smelling rusty metal springs inches above his face, listening to her breath guiding her into sleep. In so many ways he was completely at home: hiding, close by, waiting for the right moment. But that moment had passed. He trying to move— to seize the moment; but every sense was telling him he had missed it. If Jacques Normand rolled out from under her bed to wake her and tell her he loved her—what would she do? For every impulse pushing him forward, into action—Action!—there was another, stronger one keeping him from making a move. The risk was too great. No self-respecting woman would give credence to such an entrance. She would boot him out directly. She would drop the net and throw him back in jail!

Jail. Where he'd sat paying for the life of Jacques Normand.

He was stunned. Quivering. Cornered. But there was no stone wall and no one to fight: no enemy, no betrayer, no one to bounce the bitterness off. Just this fear. All he could do was lie there like a man on his death bed, giving in to the trap that was *his* life, not hers. She was only sleeping.

Time disappeared on the far side of his turmoil, deep inside a dark and wretched despair. After a while, he was aware of tears rolling down his face and, by and by, the white cat, Piaf, she called him, came over and nestled in against an outlaw's salty, bristly cheek.

Then the morning came and with it, shame. Such shame. Such an unknown paralysis of will. He watched her feet touch the floor. Her hand came down, inches from his face, yesterday's underwear was gathered up and tossed in a hamper in the corner. Drawers were opened and shut. She moved around at a measured pace, silent, selecting, putting on. She hadn't sensed him—neither the hero without the face, nor the actual man under her bed. Then she left. Another day. Find that Jacques Normand and put him away. Just a matter of time.

The pages were still in his hand. Jacques uncrumpled them and read it again. "Success depends on a couple's mutual motivation and loving co-operation." He heard her voice now as he read it—the voice of Aliette Nouvelle, and he felt that something was going to burst. Something did.

Howling after her from her balcony.

Then chasing her like a madman, into the middle of the world.

19

CLAUDE'S FOLLOW-UP SESSION

What's worse: chasing poodles or sitting in trees?
In response, Jean-Paul Blismes merely nodded in a professional manner, thus deflecting the question back to the man who posed it.

━ ━

Okay, so I followed Inspector Nouvelle from the Institute, watched her drink with the butcher and actually give him a kiss when he left her at her door, then spent the night meditating on that very central question but failed to come to any hard and fast conclusions. My only way around an encroaching sense of despair was the constant recitation of the mantra-like phrase Monsieur le Commissaire had shared with me at our breakfast meeting: you have to be tough…you have to be tough.

Thus fortified, I survived the night. But over the course of the dark hours, her room—directly across the street from the branches in which I had concealed myself—somehow became much more than the mere object of my surveillance. It was now the enticing thing, the private place wherein was steeped that elusive mix of interpersonal skills, quirky technique and maddening separateness that was Aliette Nouvelle, star of the *Police Judiciaire*. When dawn came, my nose throbbed, my ass ached and I longed for coffee. Yet there I remained, fascinated by shadows: the movements of a woman in the morning.

At eight-fifteen the balcony door opened. I saw the white cat trot out into the sunshine. In another moment, there she was, waving back up to her pet as she locked her front door and headed off to the edge of the traffic circle. I trained my binoculars on her. She greeted that traffic cop and crossed to the other side. Then, automatically, my eyes drifted back to her room.

There was a man, standing where the cat had stood.

I fiddled with the focus and the man came clearly into view. Jacques Normand! Hmm. I admit: no real words or thoughts were manifest in my mind. The binoculars misted up as I unconsciously tried to screw them through my eye sockets—making sure. The pressure was relayed to the traumatized nerve clusters around the nasal bridge. I realized I was hurting myself. "God...!" Did I yell it? Squinting, twisting my body to gain a better vantage, I came dangerously close to dislodging myself from my perch. Then I saw her, that poodle! directly below, watching me. There they were again—the dark eyes I had glimpsed as she pulled away from me in the street. Those eyes did not look surprised. Or angry. Or mean. It was if they were seeing a new kind of bird.

"Aliette! Aliette Nouvelle...!" A voice roared it.

I shook myself. Jacques Normand seemed to be on the verge of ripping the wooden railing out of the balcony as he bellowed her name, clearly in some kind of pain of his own. A glance showed the anguished cry had fallen short; she was just turning into the quarter, going out of view, while the Public Enemy was hoisting himself over the railing, lowering himself earthward, from eaves to brick to window. I saw him jump from halfway down the side of the building, land with a bounce and a roll, then take off in pursuit of the woman who had brought him into the light. Finally!

And I reacted—just as I'd been trained to do.

Swinging down through the branches, poetic if not heroic, I was, for a series of seconds, right in sync with the fluid passage through the tangles; but that feeling of oneness ended the moment I came to ground. The poodle was there and she jumped into my startled arms, kissing me lavishly, devilishly tweaking my bandaged beak. Ah! the pain! spreading round my eyes, as if my head would implode. Then she pushed me down onto the street, an erotic wrestler with a grin on her face that would have driven any man crazy, setting me up for the kill by a bread truck that rumbled towards us at a hell-bent rate. I lashed out, kicking desperately at this gorgeous creature so intent on trapping me.

In another instant, she was gone.

I rolled clear of the truck, scrambled to my feet. She danced ten steps away, teasing. I pulled my pistol but she darted away between the flow of cars.

Fifty metres beyond, I could see Jacques Normand running full speed through traffic, aiming for Aliette Nouvelle.

All witnesses confirmed that in spite of some extra kilos, Le Grand Jacques—*was it really him?*—could still turn on the jets. He charged, relentless, through traffic that screamed, stalled and began to choke as it lost its rhythm going round the circle, all reasonable motorists being distracted by this madman running pell-mell in the midst of moving steel. The traffic cop noticed the break in the flow before he became aware of the situation. He thought it was himself—something he had done, a wrong move. Then he heard a frantic voice (mine): "It's Jacques Normand! Stop him!" He saw one man pounding straight toward him, and another man (me) waving and yelling in the distance—and what he described as "that same lithe, mop-haired angel of the other morning," now skipping over car tops, just out of reach and antagonizing the one who was trying to sound the alert (ah me—still the fool). So he reacted. He had never really been trained for it, but he took a step to the left, lowered his shoulder and put it squarely into the belly of the running man.

According to the traffic cop, Jacques Normand bounced; while he himself rebounded the other way—but only as far as his extended arm would permit. "I had a grip on the shirt sleeve of the most famous criminal in the history of modern France," he said. "I was holding onto Jacques Normand!" Who did not really struggle, who did not seem like any fugitive at all as he tried to wave the traffic cop away like some kind of nuisance, while he stared off into the distance, somewhere toward the centre of the quarter. Then the traffic cop realized, as he looked into the man's eyes, that they were filled with tears.

Seeing the two men struggling at the centre of the circle, the curly sidekick sprinted away from the flailing cop and flew *through the air!* Or so it was reported by all those watching from behind the wheel, late for work and jammed into the middle of a fairy tale: *This poodle…she flew, clear over engine hoods! and launched herself straight into the middle of it…this slobby guy struggling with the traffic cop!*

Her aim was true. She connected with the traffic cop and the jolt enabled the other man to break free.

Jacques Normand—*it couldn't have been him!*—seemed to look once in the direction of the quarter—*he had the saddest, bleakest eyes I've seen in a long time*—then he ran for the park. Of course, most people did not have time to grasp that it might actually be him— *Jacques Normand!*—clambering across the hoods and roofs of their jammed-up cars, and the first wave of general reaction was one of outrage. But when they read about the incident later in the day, most decided the slight dent might be worth keeping exactly as it had been made, on the off chance that a famous foot...

For her part, the other one—*a poodle? yes, there was a kind of resemblance*—put some special moves on the traffic cop, then deftly drew in the late-arriving detective so that cop and cop collided. (No, I can't say I looked very good through most of it.) And it might have been a clean break all around, but as she gained the sidewalk and the border of the park following her boss, she noticed something in the traffic cop's bag where it hung on a hook in his small shelter. It was a sandwich, and she backtracked to grab it. We have no idea why other than it looked like she had to. Perhaps she felt she had earned it.

It was her one mistake. Whomp...! A shroud suddenly fell around the dashing figure. She was on the ground and struggling under a coat held frantically in place *by none other than the Commissaire of the Police Judiciaire!* But she was a real fighter (I knew!) and he could not hold her down. She squeezed her head back into daylight and in the second they were face to face he appeared to be grinning. *Like a private joke between them, like refs and players in the middle of a match: you kind of wish you could be privy.* Then she sank her teeth into his wrist, and—as he clutched it in pain—broke free.

"Bravo! Brav-O!" *We heard a voice, echoing from a safe point in the park*—choked on as Inspector Claude Néon leapt from out of nowhere to tackle her again. (Yes!)

She went down. The sandwich went sailing. But then the traffic cop appeared, horizontal, as he dove and caught it in his arms—*like one of those overpaid American football players!* And here was the Commissaire again, hustling to lend a hand in subduing the accomplice, wrapping her in his coat once more, *so all any member of the public could really see was a lovely poodle nose protruding, and a pair of wildly kicking feet.*

Gendarmes showed up and gave assistance. Commissaire Moreau stepped back and into control. "Where did he go?"

"Into the park!" I was gasping, lungs sucked dry, face throbbing. But the park gave no hint of Jacques Normand's hiding place. "Doesn't matter," he said. "The die is finally cast. Good work."

"Thank you," I replied, straightening my tie, dusting off my elbows, ignoring the pain. "But Inspector Nouvelle—where is she?"

"Yes...where is she?"

We turned in the direction of Inspector Nouvelle's apartment, where we saw the white cat crouched on the balcony railing, looking beyond us, conducting its own slow sweep of the park.

— —

Monsieur Blismes said, "So, now you've got yourself in this parenthetic mode, and I hear these other voices popping out, apparently at random. And you put yourself in the third person again—just at the climax, there. Was this another vision that you had?"

"What do you mean, vision? Didn't you read about it in the papers?"

"As a matter of fact, I did. I mean Claude Néon's sense of where he fits in."

"Oh."

"And this idea of climbing up a tree."

"I was told to watch her."

"Yes. Perhaps we should talk a little more about limits... boundaries..."

"But I feel better now," said Claude; "I really do."

"It's as you wish, Inspector."

20

DISAPPEARING EYES

The front page of that afternoon's *Le Soir*, usually the more down-to-earth of the city's two journals (*yes, but maybe we're onto something here!*) carried a photo of Commissaire Louis Moreau and Inspector Claude Néon displaying their prisoner in the aftermath of the scene at the *rond-point*. Her face was obscured in the rumpled folds of an overcoat, but you could see a poodle nose protruding and just a hint of darkly beautiful eyes peering out from inside. The headline read, "She Did It For Her Man!" It was a profound bit of poetic realism, ensuring that day's plates would be kept in the special archive.

Jacques Normand was absorbed in the photo, to the point of ignoring the fact that he had succeeded in injecting his name back into the news. A full page had been devoted to quotes from people describing what it was like to have someone alleged to be Jacques Normand jump over their car. Still dirty and dishevelled from a horrible night and a frantic morning, he could not have cared less. He sipped coffee and studied the image, trying to discern more in her barely visible eyes. He was looking for the love behind this terrible sacrifice. The photograph would mesmerize the entire country. People would eat it up. But few would understand how difficult it is to find true portent in the dry description of "major events."

Nevertheless, Jacques Normand was again a major event.

And Georgette was there to give it context. "This is your fault!" she hissed, yanking the paper away.

He had to face her. "It's Moreau's fault."

"No! You allowed yourself to be drawn into his silly game. You just had to play it his way, didn't you?"

"No!"

"Yes!—and you don't care what happens to anyone else. That should be you," snapped the artist's model, smacking the front-page photo. "That should be the end of it. They should put you back inside! End of game!"

He protested, "Louis Moreau be damned then...I love her!"

"Bah...! You're no lover. You're not even a man. You're just a toy."

"If you don't want to help me, then get away from me!"

Georgette would not get away from him. "Can you get her out?"

"Yes, yes...of course."

"When?"

"Soon," he hedged. "It won't be easy."

Georgette was not a fool. She practically spat it back at him: "She'll die in there!"

Jacques looked away, confusion boiling up once more. "I need to do this, Georgette! She's safe."

"She doesn't want to be safe. Safe means nothing to her. She'll starve herself...Jacques!"

"No!...she won't. Anne-Marie will never starve... It's only for a while. It's only till I can sort this out."

She hovered over him, inches from his face. "You're going to leave her in there...aren't you? Look at me!"

He could not.

"You're just as much a bastard as Louis...you're worse! How could you?"

Good question. Still no answer.

"Does she love you? Eh, Jacques...does that detective love you?"

He refused to talk. Talk was useless now. He had missed his chance to talk.

"Surely you can tell...can't you Jacques? Was it wonderful? Was it worth it?" Georgette's questions were carried on her coldest voice. It cut through momentous headlines; had no regard at all for passions.

Passion? A night spent frozen with fear like the meekest boy. Impossible to tell her. Raising his paper, such a flimsy shield, Jacques sat there staring at Louis' victory, pondering his dilemma and the meaning in Anne-Marie's disappearing eyes.

      — —

Georgette was right; but so was Jacques—in the sense that he'd never really had a choice.

Although he had tried. Given Le Grand Jacques Normand's lethal side, Jacques truly believed it was out of an evolving sense of responsibility and any man's need to go forward that he'd objected when Louis put it to him. His proposition. His game. He'd objected, then rejected it out of hand. They'd been strolling across the plaza after the group that March night, under a clear sky beginning to hint at spring. During a lull in an already dragging conversation, Louis looked out into the night and said, "I've got a woman for you."

"A woman?" replied Jacques, "*Mais*, I don't need a woman. I have Anne-Marie."

"She's a detective. I've chosen her to hunt you down. Her name is Aliette Nouvelle."

It was hard not to laugh at something like this and Jacques did. "What do you mean, hunt me down?"

"I mean to say it's time for something meaningful in your life again, Jaki…before it's too late."

"That's your diversion," he told him. "You just don't understand. I really wish you'd leave me alone…"

Louis Moreau ignored the wish. "You've got that one right…I don't understand what could have happened to the wonderful myth that was our Jacques Normand. It's a complete mystery the way he has allowed himself to fade into the grey sky of nonentity…and predictability!"

"I thought you enjoyed a good mystery."

"Of course I do. But whatever happened to my old arch-enemy? Those grand gestures? The life that left a trail of awe and fear across the entire country? Where did it go, Jaki?"

It always left him perplexed. "Louis, you've known me all along. And you won! You're the one who made my reputation too much for me. You're the one who created it...you brought me to it. I had to leave it. If I've tried to go on to the next thing...change—what of it? Why does this bother you? There's nothing more for you to gain here."

"Now you misunderstand. Me, I was always the one to follow Jacques Normand. My friend...I didn't bring you anywhere."

Friend?

Oh Jacques, oh Jacques, oh Jacques. One surreal moment in the dim past when he'd allowed his sense of the theatrical to get the better of him, expressed through the sharing of a glass of champagne and the absurd sentiment that they were soulmates. Louis Moreau had believed it. But so had he—then. And later, free again and safely lost at the edge of the world: what had possessed him to sign JN on one of his early attempts at Georgette's face, wrap it so carefully and send it by registered mail (*recommandé*) c/o Louis' Paris brigade? Why? What was he still needing from that cop? *Ben*—the story. The myth. Because Louis Moreau had believed it. There had to be someone who did. Someone who would keep it alive—tell everyone, "He's out there somewhere; France cannot afford to rest!"

It wasn't long before Louis showed up. Of course it wasn't— Louis was a professional; he'd walked into Georgette's group one night, taken a place beside Jacques and started to draw. And then there was the next moment of truth, but Louis let it go by. Instead, he rearranged his life. Yes. Two friends somewhere in France who shared this story, who knew it all by heart. So Jacques had no fear of Louis Moreau—the man's very presence meant he was safe, the laws concerning aiding, abetting, concealment, et cetera being what they were; but he had been obliged to tolerate, to listen, to share drinks at the Rembrandt and sit with him at the group—and generally allow their bond to develop as it might. Well, nothing's perfect. There had to be one man who could pass this stranger on these quiet provincial streets and nod with knowing respect.

But Jacques had grown past that need. He had! And lately, Louis had taken to musing how easy it had been to trace that package. He had forgotten that it had been a gift. He had lost that respect. Jacques had come to decide this was fate's punishment. Looking at Louis Moreau, cosmic retribution was what he saw. Now Louis was turning it into a game. Jacques told him, "My life is none of your business. Not any more."

Louis' tone was bemused and a bit disappointed as they faced each other there on the step. "You're still a wanted man, Jacques. That's right up my line—has been for forty-five years. Or have you forgotten that as well?"

"Ah, the law." Jacques flipped a hand toward the night sky, as if to toss the law amongst the stars. "Always the law. Does the law have anything to do with it? The law had me where it wanted me, three times for all the world to see, and the law gave me back to the streets through its careless neglect. You know better than anyone that the law has precious little room for diversions. That's why I'm standing here talking to you right now. Eh, Louis?"

Louis nodded in earnest consideration of this point. "Perhaps it is. Perhaps it is... Speaking of the streets, how is business, Jaki?"

A thief stays silent. It was with narrowed, night-sensitive eyes that Jacques reminded the man of the gap which would always be there, and of the fundamental contempt that sustained it.

But Louis Moreau had never been one to be deterred by the hatred in men's eyes. "What about some action? Remember action, Jaki?"

"Sure, Louis..." opening the door to the van and climbing in with a kiss for Anne-Marie.

Louis stepped close, conspiratorial, offering a secret. "You're getting older, you know..."

"I'll never be as old as you are."

"Aliette Nouvelle, Jaki...a challenge for you—to help you stem the tide."

"Stem the tide?" What are you supposed to say to that sort of dross?

"She's going to track you down and I am going to enjoy every minute of it."

"I believe that... But why?"

"Because we need you! It will be good to see you run again...and fight!"

Louis was excited. Jacques knew he was looking at a "friend's" smile: confident, warm. "But our trust—"

"—is perfectly safe. But you see, Jacques: already, there's a spark right there. Stay on your toes...be urgent!"

That night, as Anne-Marie started up the old VW motor, Jacques had watched Louis rush urgently around to the other side of the van. Anne-Marie leaned out and he gave her an urgent kiss. "*La belle* Anne-Marie...I love to see you!"

"She'll never find me," he said. "She doesn't have a chance, this..."

"Aliette Nouvelle."

"Aliette Nouvelle."

Louis' star. To act out Louis' game.

Now Aliette Nouvelle had brought him to this unimaginable *crise d'ésprit.*

His first impulse was to hurt someone.

Night came. At three minutes to half-past eight, Jacques stepped out of a shadowy corner and met Louis Moreau as he arrived at the Institute for Georgette's group. He felt his fist break through the man's face. He demanded Anne-Marie's release. Then he lifted Louis's body, shook it, threatened it, and pushed the back of his official head into the wall. It wasn't working; despite the physical damage, Jacques could not shake the light out of an old cop's eyes or wipe the knowing half-smile from his lips.

"It's your own fault, Jacques. Do you think that the Commissaire could just stand by and let her escape? I value my reputation even if you don't care about yours. It was you who set her up. You gave her to us. And the things people are going to say about that... They're going to hate you for it, and they're going to laugh at you because you're making it easy for us. Falling in love with a cop. That's too stupid, Jaki, and it's how they'll remember you."

No, Jacques could not fight his way past those words.

Leaving the Institute—and Louis Moreau on the floor—he drove to the hardware store, entered illegally and stole a ladder. Then he drove two more blocks. The Rembrandt was dark, locked up tight as usual, Willem van Hoogstraten having long since chosen the rewards of drawing Georgette over the profits garnered from an evening's trade. Jacques broke in and looted the deserted pantry: some cold roast chicken, pâté and pickles, three different kinds of mustard, odds and ends from the cheese plate, loaves of various description, half a chocolate cake, three bottles of wine. Proceeding to the lonely alley behind the cellblock, he ascended to Anne-Marie's window carrying a hamper full of her favourite things. Food. What else could he bring her? They dined in a leaning position, nose to nose. He tried to secure her forgiveness.

He drank long and hard, put the bottle down on the ledge and faced her. The prisoner looked through the bars of her cell window. Anne-Marie's sadness was nothing like a concrete wall or some enemy's flesh. She was more drunk than he and in this state of altered consciousness her silence had become kaleidoscopic: tragic, sentimental, whimsical, teasing, lusty—all coloured by desolation, a complete separation from hope. His pleas, his cajoling, and the explanation of the seasons of his life had all been considered and washed down with the wine. Now one hand groped unsteadily for a balance point while the other carefully offered yet more wine through the bars. She sipped and swayed as she stood there on the springy cot. Jacques followed her dark eyes. He continued to ask for answers she would never be able to give.

"But what should I do? If I go to her again, they'll be watching. And if I don't, Georgette will know I failed. She's against me. Completely against me...she wants me to fail!" Pulling out another *petit pain*, he handed it through.

Anne-Marie bit and chewed, automatic now, being full to the brim but unable to resist.

Jacques, desperate for sympathy and guidance, encouraged her. "Good, eh? Your favourite mustard... No, Georgette thinks I'm acting like some middle-aged lawyer whose balls have got the better of him...who runs away with his secretary! That's not me. You know I would never be so thoughtless. So careless. I couldn't be. It's not my way. Yes...she's a cop. Do you think I don't know what that means! Anne-Marie?"

Anne-Marie wasn't listening. She was spinning slowly, curling down and away from him, onto her bed. He watched as her woozy grin flattened into stupefied sleep. He would bring her treats and wine forever and she would let him. She had no choice. But she would never approve, and that was the reason he stood at her window. It would change nothing; it meant everything. It was, he now knew, what a marriage is about, even the unofficial gypsy kind—the tough dynamics of a relationship lived in a van. "You're the only one who knows," he whispered. "*She* doesn't even know!"

Anne-Marie turned over and drifted into her blankets, leaving him swaying on a ladder, there above a dirty alleyway.

What was on the far side of this marriage?

Capture the Public Enemy. Captivate the man.

Aliette Nouvelle may not have known about the previous night but she knew about him.

And who was she? From the bank to the butcher; from the image of a straightlaced, well-brought-up career girl to the unhurried musings of a naked cop on cake and heroes, she just would not be who he thought she was. Whoever she was, she knew him and was reaching out for his life.

Not the one Louis Moreau held in his pocket.

His own.

21

FRIENDS?

What I needed from this prisoner was information on the man that only his woman could properly tell: Could Jacques Normand get along without her while she sat here in jail? Had he really killed someone for her love? Was she his wife in the legal sense...the mother of any child that might be his? "Can't you tell me anything? Were you doing all right—together, I mean? Is he still your friend? This is something to consider. I don't mean to be mean. Believe me, I have the same thing happening here. My friends don't trust me at all. They won't believe I'm a loyal girl. They think I'm hiding him. They think I slept with him. I think it's because I'm alone. Solitary. You know?" Searching the dark eyes—rather red this morning; from tears? "I didn't. Never even seen him, let alone touched him... Won't you even tell me your name?"

But the prisoner was not talking. She sat in a void of silence.

Ah. Well, perhaps there was a message she might want to convey to Georgette? "...Of course, we know about you and Georgette. Matter of fact, I'm seeing her this afternoon."

This brought what might have been a glimmer of a smile—but only that.

So I went back to my desk and my notes, where I sat in another kind of void.

Claude was lurking, to be sure, but discreetly, keeping to his own end of the hall. It did not matter; Claude's eyes travelled with the rest of them, passing by, glancing in, glancing away, moving along: *How are things? Business as usual. Me too...what's the story with her?* While the Commissaire's door remained shut. If Monique, his secretary, came out—as she did a thousand times a day—I might waylay her and pry loose a hint. Monique had always been an ally. Or had it been more the helpful magpie, merely friendly to the boss's favourite? And now? I could call, on the pretense of seeking an appointment. But no, I couldn't, could I? Because hitherto I had always just walked right in and asked. Working alone under the benevolent eye of *le patron* is not quite the same as working alone. Difficult to concentrate.

Yes, hitherto, the career of Aliette Nouvelle.

I had a suspicion Louis Moreau wasn't in there at all.

He had not been at Georgette Duguay's group last evening. Nor, for that matter, had the sulky, puffy-faced man who had worked beside me the night before. What? White hair, large belly (like so many men), intense eyes framed in tortoise shell rims. Two faces missing from the remembered ranks. Was that important? Georgette's pose had been odd—as if she were trying to fly or something, her expression woeful, lost—nothing like her heroic "runner." Still perturbed by the thought of a flesh-and-blood night caller, still angry with the notion of prying eyes and strategic machinations, patience close to zero, I had given it up when the model paused to stretch. Useless. On my way out I had approached the front and dared to break the rule of silence. Presenting the model with a strand of silver hair which I had been keeping, I told her, "Tomorrow…" and, noticing Willem van Hoogstraten watching us as he stood at his easel, suggested, "That Rembrandt place would be nice. Let's say half-past one? We can talk more about this friends idea. Please be there, *madame.*"

A hair: not much, but solid physical evidence. I was willing to trade, gamble it for something more. Georgette Duguay had let it fall to the floor, replying flatly, "You should only come here if you are interested in drawing," then had turned away and taken a deep breath before resuming her desolate bird-like stance.

Later, after prowling the streets with no particular destination, I had returned to the Institute and watched from the shadows long enough to establish that Georgette Duguay came home alone to a basement studio apartment in the rue Danté. I had seen no evidence of the old camper van. And I had confirmed that Claude Néon was also working late. But I had left him in his hiding place and gone home to bed.

It took ten minutes to note these things.

Monique did not come out all morning.

While I sat as I had slept: empty, expectant, not knowing. Alone.

— —

"Her name is Anne-Marie."

"Well, at least that's settled... And what is Anne-Marie to Jacques Normand?"

"A friend."

"A lover?"

"Of sorts."

"I see... Is Anne-Marie your friend?"

"We walk together all the time."

"And try on people's hats..."

There was no sign of that one hitting its mark. Georgette's way was dry. I understood there would be no games, no emotional floodgates bursting, no confessions pouring over the tablecloth and diluting the flavour of our tea. The woman was curious about my love life, but this was to be a business meeting nonetheless. Yet in those first moments, in the afternoon light of the café, I found I was more intrigued by the beauty of Georgette's face. Softer now, and older, tired, in a way—if I was seeing it right. "Can you help me?"

"I think I can. Can you help me?"

"Georgette, we're going to try to help each other."

Willem rolled his trolley up beside our table and laid out the tea service. We each selected a dessert—the *gâteau royale* looked good. I watched his face as he worked: smooth as plastic, eyes focused on the job. Then he withdrew like a spirit. Absolutely professional.

"He was never there, *madame*."

"I saw him. He came out on your porch."

"You too? Well...even if he was, he wasn't. At least not as far as I'm concerned." I poured a drop of milk in the bottom of my cup. I always liked to see where white milk meets bone china. "But tell me about him. We haven't got to the stage where we actually talk much yet, if you know what I mean."

"I'll leave," threatened the older woman, hands on the table, as if to stand.

"And so will I. What's the point if you won't believe me?"

Georgette stared at me then peeked inside the pot. The tea was not quite there yet. "He's a thief. He sneaks around and steals things. That's all that really matters here."

"Does he draw well?"

"Yes. When he's paying attention."

"To you, Georgette?"

"To himself."

"Was that him—beside me?"

"Yes."

And I didn't even feel him! Chiding myself and demanding, quite rightly, *Then how do you know he wasn't in your room?* "Does he, um, lose track, then…sometimes?"

"For a while he was doing fine. He managed to separate himself from all that ridiculous notoriety and he just did his work."

"The work of a thief."

Georgette nodded and poured herself tea. Seeing the orangey tints now had substance, I indicated that she might pour for me as well. We sipped, and savoured for a moment.

"Then what's his problem?"

"Louis Moreau."

"He's an excellent cop—worth worrying about."

"He's a dinosaur."

"Ah." I recognized a certain tone of voice. "How personal is it, Georgette?"

"Nothing I can't handle."

"Not dangerous, I trust…"

"Not for me."

"What about for me?"

"You're a cop. You're part of the game."

"The object of the game."

"No, Jacques Normand is the object of the game."

"Oh? …Then why is everybody hanging around my place all the time?"

"Because the game is skewed."

"How?"

"He thinks he's in love," scoffed Georgette, taking a bite of cake.

I was thrown—found myself fighting to keep my cheeks from glowing. It was a one-two combination, so to speak: the revelation, and the complete contempt with which it had been delivered. Fortunately, there was cake in front of me as well. Slowly, I took a forkful and did my best to taste every crumb as it fell apart inside my mouth, to diffuse my senses which were spinning frantically again— around the notion of love. "These men…" I mumbled when I could speak again. Then I ate more cake, refilled our cups and sipped tea until the shock had passed.

I found myself luxuriating in the thick atmosphere of the Rembrandt: dust moving, pages rustling, glasses shifting, china chinking, and the myriad voices; all of it surrounding me—me and this Georgette Duguay, attempting to talk to each other. I realized how far inside it all I had slipped and had to remind myself: it's business, and this love thing is a problem. "What do you think it is they see? What is it that makes them circle around the way they do? I certainly don't ask…my body?" Chuckling, trying to lighten it up; "I mean, what's the big attrac—"

"Your life."

"My life? At this point, my life is my job…and Piaf. My cat."

But Georgette was not inclined to elaborate.

"You want to know a secret, Georgette? He's not the only one in this…game…who's fallen in love with me."

"That assistant?"

"Him too. Poor Claude. When I take two steps back from this thing, I can see how he's locked in far worse than me. But no, there's someone else who has been in love with me ever since my very first day in this town…since the day he assigned me to the second-best room on our floor. Why did you walk away from your dinosaur, Georgette?"

"Because he's extinct."

"Mmm. But I kind of like it."

"What?"

"The thought of you and him."

"Forget about it. It's gone."

"He's been my teacher…almost a father, you know?"

"No."

"Oh…" I dropped the sentimental line. The woman was utterly freezing. Could she really be? "…but where was he last night?"

"Went home. He was in bad shape."

"Ah. Broken heart?"

"His face. And the back of his head, from the looks of it."

"Not you…"

"Don't be silly."

"I see."

"I hope so."

"Georgette, I can't stop now. I have to find him, regardless of the Commissaire…or Claude, or even you or Anne-Marie. I want Jacques Normand."

"Of course. Do what you have to do…I don't care."

I took another bite of my cake, but could not taste it at all. "Sorry, *madame*, but I don't believe that. I think you do care. What is your problem with a love affair? What do you lose if I hook up with that man? Or are you just taking the part of your silent friend? Is that the only reason you came here?"

"She doesn't belong in there."

"Meaning she's innocent?"

"Meaning she doesn't belong in there. It's not where she should be. And he doesn't belong with you."

"How do you know? He might be exactly my kind of man."

"Get yourself away from Louis Moreau…don't be seduced by that!"

"It's not Louis Moreau. It's him—Jacques Normand."

"Why? There's no more mystery in that kind of man. Now that the psychologists know all the reasons there's nothing left for the larger crowd except some adrenaline…sometimes a taste of envy. Is that what you want?"

"What kind of man are you talking about?"

"The kind you think you want to find."

"No...I'm not part of the crowd, Georgette—I am someone in his life, and he's in mine. And I need to find out why!"

Georgette Duguay was visibly tense (a detective is trained to notice) as she tried to spear another morsel. Then she put her fork aside and leaned across the table. "Forget about the hero. Catch the thief. Just do your job."

"Do you think I'm going to shoot him in the head?"

"You might have to."

"I don't carry a weapon...I want him alive."

"He won't be much fun in jail."

That stung. I pulled out my credit card with the thought of waving down the waiter—and to signal bad faith. "You don't believe I didn't sleep with him, do you?"

A shrug. "I believe you're not part of the crowd."

"Thanks."

A second shrug.

But she was apologising, somehow, this crusty old woman, and so I put my card back in my case. "Have you always been an artist's model?"

"More or less."

"How did that happen?"

Another shrug.

"I'd like to try it sometime."

And another...

"I could do it...I bet I could do it."

"Maybe."

Maybe? If I could stand those ancient eyes, green as the web of the deepest forest, folding back the layers of my soul, surely I could stand the scrutiny of people drawing. So, what else were we supposed to talk about—if we were going to become friends? I sipped at my tea again, but it was getting cold.

22

SALUT, BEAU CRÂNE

As noon approached, Jacques left the van and headed out, carrying a briefcase full of cash—a small fortune's worth. His stride was brisk and purposeful, stoked by a sense of urgency, a gut twinge that told him he had better make some preparations and put some things in order—to be ready for the clean break he felt was imminent. First he returned to the alley beside the cellblock. Positioning himself so as to be invisible, he waited; and before too long, Willem van Hoogstraten came walking by.

Fear, and one man's ability to create it; it had always been the great crystallizer. Jacques held his breath and remembered... *"I knew they were afraid of me. With each of my movements I could see their fear."* And it still was: one moment this Willem was oblivious, lost in his calculations concerning the fresh fruit he toted back from the market; the next, he was on the other side of life. *Bon...* Jacques saw it and realized he still had a feel for terror. Maybe not against the likes of Louis Moreau; but this man—he held the waiter tightly round the throat and told him calmly, "No screaming." He watched the back of the man's head nod OK and felt his wiry body slowly acquiesce. Taking his hand away from the man's mouth, he turned him around, asking, "Do you know who I am?"

Willem studied him carefully. It seemed he was peering into Jacques' mouth, that Jacques might have been a horse he was thinking of buying. "Well," he ventured, "at Georgette's class...at the café..." But he finally had to shake his head. "No. Who are you?"

"I'm Jacques Normand."

"No!"

"Yes!"

"Oh no...no!"

Jacques grabbed him as he saw the fear reflex register. Covering his mouth, again he felt the softness of the waiter's face. "I said no screaming."

The man shook, breaking into a sweat that poured from his brow and through Jacques' fingers. Then, like a bird about to be eaten by a cat, the panic passed and he only waited. Jacques sensed this docile mode taking hold as if a drug had been injected. He released him, bent for the battered old case and shoved it into the limp hands.

"Wha...what's this?"

"Money."

"Yes?"

Jacques turned and pointed. "See that cell window? There's someone in there I love. She requires a certain service."

"Yes."

"This is what I want you to do..."

They took a stroll along the alley off the rue des Bons Enfants, a grimy and forgotten passage between the Gendarmerie and the Édifice de Carufel. Jacques pointed out at least three perfect places where a ladder might be conveniently hidden. He told Willem all the things Anne-Marie loved, and those—overly fatty meats, anchovy, carp and canned sardines—which she did not. Willem van Hoogstraten was obliging, naturally, but the more his fear dissipated the more he appeared to understand exactly what would be required. When Anne-Marie peeked out through the bars, the waiter knew her at once and could not help but smile. And Jacques knew this man would come through.

As he walked away, Jacques began to imagine Anne-Marie's new life in her cell. The slow build-up of things which would make it become her world: a blanket, a pillow, a special cup for her coffee. The guards, other prisoners, everyone there would grow to love her. Surely it would be everything she could ever want. And safe. He felt that in many ways jail could be a natural habitat for a creature like Anne-Marie. He thought he could feel a warmth kindling at the core of his guilt as he envisioned Anne-Marie feeling good—eventually.

He heard the bell ring above his head as he stepped into the tailor's shop. Alone in the front for a long moment, Jacques allowed his fingers to touch Italian silk. Then the tailor, wiping soup from his lips, appeared from behind a draped partition. He stood there, a silent magister who knew all the longings of the mute male heart. Jacques asked, "Remember me?"

The man looked him up and down with a skeptical eye. "Well, I suppose I've seen you at Georgette's the odd time, whenever I go—don't go as often as I should, actually...but no...not really."

Jacques turned coolly away, refusing to give in to the rising anger. He looked here, then there, at the materials and the styles, determined to fix his attention on the trappings of a world (and a man) he had been away from for so long. He told himself, "Relax, this is only one small tailor..." But, facing the man, his pride had to say, "Jacques Normand, goddamn it!"

The tailor was too experienced to respond in kind. He smiled in his thin way and stepped closer for a better look. "Unbelievable! Jacques...forgive me, but you look horrible."

Jacques absorbed this comment, perusing himself in the large mirror. "I want you to fix that."

"At your service," came the stock reply. The tailor began to go at him with his tape.

Submitting to the process of being dressed, forced to listen as the tailor nattered on about the man they had loved—it served to loosen something he thought he had got a grip on during a morning of hard consideration: how to change, how to step out of hiding and become the right man, the one who need not be afraid of a blonde detective. It was a question of dignity, built upon the reasoning that love was drawn from the essential man, and that the essential is "good" because it is the original thing. He could not find a reference amongst his books and notes to back that reasoning up, but...*mais oui!* Damn all the shrinks and criminologists. All the journalists, too. When a seventeen-year-old Jacques Normand had started out, the impulse had been a fine and noble one. Well, that impulse still existed. *Alors*, get it out and show it to her! It's what she's waiting for.

But Jacques' self-esteem wavered, came and went in the tailor's mirror like a number on a spinning wheel. So much control in a grungy alley; all of it suddenly nebulous here amongst these beautiful things. Was this what he had done before? Had he really got himself all suited up for spectacular crime, and then seduced all those fabulous women? Or any? *"I adored the night life, the sleazy bars and the sluts."* Sluts? No, no, that was not right!... *"I live off the harvests of the bourgeois. I love the girls and the bistros and I just don't need all your shit!"* Not much better, that...no, no, that was a tirade directed at a clinging wife. That was when I couldn't think straight. No! There was something clean and strong about my life. Something right!... But Jacques was too far out of touch with the way it had been and his memories were merely random. And the thought occurred: who did the tailor see? He could have no idea if this man's smooth fashionings might be right or wrong for him. He had to take whatever the tailor might suggest. He had to believe it would be something good.

They arrived at a dark blue, broad-shouldered, baggy-panted number—off the rack, a popular look, and appropriate for most anything including a wedding if you wore a white shirt and a dark tie. He took it, but with the nagging feeling that it made him look like a porter on a train. Because Jacques was Jacques, the tailor promised to have it altered and ready to go by the end of the day. "You've been out of the picture for a long time, Jaki. Back for another kick at the cat, then?"

Jacques managed a smile but did not feel compelled to explain his life. He made certain the tailor was aware that he would be back in a few hours. Then he left and found a barber.

As the barber's scissors clipped away the soft edges, he watched a younger version of himself emerging. It hadn't been that short since his military service. A soldier! A soldier had fit comfortably over his instincts and it had been a happy time. He remembered that part perfectly: "This war was an absurd situation: France fighting to keep a people from reclaiming their natural home. I stayed away from the politics. For me, the war was only a field of action where I could explore my dreams of risk and adventure. Combat, forced marches, the kick of an automatic rifle; standing atop an Algerian hill cradling a carbine and sending a gallant snapshot home. For the first time I felt good inside my skin..." And now, the civilian who had stood at the top of the news with a gun in his hand was heading home as well. Jacques could feel it and he dreamt of a warm reception.

But he squinted in disbelief at the new-age man, sleek and boyish and cleaner than he had seen himself in twenty-five years.

"It's the way they're wearing it these days," explained the barber, who might have noticed his customer's ears growing warm with creeping degrees of embarrassment and doubt.

He paid the barber and gave him a twenty franc tip. Then he propped himself up with a dozen pale yellow roses from a corner kiosk—inhaling the scent with a passionate whiff, feeling the sunshine on his face as he went on his way through the quarter.

Glancing inside the Rembrandt as he passed, he was hit by another ripple of queasy disorientation.

Just as quickly, Jacques realized he was not surprised at all.

There they were, the two of them, taking tea. Didn't they look just like so many other handsome women, out and about on a busy afternoon, bound neither to an office nor a child, but only to the never ending search for more information about their lives. He watched Georgette studying Aliette's face. She seemed to be studying Aliette's face in the same way so many had studied hers. It was clear this detective was something new, compellingly so, even for Georgette Duguay. He imagined them chatting, discovering each other in ways he could never know from his side of the sexual fence; discovering, comparing, cooking up some kind of bond. And they would be deciding something about his life while they ate their cake. A deal? Certainly. Georgette would sell him out and cross over. In the middle of one of those imperceptible nods he would lose her to Aliette Nouvelle. But information bought and sold did not matter—not any more. It was the attraction that was the important thing. If Georgette Duguay was entertaining Aliette Nouvelle, then he must be heading in the right direction. Their meeting was the confirmation he had been seeking! Jacques' spirit surged.

When he saw his new friend the waiter roll up to their table to see if everything was fine, Jacques was gratified by the man's professional grace. It was working. He was doing the right things.

Walking on: ah...the flowers in spring!

"Pretty daring, Jaki," said Louis Moreau, stepping from a doorway as Jacques approached the van.

Jacques thought he meant the haircut. Self-conscious, he brushed his hand along the top of his head. "It's the way they're wearing it these days."

Louis was dressed in Saturday clothes, all corduroy and plaid, with a windbreaker in place of the *imperméable*, his lenses obscured behind shaded clip-ons, and a beret. A regular navy blue beret on Louis' balding head? For a moment Jacques could only gape foolishly as he tried to figure it. And Louis' car and driver were nowhere to be seen. No agents were placed where Louis would place them. There was not a single gendarme strolling the beat. So! Monsieur le Commissaire had gone undercover. "The lip's a dead giveaway," mocked the outlaw. "I'd get home fast if I were you."

The old cop automatically brought a finger up to touch the bandaid-covered swelling under his nose. Then, just as automatic, he folded his arms across his chest—stolid and slightly bored. "Flowers. Is that really all you have to offer, Jaki?"

"She's a woman—she'll love them. What do you want from me?"

"I wanted to offer you the chance to get out while you still can."

"That's big of you, Louis... For old time's sake?"

"Not really. Practical reasons. You can't win. I can't let you."

Reaching over and adjusting Louis' beret to a more anonymous tilt, Jacques exhaled a studied sigh. "But you can't stop me either, can you?"

Louis slipped a revolver out of his pocket and aimed it at Jacques. "I could leave you dead right here and now and they'd retire me with the Order of France."

"Come on, Louis, too many people know... She knows. She's sitting in the Rembrandt hearing it all from Georgette right now...everything. The drawing I sent you—is that at your place or Georgette's? Maybe she brought that along too... You're out of it, my friend. It's me against her. Exactly like you planned it."

"I want you to disappear, Jacques."

"Sorry, Louis. Game's not over. The resolution, remember?"

"This is the resolution. The only one that will keep you alive and her life worth living."

"And the Commissaire still waiting? I'm not going anywhere until it's done."

Louis brandished his weapon at arm's length and opened his stance. He commanded, "Run, Jacques! Once and for all…"

Now people were noticing, and stopping, crouching behind cars and doorways. *Here were two men, face to face: no longer the Public Enemy and the Chief of Anti-Gangs, but two hardened fighters who knew the value a man's word.… I always respected an honest opponent.* Oh, yes! And Jacques had always played it expertly to an audience. That day he stood his ground and taunted, yelling, "You don't have the balls!"

Moreau fired. A woman screamed. It seemed Moreau smiled with this first shot, as if it were familiar, the sound of a lost place finally found again; but the nostalgic glimmer was instantly replaced by the hard look that comes with the killing mode, and he pumped four more rounds in the direction of Jacques' feet. Jacques danced, his flowers held high. "Run, Jacques," Moreau repeated calmly as the smoke cleared away.

A voice in the cowering crowd demanded, "Where the hell are the police!"

"Police!" bellowed another concealed man.

And the chorus began.

Louis spun, waving his gun, as if demanding silence. Jacques stepped forward and dropped him with a swift kick to the kidney. Kneeling, one knee pressing in the small of Louis' back, one foot on his gun hand, he pried the pistol loose, disengaged the action and put it safely away in a deep pants pocket. The crowd came out from hiding, applauding.

There was no further reason to struggle. Nor to invite the public to get too close. He saw them watching; it was as if they knew they were on the edges of another world. Of course, he thought—everyone has an inkling; because it's all around them every day and everyone believes they understand it. But a bullet delivered or received can never be virtual. It is beyond the imaginary. Catharsis, and dreams of the life of guns and roses—these things happen only after the fact, not before. How could these bystanders ever come near the soul of man who is still on the verge? They could not. It was too late; he had no more of what they wanted to see. And if they tried, and saw a face they recognized, it would only complicate the matter. Jacques helped the misguided gentleman to his feet. "It's not safe for you to be out on your own like this. I guess you didn't make it into the office today." He leaned closer for another look at Louis' wounded lip. "Is it sore?"

Louis patted his lip again and murmured, "You'll never have a moment's rest...I promise you."

"That's nothing new, *monsieur*." And that's the problem with you and me, he thought, as tipping his bouquet toward Louis in the manner of pointing a gun, he whispered, "Pow!" and left him standing there in his blue beret.

"*Salut, beau crâne.*"

"*Salut, beau flic.*"

"*En forme, Jacques?*"

"*Ca peut aller, Commissaire...*"

(Page 587, or thereabouts, I believe.)

23

SHORING UP THE DEFENCE

I enlisted the traffic cop. That day, when he smiled as I crossed the circle, I stopped. I stopped, looked into his startled eyes and invited him up after his shift. When he arrived at quarter to seven, I sat him down, gave him a beer, then put it to him as squarely as I dared.

"What kind of help?" asked the anxious traffic cop, with that toothy teenager grin again, while—maybe he'd been expecting something else—unable to meet my gaze, he followed Piaf's pre-supper pacing instead.

"Watch my place, that's all."

The grin dissolved. He finally tasted the beer I had placed in front of him—one gulp, to be polite, and rose. "I was already doing that, Inspector. Although I could lose my job for telling you."

"Then why did you?"

"I'm not sure. Perhaps because you walk by and say hello each day. That's worth something, I suppose."

"I suppose it must be. Please sit back down," I asked in my calmest voice. "Please…"

He did, but his misgivings remained. "I don't belong in something like this," he complained. "I'm just a working man. Not an inspector. Not smart like you…I'm married."

"Something like what?"

"Whatever it is that's going on. This business with Monsieur le Commissaire and Inspector Néon…and you. The other morning, Jacques Normand…I actually tackled Jacques Normand. I could have been blown away! I don't know what's going on…"

"But now the Commissaire has asked a favour."

By way of saying yes, he swallowed more of his beer.

"Do you think you'd ever want to take off the uniform and try it with us?" The question had to be posed carefully. Members of the gendarmerie work for the Ministry of Defence, not the Interior, and many tend to look askance at the unruly methods and members of the *Police Judiciaire*.

"I don't know," he mused nervously. "...Like I say, I'm not smart—wouldn't likely even make it into the Academy." Another swig. "And I'm happy enough out there..." looking over his shoulder and out my window, "you know?"

To which I merely offered a judicious nod. "Can't argue with that."

"What would you have me do?"

"Watch my place."

"Who would I be watching for? ...For you, I mean."

"For them. The Commissaire...Claude...I mean Inspector Néon..."

"Jacques Normand?"

"Of course, Jacques Normand," I said, oblique and careful, attuned to his every reaction. "...But you know, no one's really sure it was him. Did you recognize him?"

"Well, no," conceded my guest. "But the papers...and the Commissaire. And Inspector Néon was screaming his name."

"But have you wondered why my name wasn't in the paper too? And why did they leave out the part about where Jacques Normand was coming from?"

"Maybe he wants to protect you...your cover."

"My cover?" I tried out a smile. "Forgive me, *monsieur*, but I fear you've been watching too much television. I'm not undercover; I'm conducting an investigation. I know you people sometimes think we're a bit shoddy the way we do things—but I get assigned a case just like you get assigned a circle. Find Jacques Normand: it has my name right beside it... Did Monsieur le Commissaire happen to mention that?"

My traffic cop indicated no.

"Well, it's so. Go down to the Palais...it's on the books." Would he do that? No. I pressed on. "Look, Jacques Normand hasn't been around for years. Most people don't remember him...wouldn't know him from Adam. And suddenly he comes flying out of my apartment—him and his poodle. Did any of those people in the paper actually see Jacques Normand when he went running over their cars? You were nose to nose with the man and you didn't even see him. The whole thing was based on one man yelling another man's name. A rumour. He appeared...but nobody saw him. And now I'm under surveillance."

The traffic cop's eyes tightened somewhat as he stared into his beer. "But the night before?"

"*Monsieur*, I admit that sometimes it's true what they say about us. Sometimes there are cases on top of cases, and cases inside cases, and too often there will be people working on a single case from several different directions without each other's having the faintest idea. It can get to be a nightmare, believe me. But ask yourself, please: would he be so stupid? The smartest, most dangerous criminal in France? Sleeping with the investigating officer? And would he bring his poodle with him? Do you understand why I want some help here?"

"It's a bit complicated..."

Nodding "yes, indeed" to that, I stood and fetched myself a beer. Sitting back down, I looked into the puzzled eyes which now dulled all other aspects of the handsome horsy face I had enjoyed so many mornings. "Somebody's setting me up—using me and Jacques Normand...wherever he is, for something else."

"The Commissaire?"

"Would he?"

"I don't know."

"Well, neither do I, and nobody's saying that. But I cannot afford to have my investigation sabotaged by a cheap sideshow. This thing is too important. So much history...you know?"

"But—"

"All I need are your eyes... You can see my balcony?"

He nodded, wary.

"...And, if it comes to it, maybe a hand."

"But the Commissaire? What if—" And then it got the better of him; "I mean, I need to know more…look at the way you live, all alone here. I have no idea who you sleep with… What I mean is, what kind of woman are you after you get home from work?" Shaking his head, rueful: a man who just did not feel good about it at all.

It was debilitating, that kind of question, and I had to close my eyes momentarily to keep my patience intact. I knew the answer—his answer, at any rate: some women ask for trouble and they get it. Georgette's description of Louis Moreau was reverberating. Dinosaurs—they were all over the place and some were so good-looking. I repeated my request. "I need your help. That's all you have to know about me. You don't need to worry about anything else."

"I—"

"Please! Too many people are presuming too much already…don't you see! And I hate it. I really hate it. Do you understand that? Don't you hate anything?"

He shrugged a working man's shrug.

I did not push it further. I needed an ally but there was no point in pressing someone into service who could not handle the job. Calming down, sipping some beer, pouring out a bit for Piaf, I asked myself: what would a man like him hate? His wife when she told him to leave her alone? Forgetting his sandwich in the morning? The traffic lights on the other side of the city when they went out of phase? Foreigners who did not know how to drive? "It would be for France," I said. A last try, appealing to his larger sense of duty, as I offered him a second glass of beer.

Which he accepted, with a guilty shrug this time. And then another nod to say he would. Help me, that is. And try not to presuppose.

24

So Much More to Know

The rush of new beginnings and the flush of a (public!) victory over Louis Moreau lasted till approximately six-fifteen that evening. It lasted until he saw her stop and make a date with the traffic cop as she crossed toward her home. What the hell was happening here?

Jacques was circling the *rond-point*, the lowering sun glinting off chrome and windshields streaming past him. Aliette Nouvelle was stopped halfway across and was trying to relay something to the traffic cop. The man was smiling at her as his arms spun and his whistle blew. Then he suddenly ceased his motions and bent an ear, leaving the flow of homebound motorists hanging in the balance for an awful moment while he heard her message, taking note of her apartment when she pointed to it, agreeing to a time as she brandished her wristwatch an inch away from his nose. A rendezvous. Clearly, she was inviting him over!

The cop stopped traffic and parted the way. Now she was crossing to her side. Now she was passing right in front of his face—and looking straight at him for a blank instant with no hint of recognition and walking on.

Jacques was thinking, it's the sun! He compulsively inspected himself in the rear-view yet again—the new spiky hair atop the bristle-free face—while ignoring absolutely the swell of impatient honking behind him and the traffic cop's sarcastic gesturing. He didn't hear it. Couldn't see it. The only thing beyond himself was the detective.

She was disappearing through her door.

The citizens all blasted their horns at once and the traffic cop pointed his finger: Move it! Only then did he feel the swell of panic rise. He stepped on the gas, left the *rond-point*, circled the park and returned. How could he not return and face up to the fact of love?

And what was she doing to him now? To his love.

Jacques circled and circled, sensing his gains all flowing away.

After the bank, Louis had known it—probably with Georgette's help. It had been in the van, just the two of them. "A love affair is pure fantasy, my friend. Whatever else she is, she's a cop. It won't work."

Jacques had blanched, then recovered. "Louis... Of course it will."

"How could it?"

"The attraction, man! It doesn't care about cops! And you can't do a damn thing about it."

Louis, pensive, finally said, "Jacques, all you are to the likes of her is just another face on a Ministry circular. Forget about love."

Jacques remembered his own silence—that unresolved thing, echoing. And how Commissaire Moreau smiled as he offered his professional opinion: "You know, Jacques, you can't undermine a woman like Aliette Nouvelle... I've been monitoring her progress. She's got you pegged my, friend. It's just a matter of time."

"Oh yes? What happened to the bank, Louis? Does anybody have the slightest clue?"

"This isn't going the way I expected, Jaki. It's a shame."

"But that's the thrill of it, Louis. Isn't it? I'm enjoying it."

But Louis had sighed, "*Bon*, perhaps I should be getting out here." Jacques pulled over. Louis stepped out. He said, "Consider yourself warned."

The warning had got a wan smile.

Louis had slammed the door.

Jacques had driven away laughing, the *bon vivant*, unable to accept the other man's words. That day Jacques Normand could've been twenty-three and headed for a beer at Pigalle, some fun with some *pute* who'd struck his fancy. This day, despite the humiliation of Louis Moreau, Jacques found himself in the process of going round and round and round, watching the Inspector's porch, seeing her cat, seeing, for an instant! her arm reflected in her window, while obsessively checking his own used-to-be infamous face far too many times and wondering what it was he didn't understand about himself—that Louis might. And why his love was a thing so casually mocked? New beginnings? Just another face issued by the State.

My face?

Like saying a word over and over again, it began to seem his face must change each time he took a look: First he saw a pig, all nostrils and red beady eyes, only intent on keeping what he has claimed as his. And then a dog: a stupid, loyal dog who would do anything for her—a cartoon hound. But the amiable hound transformed easily into a devil who could, without remorse, obliterate the dancing traffic cop with a simple turn of the wheel. Or he could use Louis' gun. He had killed before; one more notch would do no more harm at this point. Then Jacques saw the image of a sad man forming—a sad man who was obsessed and without understanding. And from the sad man emerged a black, crow-like bird, looking into his eyes, telling him that the killing would matter, not to the world but to the story—*Aliette Nouvelle does not want you to hurt any more men,* the crow told him. After the crow, a bear: a stolid bear who would drive the circle forever if need be. And then the bear delivered forth a man plotting, but with nothing much behind his nervous eyes, like a squirrel in the park, sussing out the crumb-and-crust situation on a day in early spring.

Lost in this whirl, Jacques failed to notice the passing of evening into dusk—became aware only belatedly as the traffic cop sidestepped the van, collected his bag and jacket from his shelter and made his way to Aliette Nouvelle's apartment.

He pulled over across from her place, cut the motor and sat, fixated on her window. Soon he was certain the Inspector had her guest comfortably aligned and was revealing to him the soft curve of her shoulder, her breast, her belly, her hip. Jacques could see her kneeling over him, meditating on a traffic cop's firm positioning with those wondering, ice-coloured eyes. What could she be telling him, in that serious well-bred voice? Not a lot. Difficult to speak while swallowing a man *in toto*.

Then releasing him, her gentle ewe-like grin quite pornographic and very content.

But that was not right! No!...pounding on the wheel. Surely that was his reward being too easily offered, so casually usurped. Not right at all! What kind of woman was she? The question was directly related to the larger problem. It sent him scrambling to the back of the van, where he pulled the soiled dog-eared volume out from under the musty sediment of his former life. Yes: page 133—one of his first mature observations on the subject, courtesy a long-forgotten *pute* called Paule. "Women are a complete mystery when it comes to sex: they can resist a man they've known for a long time…forever, if they want to; and they can give themselves completely to a stranger two hours after saying hello." He read it several times, trying to square the current woman with the vintage thought, and the sting of the thought with the pang of his feelings.

Resuming his place behind the wheel—there was that other cop, that Claude Néon who'd been in the picture with Louis at the capture of Anne-Marie, camped now on a bench at the edge of the park with the usual page of news as a blind. Jacques saw him abandon his newspaper. Now he was pacing in a highly distracted and in no way subtle manner along the walk, gaping up at Inspector Nouvelle's window. Anyone passing would have noticed that he was a deeply worried man. Then this Claude suddenly reached out, scaled the fence, jumped into the yard and began to climb the plane tree that stood behind the tulip bed. Seeing it, Jacques was forcibly yanked from his own erotic distractions. Another instinct took over. Havoc— a thing he used to be great at. He started up the VW van and blasted off, circling the *rond-point* once, twice, watching with a cold heart as the man shinnied out along a bough which would lead him to her room.

Picking his moment, Jacques turned the wheel and began to veer out of his lane and off the circle, arching toward the yard, deftly collecting three terrified motorists in his sweep and herding their vehicles over the curb, through the fence and into the garden. He redirected his own trajectory just in time, squealing ninety degrees and back into a proper lane. He circled once more: all headlights and honking were focused on the man hanging suspended from a branch over the third-floor balcony. Then the man dropped.

When Aliette Nouvelle and the traffic cop emerged, stupefied in the face of blaring horns and an eagerly converging crowd, Jacques took note of the fact that they had their clothes on…all on. She was directing her guest's attention out past the mess below, toward the park where one man stumbled in a desperate effort to take himself out of view. And it was obvious, if only in the simple gesture of showing, that she and the traffic cop had been nowhere near the advanced state of intimacy his fevered brain had conjured up.

Stupid Jacques...pretty bloody stupid. Very bad timing, mon ami.

Then the fingers of bystanders began to point toward the circling van. He took his cue and sped off into the quarter.

Breaking into the tailor's was no problem; the sticking point was the unfinished suit. The pants lay across the tailor's table, still ripped wide in the behind where they had to be let out. And the jacket sleeves still rubbed against his knuckles. But the tailor promised...!

But apparently something more important than a suit for Jacques Normand had come up.

A copy of *Le Soir* had been left by the phone. He stood there staring at the headline: "Le Retour du Grand Jacques!" Under it, the face from the old Wanted poster gazed at the world, dangerous and mean, while the cutline asked, Could it really be him?

The lead story wondered if the modern Republic's most notorious man had somehow walked back out of hell and onto a traffic circle in this fair city. Why? How? The police claimed to know only what the people in their cars had told them. Commissaire Moreau of the *Police Judiciaire* had not returned a reporter's calls. The statement from the Palace of Justice was in the form of another question: what would he be doing here? Then the writer turned to the hole in the wall of the Central Bank. "*C'est bien possible...*"

"Stupid ass," snarled Jacques.

He had to read the other side of the page, which was a history of himself. Impossible not to read it. This writer, one Rose Saxe (better known for her "Society Notes" column) was not so sympathetic in her conclusion. "A generation grew up with Jacques Normand, and the same generation left him behind, hidden in his own oblivion. At this late date, why would he bother?"

"Bitch!" The last journalist who provoked him like that had ended up bound and gagged, sitting in a cave listening to bats. In his frustration, Jacques lashed out at a fitting dummy modelling a banker's pinstriped vest. With a bitter fist, he knocked it flying. With a hate-filled foot, he kicked it round the room. With contorted rage-rent hands, he picked it up and made a move to throw it through the fucking—

But the steam went out of him An angry spirit departed, saying I won't be spent on a tailor's dummy; this thing is all a waste of time.

Oh yeah, time. In due course he found himself standing there embracing this dummy, awkward and vague, like a tired drunk hanging on for the last dance. In turn, the dummy supported Jacques as he paused, outmanoeuvred by dull time, completely in thrall to its circumstance. Emboldened, the dummy whispered in his ear: *Si tu vis dans l'ombre, tu n'accèderas jamais au soleil.*

Well, that was right out of his book! Why didn't the rest of them read his book? Again! Read the thing again! There was so much more they could know!

25

TIME TUMBLING OVER

It was Georgette Duguay's finely honed and often intolerable opinions concerning certain people's way of living their lives which had kept a worn-out Public Enemy coming back to her group, night after night, year after year. He could draw (as Aliette had observed), but Georgette did not care about that. The tailor was also very good at rendering her likeness and she had no use for him at all. It was the man Jacques' plight was a challenge that had grown into a relationship. But of what sort? She knew that Jacques often felt she bullied and (worse) mothered him. She, however, was no one's mother and had never wanted to be; and so she had always put it down to an attraction to someone who lived, like her, just beyond the pale, and who deserved and needed a place like anyone else. It was because of this attraction that she had demanded of the butcher, "Who?"

That strange day—it was right at the end of March.

"Two of them," he'd stated, while his eyes remained unabashedly fixed on Anne-Marie as he wrapped another package of meat. "A young woman. Inspector Nouvelle. And a strange young man. Claude…"

If nothing else, Georgette was patient. When the butcher pulled his gaze away from the lure of the Anne-Marie's charm, she quietly insisted, "Yes…?"

He was perplexed. "She showed me an old picture of Jacques Normand, then began to question me about my male clientele—and if any had companions… I mentioned that your lovely friend here comes in with a man…a completely forgettable man, compared with her..." smiling shyly at Anne-Marie. "She has been in a few times. Has this odd idea in her head. It's not really Jacques Normand, is it? Surely he's more... I mean, I would have expected someone more...more..." The butcher had not been able to find the word, so made a grand, barrel-chested gesture in its place.

As the butcher offered up this wordless conception of the Jacques Normand he thought he knew, Georgette had felt something. What was it? Like time tumbling over—and a door opening. Someone was actively seeking Jacques Normand again, after all these years, and the butcher, who saw him, served him almost every day, had no idea. The man seemed disappointed that one of his valued customers might actually be the notorious outlaw. "Exactly, *monsieur*," affirming the butcher's disbelief with an old woman's clucking refutation of the patently absurd. "It's odd what some people think." But Georgette had felt uneasy, strangely unsure, there in the butcher's shop as she handed over payment for her meat.

"It certainly is, *madame... Merci, bonne journée.*"

Walking away, she asked, "Does he know about this search, this Inspector Nouvelle?"

Anne-Marie had shrugged: "Yes...but no big deal."

Later, in the Rembrandt, Georgette had been an eyewitness as Jacques and Louis taunted each other.

"You sent her there!"

"I didn't send her anywhere. I gave her the file and let her go. But look: a month ago she thought you were in heaven; today she asks for you in a butcher shop... Meat-and-potatoes police work, Jacques, not unlike your B&E's. But *the* butcher's shop. She's zeroing in, isn't she? Just like I said."

And Jacques had turned to Louis, mocking. "Does she really think I'd be out robbing a butcher's shop?"

"Jaki," came Louis' wistful response, "a dentist's house, a butcher's shop...what's the difference? But it'll pick up. It'll get bigger—as big as you want it. After all, you're the one who leads the chase." Smiling as he'd sipped his Pernod. "It's your move."

Jacques' move? Georgette had felt a need to get something clear. Turning to Louis, stone-faced: "This is obviously something you created. You'd better buy us another drink. I'd like to know more about this Inspector Nouvelle."

"Certainly," catching Willem's eye, signalling for another round. Louis was inured to stony looks in a way a former Public Enemy could never be. That day he seemed like a man with profit on his mind as he'd taken her hand in his. "You have never been part of the hunt, have you, Georgette?"

"No," she conceded, "I suppose I haven't…not lately anyway."

"Of course you haven't. The hunt is for a different type of person. You live the contemplative life, and you live it well…"

"Thank you, sir."

"Not at all…But what I mean to say is, it's not the style of life for our Jacques. Yes, I created it, although it is really more of a re-creation. I have brought the hunt back to the life of a man who needs to run. The chase…You just watch the chase as it unfolds. My inspector, Aliette Nouvelle, will bring Jacques Normand back to life again." Letting go of her hand, he patted Jacques' forearm. "This man is an institution, a cultural treasure… I intend to keep him shined up, as it were."

"I thought he was a thief."

"Public Enemy Number One. You can never go back on history."

Georgette recalled sipping her drink before commenting. "But this is bullshit…bogus. Surely just something for boys still waiting for their testicles to fall into place…no?"

"Georgette," said Louis, beaming, as if charmed by her spite, "you may understand form and shadow, but apparently you have no idea what it is that makes a great man. From now until the resolution—and who knows what or when the resolution will be except that it will be—Jacques, here, will be existing in a state a person like you can only dream about…"

"Absurd," she announced, compressing the force of her contempt to the size of the hardest diamond.

Because, seeing this—Jacques: insulted and suspicious; Louis: so smug—it occurred to Georgette Duguay that this Inspector Nouvelle had undermined the both of them. She had proved there was nothing to Louis' silly challenge; had proved it just by walking in the butcher's door and coming out with nothing. Georgette had seen it herself: the butcher's disbelief. There was no Jacques Normand. There was only a forgettable man with a poodle.

That night, after the group, she had pushed the issue. She and Louis were settled in front of the fire's glow in the *salon* in the elegant but rather empty home in the north end. Accepting the usual drink, sitting back and taking off her earrings, she said, "You told me you came to me because you wanted to draw."

"I've been drawing you for ten years…" And making love to her, quite competently, for nine. "You have to admit I'm progressing."

"I'm wondering…" She sipped her drink. "It's meant to be an exercise in seeing clearly."

Louis had chuckled in his quiet way. "You mustn't worry about Jacques and me… I told you, it's another world."

"There is only one world," she told him. And she wasn't worried about them. It was about herself. Her judgement—her own ability to see. From one man to the next, if she wasn't clear in what she saw, then where was the value in what she showed them every night? What was the point of her work? Because her work was her life.

Louis seemed to read this. "We have an understanding," he said. "We trust each other."

"How much?"

"As far as it goes. There is trust. And there is duty. A man knows where to draw the line… Chin, chin!"

Their glasses clinked.

"What if she catches him?"

"I suppose she'll be a hero."

"No—to Jacques…"

"The risk comes with the territory…" pensive now, staring into his drink. "Georgette, you're not wrong about seeing things clearly. Our Jacques thinks he can just walk away from reality."

In many ways this was true. But… "He doesn't seem to trust you much these days."

Louis nodded. His mind was on sex, not work. (And, to be honest, so was hers.) "He doesn't seem to trust himself."

"Mmm." Letting it go for the moment; letting the moment be what it was supposed to be as Louis' strong fingers massaged the back of her neck.

Then the hole in the wall of the bank. Stupid Jacques, playing into Louis' hands.

Yet this detective had come to her instead. Then to the group. She sensed him. Aliette Nouvelle sensed the man.

The visit to Aliette Nouvelle's apartment—childish, foolish— had brought light to the matter. Love: childish and foolish. The spectacle at the *rond-point* had showed how serious— and seriously deluded—the man could still become.

And Louis—pouncing on Anne-Marie like that! How could he?

And now the woman herself, bright-eyed and direct, saying she would like to give it a try up at the front some time. Apart from the fact that no one else had ever asked or even remotely suggested it, it was the way she had said it, the tone of her voice. Purposeful.

Since leaving Aliette Nouvelle at the Rembrandt a few hours prior, Georgette Duguay, the artist's model, had walked through the quarter, up and down, forgetting her supper, taking herself far from the kind of quiet calm she needed in order to do her work the way it was meant to be done. She kept seeing two things: the woman called Aliette Nouvelle standing beside her up at the front of the group; and the killing of Jacques Normand, which had something to do with running. But neither of these visions was clear, and Georgette herself was only a silhouette against the last light of day as she crossed the plaza toward the Institute door.

She heard Jacques slam on his brakes, then the door of the van and his steps as he sprinted after her. She did not stop or turn to greet him.

"Wait!" catching her at the door. "...We'll go up together."

"It's not a good idea."

"Why not? I saw you with her this afternoon!"

"There's no place for you tonight, Jacques."

"Of course there's a place for me...I'm a regular."

"Look at the paper. If you come, the rest of them will go. The group is all I have. Will you wreck my life too?"

"What do you think I'm going to do? Start shooting?"

"It doesn't matter what I think. It's them."

"She's coming again…?"

"The group is not just for her."

"I need to be there, Georgette! I need her to see me there, with all the others."

"No. You've missed it…maybe somewhere else. Not here. Not any more." She turned away and reached for the door.

Jacques leaned against it. "I'm going in with you." There was a mean tone at the back of his voice.

She wasn't worried. She knew that her eyes at that moment would be as cold as the stone walls which framed the gloomy entrance. And she knew Jacques. "Well, I can't stop you, can I?"

"No, you can't." Still, as he watched her, heard her speak in this way, his arm dropped and he sagged against the wall.

Georgette did not really see the ill-fitting, silvery suit or the crookedly-knotted tie. Or the out-of-kilter face and hair. She saw a man who needed some kind of answer, desperately; but a man who knew he could have it only if it were freely given. With this in mind, she considered that although he may not have been perfect in his respect for her age or the things she had tried to show him, he had tried. And he had shared with her. They had drunk together at the Rembrandt. She had her own set of keys to the old van. He had probably saved Anne-Marie's life—back then. That was worth something.

And Georgette now understood that Aliette Nouvelle was not Jacques' fault—or, for that matter, even Louis Moreau's. The artist's model had realized that this woman, this Inspector, was something far beyond Jacques'—or anyone's—control. She told him, "You want her, Jacques—steal her."

"What?"

"Steal her away."

"Well, I'm going to!"

Watching the empty eyes of a man who is lost, Georgette felt a tug, then a twist, in the region behind her breast. But that had nothing to with her role as a model. So she had to say it. "No, you're not. There was a time when you could have...now it's too late. Far too late for a man like you to pull off a job like that. The world wants her...the world needs her. Not as a lover. Not your lover, at any rate—but as a replacement. For you. She's here to take over. Succession, Jacques, not marriage. It's a shame you don't understand. But then, you're just a thief, aren't you?"

He didn't want to hear it. Of course he didn't; and the resentment surged again. "You crazy old woman...with your poses!"

Good. Fine. It would make it easier for both of them... "A thief. A quiet little thief. Accept it, and you live in the eternal. You could still do that...perhaps."

"I need her!"

She looked up at the sky. Night had descended. It had once been Jacques himself who had told her that night made the glow in her eyes all the greener. "Oh Jacques...Do what you have to do, but do it in the dark. Out of sight, but deep in mind. That's what you are, and who you are comes from there. You can make her feel it if you work with what's there, with what you know. More than that, I can't tell you..." This was a homily of sorts. Just a quick one. "If you would leave me, please...they'll be coming soon, I have to prepare."

A homily, but no benediction.

This time there was no resistance as she opened the door. She slipped inside, leaving him there with his options.

26

THE GROUP

I was late for the drawing group, having had to stay at the scene in my garden, denying any inkling of the pile-up to the gendarmes, offering solace to my shaken landlady, Madame Camus. When I arrived, the room was full (but for two again), and Georgette Duguay was posed with her arms aloft, as if reaching to touch—or signal?—something. A long and graceful line: the stance was turned slightly, giving me a three-quarter view. I set up and got to work.

It was not easy to concentrate after such a brutal move. Had sneaking into my room evolved into bashing it to pieces? There was no way I would meet him on that level. Claude either, it appeared. And would a gentle traffic cop now be too frightened to come through on his promise?

But I was dithering and my heart protested: *Come on, Aliette. You should only come here if you're interested in drawing. Get to it!*

Yes. Right. Focusing.

Same rules: Block the proportions. Understand the size of things. Interesting; when her hands are extended like that they seem to be the biggest part, depending on one or two strokes of motion in the torso and the leg. But if you don't get that, then the hands shrink back to normal—which is as it should be, literally. And yet the reach—the motion; this confounds the sense of the literal. Yes. But you have to work with what's there. Draw what you see. So what is the right thing here? What's honest? I succeeded—no, not perfectly; not at all—in depicting the motion in the model's body. I saw it, felt it, and therefore found I could not help making the hands larger than I knew they actually were.

Georgette paused for two minutes—went promenading in small circles, stretching, rolling her neck, touching her toes. When Jacques Normand walked into the room just after the model resumed her position, I tensed for the worse: a cop reaction—not that I could have offered much by way of physical intervention. Of course, with the story growing by the hour, everyone knew him and everyone stopped to look.

But when the fish is out of water people often manage to remain calm. It is like bumping into a movie star in the bathroom of a bar. Off the page, off the screen; so this is just a person. Nose hairs. Less than perfect teeth. Not nearly so tall. That evening it was the same reaction to the face of a person known to be dangerous, very possibly armed. The tailor, working beside Monsieur Bondiguel, was the only one who made a sound. A gasp—quickly stifled.

Defiant, Jacques stared past them all and straight at me. An odd sight—certainly not the man once featured on post office walls around the country. And nothing close to the one I had dreamed. He sported a quasi-military haircut and a shiny suit which gave off a rainbow iridescence under the glow of the sodium lights. Wrong colour. Very wrong. What he needed was a basic grey or blue. And it was a size too large—the pant legs had been crudely rolled up. And the hair—his hair did not make sense. Disconnected; this is what I thought.

And how did I appear to him? The way he stared made me wonder.

Georgette, however, did not budge, and the lapse—the group's lapse—was only momentary. Physical intervention indeed; the model ruled. Jacques set up his pad and began his work. Everyone else continued on with theirs. It was safer than running for the door.

But I was mesmerized. There was one thing—now that he was finally there in front of me, off a Wanted poster and in the flesh with nothing to hide—one thing that conformed to everything I had read and heard and dreamed. The intensity of the man. The way he appeared to dig into the paper, his bit of crayon lost in his hand. As it emerged, the figure he was fashioning seemed to push away from the page, as if he were sculpting rather than drawing.

Oh, Aliette, get on with it!

Yes.

Yes, yes, yes, yes, yes... Distracted, but...

Necessary!

Yes.

And so, struggling on, into the details. Her ear and her earring, her lip and her nose and her eye. Yes.

Then suddenly he was finished—and gone; just like that, leaving his work right there.

I listened to a soft trail of footsteps disappearing.

Now would be the time to do it. Be a cop. Chase him. *Get him!*

No. I knew now that so many of my Commissaire's words had been deceptive. This game. This contest. But one thing remained true. There is no need to run after anybody—and *I* had learned that quite well.

And there was the problem of Georgette's eye. Like the woman herself, the eye was a difficult thing. Perhaps there was a disadvantage in trying to get to know your local artist's model. Or being forced into knowing her. At any rate, many were leaving now, having given the man who may or may not have been Jacques Normand a good head start. But they all paused to take a look at what he'd done, and were nodding with approval as they marched carefully out into the hall. While I had to wait there, with the butcher again, who seemed to be stuck on (or could it have been adoring?) Georgette's earring.

Hold it. Georgette! Just give me a minute here.

Ah! Just the tiniest, tightest mark—there, right where the light shines through. That's it! Something stone-like and so very old, like a quiet dolmen standing at the edge of a wood. I stepped back from my page and was proud of that last touch which brought the absolute element to Georgette's eye.

27

MY KIND OF LIFE

Georgette, Monsieur Bondiguel and I crossed the plaza. There was no conversation in the wake of Jacques Normand's bizarre appearance. I looked out at the twinkling city: Piaf would be waiting, Claude would be watching; my now vague and strange Commissaire as well, no doubt, somewhere. But I had worked hard and I was tired from the mental effort. I could continue on with these two, say good night, feed my cat, go to bed, to wait, to sleep, to leave it till tomorrow. Yes. And nothing would change.

I stopped. "I have to go back."

Georgette and Monsieur Bondiguel both turned and wondered why.

"His work...he left it there. It could be useful."

"But it's his," Georgette said.

"I'll keep it for him," I promised. Then I headed back to the Institute. I would never have considered allowing them to follow. (It's the danger element, you see.)

I pulled the heavy door gently shut behind me. First impression: empty. But I was empty too. Always empty when I worked. And who's afraid of silence? Not me. I was used to it—a natural element, like water. So I waited, empty as the first page, allowing silence to envelop me and seep into my senses—waited till I heard something. There. A movement with no kind of definition. That would be him, finally saying hello.

My eyes adjusted. Phantom streams of light, strays from the world outside, added some dimension. I could just make out the shape of his face. Then he moved again. His full shadow appeared on a far wall. I moved toward it. I knew I was close, so close he could have tripped me. Or he could have grabbed me, strangled me, then left the country forever. I sensed these possibilities as I passed by and back into the dark. Where I met his voice:

"What's your hurry? We should try to make this last all night."

"No hurry...no hurry at all, Jacques."

"You said my name."

"Why do we have to go through all this?"

"Don't you know?"

"I know that I—" I couldn't help it; I yawned, "...I'm so tired." The dark was so enticing. Resist! This time, resist...it's not a dream. But I yawned again.

Several moments later, from yet another vantage point, he said, "It's not that late, surely."

"It's too late for this." I knew he knew my problem and he was teasing as he led.

"Did you see my drawing?"

"Yes, Jacques... It's good."

"It looks like you."

"What do you mean, like me?" Again: the sense that he was within touching distance.

"Inspector Nouvelle...I mean like your body, your face."

I thought about it for a second. "You *were* in my apartment, then?"

No reply.

I dashed toward something shifting, but it was nothing. So I ran farther, to the end of the hall and up the stairs and back to Georgette's room and turned on the light.

The drawing was me and he had been there—past the limits of my privacy. Claude Néon and Monsieur le Commissaire would be glad to know that. Georgette Duguay too, I thought bitterly. They had been right to suspect me. Maybe he had slept with me, too—raped me while I dreamt. I was embarrassed by the thought of it. I knew it was only a thought.

Venturing back now, into loose shadows, faint echoes:

He's a thief. He sneaks around.

He draws well.

When he's paying attention.

To you?

To himself.

I'm the object.

He's the object! Catch him and do your job.

Well, I would—but I can't find him…

He thinks he's in love. Georgette had said it in such an ugly way. But that was merely more information. Another clue. Not the final word.

It was like looking for something lost in the house, tracing the feeling of it, forward, to where it must be, while retracing the path of memory, back to the last time you held it in your hand. And he kept returning, gradually, to colour my search with his presence, his barely perceptible moves. Like that pair of gloves, that book, or that number on that scrap of paper: I knew him. Yes…just a question of catching sight, then you can lay your hands on it. Then it's yours again.

Finally, moving into the big room at the foot of the stairs, past the sculptures—in the darkness it was as if I were drifting through islands. "I thought I'd lost you."

From somewhere, he replied, "And I was thinking you didn't trust me."

"Well, I don't…" as I went creeping into a dark spot in the lee of a huge shape. Feeling it, soft dust on my fingers. "How could I trust you?" It was an honest question.

"No one can," he admitted, then was gone again.

I came upon him from behind. He was in the cover of a hippo-shaped object created by the local master, Raymond Tuche. I could make out the signature carved in child-like printing into what I would have called the left haunch. Jacques Normand was blithely keeping watch from the front end and I watched him for a moment. I reckoned he had made it easy. Yes, he thinks he is in love! That also had to mean I had nothing to fear. *Alors,* I felt no fear as I tapped him on the shoulder.

He spun around to face a cop who carried no gun.

We looked at each other. No, he wasn't beautiful, there could be no more illusion on that score. Still, here was a man whose life had captivated an entire people, a symbol of freedom, standing in front of me, looking a bit ridiculous with the hair and the suit—and so hopeful. Yes, hope. I knew it was what I was seeing—and that I held him in my hand. So, what was I supposed to do now? My decision-making process had come to an impasse. I could feel my instincts on the verge of doing a flip. I touched his face. When I kissed him, at first, up that close, he was only a man: like a butcher with a shop that never changes; or a bright Judge of Instruction I might have married.

But he wasn't. He was Jacques Normand. I was in the arms of the Public Enemy.

No. Change that: the Public Enemy was in the arms of Aliette Nouvelle. And he thought he was in love.

That first embrace went on and on. But it had to be broken and reconfigured. Because I felt like fucking. Really fucking. A surge of heat far past fantasy.

Aliette… (the lightest whisper) *it's that physical fact that history always needs.*

So: Not in a dream. In a hollow room surrounded by objects that appeared to be alive—but marooned, and lonely. And not in a bed, neither his nor mine. On a cold, hard floor softened only by our coats. I sat back on top of Jacques Normand, inside me now and on no uncertain terms. I moved on him, getting a sense of him, stirring and shoving. When I opened my eyes and looked down at him, he seemed like nothing so much as a kitten, pinned down and reacting, but not knowing. His breathing was quick and quiet; his eyes were far too serious. Even if he thinks he's in love.

I could not get away from it, and found myself, despite myself, searching again for another reason to be astride this odd axis mundi, this strangest one that could have been. It was those words and lessons that we all carry, always—yes? Yes, leaving us enjoying and worrying in equal amounts. It was all those times I had been with him in my dreams, with my own ideas of love.

But that wasn't him. It was someone I dreamed up. I never did really see his face.

Well, you don't fuck a face, at least that's what I've heard them say.

Ah, you are such a saint, Aliette, so good to have closed your eyes and given your body, so très, très sympa…

Backward and forward, and up and down, up and down. When I came, I came full well, my orgasm spreading through me, pushing all the thinking out of my mind and into my blood, and as I humped faster and faster, the vibrations focused—to a point, then hit me again and again: a light dissolving. Then the energy, the ripple of my orgasm began to flatten, folding back to where it came from, and I wanted to slow down with it, just sit there, or lie on his thick chest and sleep a bit. But his eyes would not permit it. Without a word, he was hoping for everything.

So I continued to move, gently, for the sake of self-preservation now, and because it was apparently a good pace for him. He needed me, and not for some crude conquest, I was certain of that. Exactly why, I did not know and I could not think about it any more. But there was one thing I could do for him. I could help him come too.

He grabbed my buttocks more tightly, pulling them apart and my weight forward. He shoved up inside me. And again and again; and I bent over him, letting my hair fall down in his face. He groaned as he arrived, but in a hidden thief-like way. I was aware of liking the notion that we were both very quiet lovers. Then I hovered over him, steadying myself, letting him ease away from the moment. He released my behind, and felt the ribs under my back. He leaned up, took my breast into his mouth. He fell out of me softly. Then pulled me down to him. I acquiesced and lay there, not quite eye to eye, but looking over the top of his head at this strange, strange place to make love.

No, he wasn't the type to conquer anyone. Neither had I any sense of having given myself to Jacques Normand. In fact, it was just the contrary, the more I retraced the movement of the whole affair. Even those dreams, when considered clearly after the fog of longing, the heat of confusion; they had come to me, unbidden, just as the Commissaire had handed me the Normand file without me asking for it, without the slightest inkling that it had been waiting there for me.

I had been set up for this, in spite of the circumstances out there in the street; and in spite of myself.

When we fell to talking, the first thing he asked was if I was not afraid I might become pregnant. I explained the basics of the Billings Method and assured him I wasn't fertile that night—that there was little risk. When he asked if I wanted to be pregnant, I demurred, somewhat surprised and instinctively threatened. Sometime...not right now.

We rested, then made love again, a little better, a little longer.

Then lying there talking again, wrapped in our coats; like lovers anywhere, the difficult climb back down, through words:

"...But hiding! like some strange boy. Why?"

"I was afraid of being caught."

That was straightforward enough. "What about now?"

"You're going to help me."

"I'm not going to hide you."

"No...but France is a lot bigger than this place."

"I like it here. I'm comfortable..."

"With Louis? And people watching you?"

"With my work. I'm a cop. This place is as good as any for my kind of life."

"Your kind of life?"

Rolling away from him, studying the cavernous ceiling. What to tell him? The truth. "We're here together because of my job, Jacques."

"The Normand file. It's just paper."

"It's not paper. It's history."

"It's not history yet."

"I think it is."

"What are you talking about?"

I tried to keep smiling, but couldn't help looking away, the way people do when they have sad news. "It's over. The case is finished. That's all we have between us."

"Stop talking about the case. I'm telling you I need you."

"I know."

He brought himself up on one elbow. "You know...? You would let this happen. And then you would put me away. What the hell am I doing here?"

"That I don't know."

"This is all a trap! You played me like a—"

"No!"

"Then what?" On his knees now. "Why? I love you!"

These words bounced around in the darkness and dropped back down in front of us. I raised myself onto my knees, took his hands in mine and held them by the wrists. Like handcuffs. "If it's a trap, then I'm in it with you...What are you hoping for, Jacques?"

"You!"

"No...before me. Before you heard my name. And after me...Your life. Your life has to be bigger than one person. What are you hoping for?"

Now he ripped free of my fingers and pulled a gun from a pocket in the mess that was our blanket. Holding it trained on my face, Jacques stood, naked, overweight, trying to find an answer to my question, his eyes continuing to ask me: my life? What does any man hope for? Then he turned and pulled the trigger.

There was the usual dry pop, with its echo surrounding the shattering in the corner like a wreath. Whatever that shape was supposed to have been, it was not any more. "I helped you!"

I only watched him.

He fired again and killed another piece of someone's work-in-progress. White dust spread like some defeated spirit, briefly lightening the darkness. "I walked into that room tonight for you!"

"Yes, you helped me."

The gun came back around, to speak with me again. "You would never have found me...never."

"No. Never."

Now the gun wanted to touch me. It nudged along my collar bone, hard—but warm from shooting.

"Did I help you, Jacques?"

"No... You tell me how I helped you!"

"Don't, Jacques… Please."

"No…not please… No!…give me more than that. I'm Jacques Normand!" He held the gun to my throat, demanding a response to the fact of his very name.

"Your life. It helped me—"

"My life… But you aren't even afraid of me. Why aren't you afraid? At least do that for me."

"Don't, Jacques!"

"Why not? …One good reason."

"Whatever's happening here, if you do that, it won't be finished. It won't be over."

"Not over?"

"This is right. Us, here together. l wouldn't let it happen like this if it weren't. Are you going to ruin something that's right? Don't you want to see what it brings? Don't you hope for something like that?"

"Not over." He repeated it. The anger in his eyes turned vague, as if he had suddenly lost track of something elemental. Place? Time? Hard to tell.

The gun eased away from my skin. He let me take it from his hand.

I moved so slowly, taking it out of the range of his eyes, sliding it back into the rumpled folds beside me. Away. Putting it away…see? There was no need for it to be a part of this.

"What's going to happen to me?"

"I don't know. I wish I could tell you. I wish someone could tell me…"

It took him a long time. He was trying to trust me. He was touching my shoulder…and my breast. Then my neck, where the gun had been. I did not move till I felt it. Felt the anger leave him.

But the hope? Had that gone too?

Well, he was a tired man. I let go of the gun, resting there unseen, and held him with both arms. There it was: surrender.

And for a moment, I felt full, as if I did not need him any more. Then guilty for that—guilt being a feeling that was never far from my life. Contemplating the gross and lonely hippo-shaped creature standing across the floor, I thought—all right, yes, we can be Aliette and Jacques. There doesn't have to be a reason. If the shoe fits, wear it. At least for tonight. So I wrapped my overcoat around us as best I could, tucking it tight against all the cold spots. And curled back in beside him.

As he lay there, he whispered something about La Puce. The daughter, somewhere in his past. And then: "I need you..." on a heavy, sleep-borne sigh.

CLARITY

He lay beside her, wishing for clarity. Something had happened to his sense of where he was.

Holding the gun to her neck, Jacques tried to fathom this thing about his life. Not over? No. She should pay him back with a bit of fear. At least some fear; to take with him. His just due.

Her eyes were steady. Her voice fearless. But a bullet: why not just do it? Then break out of here. He tried to decide. His hand tried to decide. His hand could do it so easily. Then Jacques Normand would be gone, anywhere he felt like, with or without a Louis Moreau on his tail.

And there would never be another one like her in his life again.

He gave her the gun—so unclear.

But as he reached out for Aliette Nouvelle with hands that did not know why, Jacques knew at least that he believed her, that all that painful, humiliating time was time spent going toward—not away. His hopes had been built around getting here. To her. And he had made it.

His life. The past. All of it so tiring. He felt sleep coming. Dozing off, he was visited by the thought of his daughter. La Puce. A lovely girl—no, a woman by now. He saw her perfectly. What was she saying to him? He listened through the softness of this sleep. Her voice—her woman's voice, it was a lot like Aliette Nouvelle's and it surrounded him like the world. What was going to happen now? Maybe she knew.

Jacques Normand had to fall asleep because he wanted to know more.

She kissed him, then lay close.

TOWARD A SINGLE MOMENT

Claude was in need of respite. Perhaps he should line up another session with the Ministry *psychologue* after all, because trying to juggle his feelings for Aliette Nouvelle with the mystery of Jacques Normand was still taking its toll. It was not her he was after, professionally speaking, but the outlaw, and so it weighed him down spiritually when she hated him. But how would she ever think of liking him, physically and/or soulfully, if he did not do well professionally? Claude's pain added to his confusion. The regions behind the bridge of his nose continued to throb with ceaseless cross-patterns of wicked pounding. The incident in the tree that evening had taken his breath away and almost cracked his ankle. There was a gaping rip in the crotch of his trousers. The case had become a vicious circle wherein bad luck was attaining surrealistic dimensions and persevering was worse than hard—it was ominous, framed in a series of what surely must have been numenistic occurrences: An accursed suit from a debauched tailor. His dumb-faced embarrassment at a butcher's counter. A poodle who had left him crying—then bleeding. And now an attack by three wild cars. Any other man would have bowed to such a relentless barrage of heavenly joking and backed off. Not Claude Néon. Ambition, fear, and the dream of finding love combined to push him forward. And he was a wreck.

Finally, after limping doorway to doorway till he saw her safely through that dark door to her drawing class, he turned around. Monsieur le Commissaire had said leave the drawing class to me. Claude had not seen him all day but saw no reason to ignore the order. Now would be the worse time to begin to second-guess. Forlorn, he found an open door where an old Chinese woman sold him some bread and chocolate and a bottle of wine. Her distant eyes were for business, not judgement, and for that Inspector Néon was grateful. He knew he was a mess; drawing attention to the fact was not going to help at that point.

From there it was back to his post: the shameful vigil.

The wine went down well. It made the night air less cold and the job less stupid. It went down well and quickly. He was not able to resist going back to the same good woman for a bit more of the same before she locked her door.

No problem, *monsieur.* Last chance for a third before I go to my bed.

No. No, *merci.* Claude laughed about it as he returned to his bench and sat back down. He laughed at the way a woman in a corner grocery, on the other side of the world from where she had been a romantic girl, just did not give a damn. Well, neither did he. Was he then on the other side of the world as well? Hmm. The heroic nurse, immortalized in stone and presiding over that section of the park— she was a different story. She was French. Her eyes were imperious, severe; gazing across at Claude they spoke only of her greatness, in a different time, when people were obviously more serious about their lives. They offered nothing by way of wisdom or comfort for derelict detectives.

Well, fuck you, lady. You're dead. I'm working.

When this bottle, this excellent bottle!, was a quarter empty, he stood and walked to the street. From there he could see her balcony. The white cat kept watch on the railing; the apartment was dark. The cat seemed to look right at him, admonishing by proxy on behalf of his sleeping mistress.

Claude got the message and was suddenly not so brash. Lowering his eyes, he slunk back to his post by the statue and the pond.

When the bottle was three-quarters empty he made a second round. No change. At such an hour, people slept, cats stood guard, and creatures like Claude were the grey ones. So, returning to the bench, quite sodden now and awash in reverie, he sipped the remaining wine. Claude was dreaming of drinking. Drinking beer with Aliette. That would be a lovely thing.

Mmm. Hic! Zzzz...

He awoke to the sound of a bird's song. The early bird stood atop the shit-and-time-stained head of the stern lady of the park, serenading the new day. In fact it was still dark, with only the barest tinge of blue along the eastern skyline; but the early bird was there for anyone who wanted to get a jump on things. He was there for Claude.

Shivering, he proceeded back to his designated position. A jogger passed him. The traffic circle was vacant. The driver of the first bus swallowed coffee and perused the front page as he sat at his starting point directly below Aliette Nouvelle's yowling cat. A pale nurse, clearly not cut from the same cloth as the role model in the park, watched the bus driver with a listless stare. She yawned, sneezed, sniffed as she waited to board. The driver kept the door shut, determined to ignore her until the proper time.

That damn cat. How could she stand it? She must have slept deep and childlike to be able to ignore a racket like that. Claude Néon had a warm moment—a split second—in which he could see her Sleeping Beauty face and the downy softness surrounding it. Then he was running, heart pounding, a man on the verge of his final mistake.

She wasn't there! Hadn't been all night! He sprinted to her front door and pressed his thumb against the buzzer under A. Nouvelle. Then, frantic, he began pressing all the buzzers. He knew it in his bones, but he had to confirm it. There was no time to explain this to the woman who finally answered the door. He rushed in past her, and up the stairs.

The woman screamed at him, then stepped out onto the walk to look again at her broken fence and scream at the cat.

Pounding on her door, calling her name! Other doors opened, but not hers. He tried kicking it—and almost fainted with the stabbing jolt to his ankle. Claude had to see to be sure. That was his job. And a cop has a few tricks—can sometimes perform them even when seeing double, on the edge of tears. He collected his wits, took his pen knife from his pocket and opened her door.

He was right. Her bed was empty. There was just her room, her things, the poster of Jacques Normand. So, then: where? He turned in grasping circles, reaching, almost touching everything, needing something to hold in his hand, to help him put it together. But resisting. Aliette Nouvelle would never forgive him. Finally, he focused on the phone...

This was a big moment in Claude's career, in his life! calling the Commissaire at five-thirty in the morning and ordering him— advising? (it was hard to gauge my tone at that point)—to get himself down to the Institute as fast as he could. The Commissaire did not argue or even complain. But Claude knew that everything was on the line as he sprinted back down, practically hurdling the woman on the stairs. She let him know what she thought of him but he didn't catch it. Something southern—Corsican? Pied-noir?— he had no idea. He flew out the door—on one foot, more or less, and ran for it.

Louis Moreau was a tough man; a fat lip was nothing. But it had been a long time since he'd had his head slammed against a stone wall and his back kicked so hard. Both ached; he had passed some blood that evening. Four or five aspirin since the afternoon had not prevented his sleep that night from being fitful at best. Yet in response to Claude's call, he rose from his bed and threw water on his face. He finally had Jacques where he wanted him; it was his duty to be there too. Words and a fist would not change that.

Two nights before, mounting the stairs to the group, with Anne-Marie in a cell and the press beginning to believe in ghosts, sure enough, Jacques Normand had stepped out from the shadows, plowed him in the face and broken his lip. It was no big surprise. Then the outlaw had grabbed him by the lapels and threatened. But this too was to be expected.

"You bastard, Louis...what do you think you're playing at?"

Playing. Yes, you could call it that; his skills, and his years of experience in dealing with the marginal elements allowed him to take a punch and bounce back with a quip. "Only doing my job, Jacques... Just doing my bit to keep things moving along."

"You better get her out of there...old friend."

"Sorry, it's out of my hands. Don't worry, they'll go easy on your poodle... She really does have the sweetest face."

So he had been lifted and slammed against the wall: saw some stars, lost his breath, felt the stinging, and yet managed to grin, to keep the edge, to let Jacques know his folly in the face of history. And where Jacques would deny, he would remember. It was his business to remember. Every word, for the record: "...You're making it too easy, Jaki...no challenge there at all."

Another fist in the mouth. Of course. He was a professional; he could take it, feel it, and still keep his own eyes clear enough to see the angry light in Jacques' struggling eyes go dim. Louis Moreau had seen that—without a doubt, even in the dark hallway of the Institute.

And he had seen it again in the street that afternoon, lying there humiliated and so close to being exposed. It was still Jacques Normand on the short end: the fear that had always been behind the bravado, that elemental touchstone the man would never, *could* never acknowledge. But it was now dimmed to a vague uncertainty writ large behind the churlish mocking, that ridiculous coiffure.

Fear you could work with; uncertainty was a useless thing.

Yes. Worse than the squalid spectacle, it was a pathetic way for them to end. Very sad. Hadn't he offered him a chance? Hadn't Louis Moreau always worked hard to make it equal and interesting? And all out of respect—a sense of honour. And of his own volition. And risk! Because an outlaw has no rights. No rights at all. Not when he's running.

Ow! Louis groaned as he bent to pull on his socks. But there was no one there to hear it. No more Georgette to lay a woman's hand against the sore spot... No, Georgette could not have shown Jacques' picture to Aliette Nouvelle; the portrait Jacques had sent was hanging in its silver frame by Louis' mirror. Would she ever forgive him? Maybe yes, maybe no—you never knew with a woman. Ah, well, that was the price of playing at this level. It always had been. Maybe Georgette would see it clearer later on.

What a shame about the Inspector. A mystery, really, and he had to admit, probably his own mistake. How many times had he looked at her and told himself, it will be her—amongst all of them, this Aliette Nouvelle is the one? Enough to feel he had raised her, in a way. Enough to feel mystified. He had no idea what she had become. But she had made the Commissaire's presence dangerously second-hand and that had to be set right.

He was a public servant, after all, and he owed it to them to be there. To the public. To see that it turned out right; to ensure that it had form and validity in the public eye; to confirm that history had been served.

Ah! More pain as he eased into his coat.

Just pain, just pain. That morning, he knew it would be finished.

And Louis was not happy that he would have to do his own driving if he wanted to make it to the scene on time. Commissaire Moreau was not fond of arriving anywhere official in the front seat of a car. The role: appearances were too important.

There was also the problematic fact that his own car looked like a second-hand police car. Of course it was not; that would have been steering too near the kind of corruption allegations small-minded journalists loved to stir up when they had nothing better to do. He had bought it, and had the papers to prove it, from the proprietor of the corner garage when his beloved British roadster had finally given up the ghost—just after moving here from Paris. It was to have been a temporary thing while he searched for the next vehicle with which he could really make a statement, but he had never got around to it. In fact his licence had lapsed, and there was another target for the wretched press. But on this particular morning it was a risk he had to take. If the damn thing would start.

Louis Moreau shuffled out his back door and across to the carport. Ten years, he was thinking; ten years, living the quiet life in this very dull eastern city. It had felt much longer.

⌐   ⌐

As time spirals inevitably inward toward a single moment in history, some people (usually Commissaires and the like) tend to jump the gun, so to speak, and begin to think in historical terms. Before it happens they are already thinking how it all *was*, and, more important, how *they were* as the time drew nigh and the event became imminent. This is probably a natural thing, especially if you sense a change is in the air. Others prefer to dream until they can dream no longer: Jacques Normand could see a door opening. He could hear its large movement...opening.

Then he was awake. Aliette Nouvelle was crouched beside him, her silvery eyes unsure. Steps echoed. A man went rushing past the entrance to the sculpture room. A second later they heard his footsteps racing up the stairs.

Jacques was on his feet in a second, pulling on his pants. He jumped into his shoes, a move he had perfected during one of his prison stays.

The Inspector pursed her lips. "Wait…it's only Claude. Let me think."

"It's never only Claude… *Salut.*" He bent and kissed those lips—quickly, yes, but it was a kiss that let her know he trusted her, that it had worked out right. Then he ran from the room.

Charging for the door— at the far end of the Institute hall the sound of feet came clattering in a descending rush. The voice called, "Stop in the name of the law or I'll shoot!" But Jacques made it through the door.

He was in the clear… Exultant! From over his shoulder—it seemed like miles away—he saw the man go down on one knee and aim his gun. Then there she was: She ran…! now leaving her feet…flying, knocking the man to the ground. "No!" her voice blending with the report of the errant shot as it spread through the square.

Then the one cop was back on his feet and running like a fool to catch up with the inevitable. The other cop sat there—as if she knew there was no more point to running.

Jacques drove himself hard into the brightness of morning. Jacques knew: it was only for *him* to run, one last time. He knew that Aliette Nouvelle had run to save him from their guns and this was proof of his life. She had given him an opening and now he soared, smiling as he sprinted for the freedom of the side streets. Oh, Georgette!…because now he understood what was happening and he would run all the way back to Paris to let them know—La Puce, and all of them!—let them know about Aliette Nouvelle! He looked again and saw her: this woman, a cop: sharp focus, amazing, amazed, before he turned the corner.

Where he is hit, spins into space, clasps hands with his waiting soul.
(There's our single moment: three-fold, simultaneous, eternal.)

When Claude came barrelling around the corner, a traffic cop was there, on his sleepy way to another day's work. Together they approached the body. Claude turned it over. As far as he could tell, it was Jacques Normand and he was dead.

The car was halfway up the side of a wall. The traffic cop found the Commissaire in a state of shock, still clutching the wheel. The man had sustained a terrible gash in his forehead; bits of skin were hanging from a bubble-like dent in the windshield. The traffic cop stepped back, incredulous. That looked like a police car. And Monsieur le Commissaire had on only his pyjamas underneath his *imperméable*. He was not sure if he should get a whiff of the Commissaire's breath before the ambulance people descended upon the scene. Leaning in— the Commissaire did not seem to notice him—he was close enough to kiss the man. He sniffed, then harder. No, no booze that he could detect, just your regular raunchy morning breath. But the traffic cop knew he should not touch the victim, so he stood there. Inspector Néon came over. As they waited for someone to show up and take charge, Claude Néon inspected the dent in the windshield. The traffic cop noticed that he seemed to be fascinated by the hanging shards of Monsieur le Commissaire's skin.

"That looks like a police car," noted the traffic cop. "Bullet-proof glass."

Claude nodded and muttered, "Yeah."

Within minutes the corner was packed with onlookers, more police and a couple of ambulance crews. As Claude was giving his version to the senior gendarme he became aware of Inspector Nouvelle standing at a distance, observing. He turned away to answer someone else's question. When he looked again in her direction, she was gone.

The Lively Spark

I met his eyes one last time, then heard the horn blast, screeching brakes, the thump and the half-scream, the scrape and crash, the shattering. I saw him go flying across my field of vision, end over end, spreading like a newspaper coming apart in the wind, and land in a heap on the far side of the road. Seeing it, I picked myself up and started to run, took three steps, then stopped. What was there to run for? It was over.

A bit later I turned my back on the accident scene and walked across the plaza, back toward the Institute, tuning out the noise of sirens and the crowd. I saw Georgette Duguay at the corner, getting into the van. Without so much as a wave, she started it up, did a U-turn and drove off. What was it? Just past six-thirty, and somehow she knew. Another one who had been watching, I reckoned, and I guessed where that old woman was headed; she would be the one to deliver the news to Anne-Marie. It was of no consequence to me that Georgette was leaving the scene. I knew I would see her again.

Morning light added a stark comfort to the halls of the Institute. Stopping at the foot of the stairs, I looked in at that room full of shapes. We had been there in the middle of it, Jacques Normand and me— moving, making love. We had been another shape that did not know quite what to make of itself, but had gone ahead and tried regardless. In fact, hadn't we been the centre of that room, under the cover of darkness—warm, defining everything around us through the act of love?

Climbing the stairs, I had to consider that love is always possible in a dark space where nothing is complete. In the morning, when things are clearly seen, there are duties to be done. And almost all investigations ended in violence of some sort. It was part of the business—as if Jacques and his kind were guided by an energy whose sole purpose in life was to blow a hole through death: *l'instinct de mort*; men whose lives appeared to be opposed in principle to the idea of a natural end. There was not much I could do about that. Listening to him explain himself, indulging his sad reasoning, I realized Jacques had probably been even more of a dreamer than me. So the Public Enemy was finally killed by a car instead of a gun; either way, the statistics were so large as to be meaningless when you tried to slot it into that category called Fate. I realized his gun was still in my pocket. And that I would have used it if his angry hands had got the better of his hopeful heart.

Many hard sentiments were entering into the mix now; but this line of thinking directed me to the crux of the matter, the lively spark, which was freedom. If Jacques had an instinct for death, he also had a love of freedom. The symbol of freedom must love freedom, *n'est-ce pas?* I had misunderstood the attraction. It had been trying to tell me not what I wanted, but what I already had. Yes: freedom lay in what I did and how I did it. Here I had just brought down the most notorious man in France, all by way of instincts and intuition. Physical. Nothing held back. Not like the Commissaire, who had to control him, had to play him along. Nor like Claude, who was a slave to his mystique. I had not compromised myself in coming face to face with Jacques Normand.

So then, what was given over—if indeed, in the touching, there was something given over—when there could be no chance of a life to be lived together, no hope of any pleasures past the moment? Freedom. It was something serious which he had carried, which I could carry on. Perhaps now better defined? I didn't know, and still don't. But what else could I make of that man's love? And what had Inspector Aliette Nouvelle given him back? More to the point: what had he taken, that hopeful thief? Freedom? But he was dead. Love, then? Something he had believed, something I had seen in that last moment. Still, I was uneasy with that: how had the love of this one cop figured in the killing of Jacques Normand? This dream love. It was something I would ask Georgette Duguay.

Feeling sad, but not bitter, and fateful, yet without any sense of having made a mistake, and uncertain, as I took his drawing down from the board near the front of Georgette's room; because that was me, to a "T," as the English say, standing there so naked after all. You listen to your heart and follow it for all it's worth, and it takes you to the edge. But will it tell you who you are? Hardly. And no point waiting for the editorials or the official story. They would tell it differently. They always did.

I rolled the drawing up and tucked it under my arm.

They were loading the body of the Public Enemy into the police department hearse. Monsieur le Commissaire had been strapped to another stretcher and parked in an ambulance. They had also sent the Commissaire's official car—Claude was sitting in the back seat making his notes. He looked up and asked, "Where is Inspector Nouvelle?"

"I'm here," I said, opening the door on the opposite side and climbing in.

Claude wanted to say something, but all he could do was look at me and scratch his morning stubble. Instead he told the driver, "Let's go."

"Would you take me home?"

"Our reports," he said. He was trying to smile. Perhaps he was trying to show me a new Claude Néon who was willing to forget everything and begin again.

We both knew there were things that would require some sorting out.

"I'll be there," I said. "I have to feed my cat."

"Right." He turned to the driver and indicated the direction.

Piaf was waiting on the railing when we pulled up in front. He appeared to be watching the traffic cop. I knew he was watching for me.

Someone had been in my apartment again. Maybe Claude had finally made it. Maybe that's why he had smiled like that. I opened the balcony door. "*Salut, Piaf! Viens ici, mon petit...*" He jumped down from his perch and raced in for his meal.

I pulled back the curtains, opened some windows to air the place. Then I paused for a moment to enjoy the morning sun.

EPILOGUE

By the cops and robbers process of attrition, the old van was now Georgette's. She drove it through the quarter to the entrance of the alley behind the cellblock. The waiter was up the ladder, fulfilling his side of the deal with Jacques Normand by serving the first of many fine meals to Anne-Marie. Seeing Georgette beckon, he refilled Anne-Marie's bowl of coffee, then descended. As he approached the van, Georgette proffered the bouquet of flowers that was still waiting to be delivered. "Give these to her, will you? Tell her they are from Aliette Nouvelle—and that help is coming soon."

"Of course." He stepped back as Georgette put the van into gear. She began to pull away, then she stopped again. The waiter looked up, awaiting further instructions.

"He's dead."

Willem blinked once, but understood immediately. He bowed with a slow professional nod and began to withdraw. Georgette looked down the alley toward the ladder and the window, but all the while she was releasing the clutch. Her lips were tight. Her eyes betrayed nothing of what she might or might not feel. Then she gave her eyes back to the road and drove off, guiding the van in the direction of the autoroute. Perhaps she was thinking of going to the river for a bit of fresh air.

Anne-Marie did not understand the flowers (although her own kind of instinct told her something was going on), but the waiter could not bring himself to tell her. A message like that was surely not his job. It had to be Georgette. Or that Inspector Nouvelle. Yes. The Inspector would find the right words. By the time he returned with her supper, Anne-Marie would have found out and she would have survived. Dealing with it. Safe in her cell, and well provided for.

The *Palais* was pleased—of course, but the thing, as it stood, posed many unanswered questions. *Maître* Souviron, speaking on behalf of the court, would be working closely with Chief Magistrate Richand and the public should rest assured. Upon his recommendation to the Divisional Office of the *Police Judiciaire* (in the larger and more interesting city to the north), Inspector Claude Néon was appointed interim-Commissaire while Commissaire Moreau recuperated. He had earned it. They were, after all, talking about Jacques Normand, and he knew the public would extend him its full support.

Then the voice of the interim-Commissaire could be heard adding his assurances. He made special mention of one Inspector Aliette Nouvelle, saying she was a credit to the force.

All this by lunch time. Law and order was well in hand.

"I don't know about this new Commissaire," said the butcher, turning the radio down. He waited for the tailor to select his meat. "I really doubt he's the right man for the pressures of a job like that."

"I was thinking the same thing," concurred the tailor, his wandering imagination finally zeroing in on a tender New York cut. "But his tastes in fashion might have nothing to do with abilities as a cop."

"Style is substance," mused the butcher. "He was in here one day with that Inspector Nouvelle. He seemed lost. If they were just another couple, I would say that she definitely wore the pants."

"I'd like to sell her a suit."

"I'm sure you would... But she was odd as well. Capable—you could see that...but ...well, different. We talked one night. She had been following me. She thought I was him."

"Normand!"

"*Mais oui.*"

"*Incroyable*! ...No wonder they gave it to him. I don't think she likes me. Just the way she looks at me in the group. That one there." Pointing to the steak in the window.

The butcher shrugged as he took the meat and wrapped it. "Who knows what they're thinking..."

"Women?"

"The police."

"How true," agreed the tailor, paying for his package and wishing the butcher *bonne fin de journée.*

— THE END —

JOHN BROOKE

John Brooke lives in Montreal, where he earns a living as a freelance writer and translator. He has worked as a film and video editor as well as directed four films on modern dance. Brooke's poetry and stories have been widely published and in 1998 his story "The Finer Points of Apples" won him the Journey Prize.